# THE
# MISTRESS'
# HOUSE

# LEIGH MICHAELS

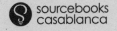
sourcebooks
casablanca

Published by Sourcebooks Casablanca, an imprint of Sourcebooks, Inc.
P.O. Box 4410, Naperville, Illinois  60567-4410
(630) 961-3900
FAX: (630) 961-2168
www.sourcebooks.com

Printed and bound in the United States of America
QW   10  9  8  7  6  5  4  3  2  1

*To Michael, for always believing in me.*

# *One*

## The Earl Buys a House

The Earl of Hawthorne looked wistfully past his man of business. At the far end of the library, a pair of long windows stood open to a glorious autumn day, and in the distance he could hear the bark of a hunting dog. It was a perfect day to take a gun and a dog and go for a long tramp across the parkland and into the woods of his Surrey estate. But here he was instead, sitting at his desk and listening to Perkins prose on for hours about the benefits of investing in a canal somewhere at the far end of England.

Except, now that Thorne actually pulled his attention back to the library, Perkins appeared to have finished with the canal and moved on to the benefits of buying a house in London.

"Perkins," Thorne said gently. "I already *have* a house in London. A *big* house—right on Portman Square. You can't have overlooked that."

"No, my lord."

"Surely you're not suggesting I sell the house I already have and buy a different one?"

"No, my lord."

"And surely you're not suggesting that I need more space in London."

"No, my lord." With each repetition, Perkins' voice grew more wooden.

"Then you're suggesting I buy another house and lease it out?"

"Not *exactly*, my lord."

"But if I'm neither going to live in it nor rent it, what on earth would I do with another house in…" Thorne paused. "Perkins, exactly where is this house?"

"At Number 5 Upper Seymour Street, my lord. It's…"

"I know where it is. Right around the corner from Portman Square."

"The garden of Number 5 backs on your own, my lord. It is not a large house—only six bedrooms, four main reception rooms, and all the usual arrangements for servants. But the location and the situation are quite salubrious. Unlike the other houses in the row, Number 5 has windows all along one side, as well as in front and back, because it lies next to Berkeley Mews."

"With horses coming and going all day," Thorne observed. "Not every tenant would like that."

"Since they are mostly your own horses, my lord," Perkins observed, "I felt it likely this would not disturb *you*. The location alongside the mews, plus the large number of windows and the consequently high window tax, does mean that the house isn't in quite as much demand as it might otherwise be, and that has kept the price reasonable. And it is a very convenient situation, should my lord wish to come and go without being observed."

Thorne leaned back in his chair, tapping his index finger against his jaw. "You make me sound like some kind of spy, Perkins," he said dryly. "Surely you're not laboring under the delusion that I'm part of an espionage ring."

Perkins coughed. "Certainly *not*, my lord."

Perkins' tone, Thorne thought wryly, was unnecessarily acerbic. It wasn't, after all, that Thorne didn't have the right talents to be a spy. He'd just never been called upon to use them in that particular way.

"I merely meant," Perkins went on, "that your lordship is a figure of interest in London society, and therefore your... actions... are noticed and often remarked on."

"*Actions*? Why, Perkins, you old dog. You're actually volunteering to help me to keep my affaires under wraps? If I didn't know better, I'd think you were blushing."

Perkins shuffled his feet and looked down at the carpet.

He hadn't been mistaken; Perkins *was* blushing. Thorne had never seen anything of the sort before.

He considered the idea. There was certainly merit to the notion of buying a house just off Portman Square. If he could tuck a mistress into a trysting place just a step from his own garden, he could avoid a long list of inconveniences. Kicking his heels for hours while messages were delivered and answers returned... Riding halfway across London for an assignation... Finding new, safe, and very secluded meeting places... Wandering around the halls of a country house trying to locate a particular lady's bedchamber... Keeping his horses, and the grooms who cared for them, waiting outside a private house on a cold day...

"Very well," he said and stood up. "Buy the house. I'll look it over when I come up to town for the Season."

"Yes, my lord. I shall put the transaction in motion immediately."

"I have the utmost faith in your judgment, Perkins." Thorne clapped his man of business on the shoulder and escaped to the gun room before Perkins could wax poetic about his canal once more.

Of course, there was one drawback to the scheme, Thorne thought as he started off across the lawn, a shotgun on his shoulder and his favorite hound rollicking at his heels. Once a mistress was actually in residence in a house right around the corner from his own, he might find it a bit of a tangle to move her out again when he tired of her. But he could deal with that when the problem arose.

Or, he thought with a twinge of humor, *Perkins* could.

# *Two*

## My Lady Wilde

The Earl of Hawthorne paused in the hallway of Lady Stone's London town house—feigning interest in the portrait of a long-dead Stone ancestor that had been painted in muddy shades of brown—until a footman had passed. As the footman opened the doors of the ballroom at the far end of the hall, the strains of a waltz swelled into the hallway.

Thorne waited a moment longer, until the doors had closed again and the sound had dropped to a murmur. Then he slipped through an anteroom at the back of the house and into a small morning room that was never used during Lady Stone's parties.

At least, it was never used for *organized* portions of Lucinda's parties, he thought as Charlotte surged forward and threw her arms around him. "You took forever, Thorne," she whined. "I thought you'd forgotten about me."

Forget Charlotte Barnsley? Hardly, especially when her very generous breasts were pressed so firmly against his chest that the diamond stickpin in his cravat might actually wound her. Then she moved even closer, slipping her thigh between his legs and dragging his head down to kiss him. Her mouth was hot and wet and hungry, and her fingers roamed over his hair, over the shoulders of his coat, and down his back.

He captured her hands and pulled them away—and was startled at the strength and suddenness of his antipathy. What kind of a rake was he, anyway? With a woman in his arms who was not only willing but eager, what was stopping him? Perhaps it was just the fact that she seemed to be in such a rush. Out in the ballroom, the dancers were still going round in circles, and the supper break was an hour off. What was Charlotte's hurry?

"Thorne," she whimpered and wriggled up against him again.

This wouldn't be the first time he'd put Lucinda Stone's morning room to a use her ladyship didn't intend—though never before with Charlotte, for she wasn't his usual type. Even a rake, he thought, ought to show some discrimination, and he much preferred to be the hunter, rather than the prey. Obviously Charlotte hadn't noticed that—or else she'd opted to ignore it. She'd actually hiked up her skirt to get a trifle closer to him.

Why had he agreed to meet her here? Sheer boredom? The fact that she'd been pursuing him for weeks and seemed likely to continue ad nauseam? The lack of anyone else who had drawn his attention lately?

Was Charlotte in such a hurry because she sensed that she wasn't apt to last long as a distraction for him?

Thorne took a breath to tell her that she was wasting her efforts, and she slid her tongue into his mouth.

From the corner of his eye, he could see the door into the anteroom. Because Charlotte had thrown herself against him the instant he'd walked in, he hadn't had a chance to close it firmly. And just beyond that slightly open door, he thought he caught a glimpse of movement.

Thorne's instinct for self-preservation reared up like a cobra on the attack. Was someone just outside, about to burst in and embarrass them?

Not that he was easily embarrassed. A rake wasn't much of a rake if he gave thought to what others believed about him. And the *ton* clearly knew it, too— for no society miss or scheming mama had made an attempt to compromise the notorious Lord Hawthorne into offering marriage for... oh, several months now, if he remembered correctly.

Charlotte's teeth nipped at his lower lip in a harder-than-playful bite.

He didn't think Charlotte would be all that embar-rassed to be discovered either, especially considering the way she was kissing him. Unless her husband happened to be the one out there. But the elderly Lord Barnsley was unlikely to come rummaging around Lady Stone's Grosvenor Square mansion in the middle of a ball in search of his wife. He might, on the other hand, have simply made a wrong turn on his way to the card room—and if he had, the results would be just as untidy.

Charlotte's hands had slid down to the fastenings of Thorne's breeches. He captured her fingers and pulled them away.

There was one more possibility. Had Charlotte been just a shade too enthusiastic in her greeting because she knew someone was out there? Because she'd planned it and was hurrying things along? Though why, he had no idea…

Without making a conscious decision, he found himself standing three feet from Charlotte. She was looking up at him in puzzlement, her eyes wide, and barely able to keep her balance. "What's wrong, Thorne?" she whimpered. "Don't you want me anymore?"

All right, he conceded. Maybe she *didn't* know about whoever was watching from the anteroom. Still, what little interest he'd felt in her was long gone.

"Not the best place," he said. "Lady Stone's a friend."

"That's why it's perfect," she complained. She cupped a hand around each breast, pushing them up and out at him. "My little girls are lonely, Thorne. Won't your big boy come and play with them?"

Charlotte had a lot to learn about enticing a lover, and that inane comment made one thing absolutely certain—she wouldn't be learning it from him. "Not just now." Thorne caught another flash of movement outside the door in the shadowed anteroom. Definitely *not* his imagination.

"Tomorrow, then? Barnsley will be at his club. It has to be soon, Thorne, for in a few days, I'll be going to the Winchesters' for a house party. Though I'm sure Arabella will invite you, too, if I ask her."

"She already has," Thorne said absently.

Charlotte's face brightened. "Then we'll have a whole week together! She's got the most magnificent little gazebo in her garden. So very private… Oh, Thorne, you naughty boy, teasing me, when you had this set up already!"

"Off with you now." He considered telling her the truth—that he'd rather be roasted on a kitchen spit than attend Arabella Winchester's house party—but that would only set her off again. He'd write Charlotte a note or something later.

"One more kiss first?" she pouted, and stretched a hand out as if to caress him.

He held her off. "Anticipation is half the fun." He was looking past her, barely hearing what he said. Would the woman *never* move?

She did, finally—but toward the anteroom. "Not that way," he said hastily, and put both hands on her shoulders to turn her toward the other exit.

She shrugged, managing to brush her breast against his hand.

Thorne hastily pulled away before she could get a head of steam up again. "Go through the music room and back to the hall. I'll wait here a couple of minutes before I follow you."

There was no movement in the anteroom now. But perhaps the loiterer would stand still and wait, expecting Thorne to use the other door as Charlotte had, rather than take the chance of making noise.

"So even if someone sees one of us, they won't know we were together? You're so clever," Charlotte simpered. "I never would have thought of that."

*Because you're so inexperienced at this? Hardly.* Clearly, this wasn't Charlotte's first experience with dalliance, no matter what she'd like him to think.

And it wasn't cleverness that made him so cautious, either. It was experience. A man didn't remain unattached for long in London society unless he kept his wits about him and his eyes wide open. Now if the woman would just go away so he could see who stood behind that door…

Charlotte paused to give him a sultry little wave. "I'll be waiting," she whispered.

The instant she was out of sight, he breathed a sigh of relief and wheeled toward the anteroom, crossing the fine plush carpet in two large and silent steps. Common sense said the watcher would be gone by now. Whether she'd been shocked or titillated, the woman—and he was certain it had been a woman, because the flicker of movement he'd spotted had been light-colored and low to the ground, like the edge of a skirt—would have fled as soon as she realized there would be nothing more to see. But Thorne hadn't reached thirty unwed by being careless, so he flung the door wide.

Halfway across the anteroom, lit only by the dying fire, stood a woman in a white dress. Her face—in the dimness—was nothing more than a pale oval under a smear of dark hair.

No, not a woman. A mere girl—for her dress looked like the sort of ball gown worn by the newest members of the London *ton*, the young women in their first introduction to society. White, trimmed with bright ribbons and lace.

She made no protest, no move to escape. She didn't move at all. But why? She'd had plenty of time to retreat. If she'd simply wandered down the hall from the ballroom by mistake, why had she stayed, especially after she must have heard him urging Charlotte to go? Was she hoping to satisfy a maiden's curiosity about what men and women did in dark-shadowed corners?

"Did you enjoy the show?" he asked ironically.

She took a step forward. "You're Hawthorne." Her voice was low and throaty, almost as if she hadn't used it in awhile. "We have not been introduced."

"And we're not likely to be," he pointed out.

She didn't seem to hear. "I was looking for you. Because..." She paused and then went on in a matter-of-fact tone, "Because I want you to ruin me."

It hadn't been the smoothest of approaches, Anne scolded herself. *I want you to ruin me*—surely she could have done better than that. Still, the Earl of Hawthorne had no reason to look at her as if he'd just bitten into a lemon. She hadn't insulted him; he was the one who'd built a reputation as a roué, and nothing Anne Keighley could do, or say, would change that a whit for either better or worse.

He was still looking at her. As if he was inspecting merchandise, she supposed—and finding plenty of flaws. With her pride stinging a little, Anne snapped, "Am I that much of an antidote, my lord?"

His gaze traveled slowly over her, one eyebrow arching in haughty disdain. "You've a tongue like a fishing gaff."

*Wonderful, Anne,* she told herself. *Why not just lame your wheelers at the starting line?* She stood up a little straighter. "Your pardon, my lord. I should not have said that. A too-quick tongue has always been my greatest failing."

"Yes, I wager your mama has scolded you about that, too."

"What do you mean, *too*?"

"If you make a habit of asking gentlemen to ruin you, she must have a few things to say about your behavior, as well as your quick tongue."

"Oh. Well, I don't. Ask to be ruined, I mean."

"I should hope not. So why am I the recipient of this... honor?"

Anne shrugged. "Who better? You're the best-known rake in all of London."

"I am humbled by your regard." He moved to the hallway and looked out; then he checked the morning room again. "Your witness seems to have been delayed," he observed.

"Witness?"

"Yes. Mama, big sister, chaperone. Whoever was supposed to observe us in a compromising position, shriek in horror, bring down all the society matrons upon us, and force me into marrying you. I grant it's a nice trick, useless though it would be in the end."

The sheer arrogance of the man—though it didn't surprise her in the least—made Anne's teeth ache from gritting them. Did he truly think he was irresistible? If she didn't need him so badly, she'd walk straight back to the ballroom and take her pick from the rest of London's rakes.

On second thought, that was exactly what she would do. "It is no trick," she said over her shoulder. "I beg your pardon, my lord. I made the mistake of thinking there might still be a gentleman lurking underneath your reputation. I was mistaken."

He moved very quickly, stepping between her and the door. Anne was suddenly breathless, cursing the quick tongue that her mother had always said would get her into trouble. To tell a peer of the realm that he wasn't a gentleman… Men ended up fighting duels over insults like that. What might he do to a defense-less woman alone in a shadowed room?

"If your definition of being a gentleman includes agreeing to ruin you, I must admit to being intrigued." His hand came to rest on her shoulder, turning her around to face him once more. "Let me take a better look." He drew her closer to the fire, moving her so the light fell across her face.

Anne didn't resist. Her breath seemed to stick in her throat. He was so *big*. He towered over her, and there was a hint of brandy on the warm breath that brushed her cheek. She looked past him, trying not to take in the scent. But her gaze skittered back to his face.

She hadn't expected him to be quite so handsome. She'd anticipated that he'd be attractive—how could a man be a rake if he wasn't?—but she'd thought his appeal to women would probably lie in an aura of hard-edged masculine danger, rather than in sheer looks.

His deep brown hair was fashionably short, and the color of his eyes was difficult to identify in the fire-light. They were dark—she knew that much. Though he was well dressed in a midnight-blue coat with snowy linen and a remarkable diamond stickpin in his cravat, she thought he was too much of an athlete to be a dandy. There was no mistaking the air of power about him. She could no more have broken free of his hold than she could have ripped the mantel from the wall. Yet he was not forcing her; when he'd urged her to move closer to the light, she'd simply found herself wanting to cooperate.

"My, you are a beauty, aren't you?" he said.

"I am generally accounted to be passable, though of course not in the first stare of fashion."

"Well, it would be a shame to waste all your effort."

"My effort?" She looked directly at him.

"It must have taken some planning to elude your chaperone and leave the ballroom unnoticed. Such industry should be rewarded." Slowly, his arms slipped around her, drawing her close.

She looked up into eyes that seemed very dark, very large... very near. His lips brushed her cheek softly and then settled firmly onto her mouth.

Every muscle in her body tensed.

He didn't seem to notice. But then he wouldn't, Anne told herself. Because men didn't.

He lifted his head a fraction. "Oh, you can do better than that. If you really want to be ruined, my dear, you'll have to cooperate a bit."

She took hold of her courage and concentrated on relaxing her lips.

He kissed her again, tasting, caressing, teasing. "That's more like it," he whispered, and only then did she realize she had opened her mouth for him. His tongue gently invaded, doing terrifying things to her pulse, to her knees—how was it that a kiss could make her knees go weak?

He set her aside, patted her shoulder, and said, "There. You're ruined. Just do be careful who you tell about it, for most of your acquaintances won't believe you. Now go back to the ball and stop being such a silly little girl."

And before Anne could so much as stamp her foot—much less find her voice—he was gone.

❧

Thorne paused in the dining room, where supper was being laid out, to help himself to a brandy. Lord knew he could use one. What the hell was wrong with him, kissing debutantes in the dark? He was damned lucky there *hadn't* been a chaperone lurking.

In fact, he might not be out of the woods yet. If his little conquest wasn't as tight-lipped at talking as she was at kissing, he might find a father on his doorstep in the morning, demanding that the banns be read. Where were his wits, anyway?

And what the hell was that girl up to? *I want you to ruin me.* She hadn't the vaguest idea what she was playing at, that was plain enough.

Thorne was so absorbed in his thoughts that when Lord Hastings called his name, he jumped six inches. Hastings had daughters, he seemed to recall. Could she have been one of *them*…? But Hastings only wanted to talk about a horse he'd seen that morning at Tattersall's.

By the time Thorne returned to the ballroom, he'd had two more brandies and managed to talk himself down out of the boughs. But he lurked at the edge of the room, leaning against a pillar and looking for her.

Only, he assured himself, in order to stay as far away as possible.

Lady Stone sidled up beside him. "Are you enjoying

my party, Thorne?" Her beady gaze was still as sharp as it must have been when she'd made her own debut forty years earlier, and she used it to skewer him to the pillar.

"You're looking quite handsome tonight. Very convenient for you young bucks, the new *a la Brutus* curls. One can never be quite certain whether you've just left your mirror or you've been lurking in the music room with a female running her fingers through your hair."

He tore his gaze away from the crowd. "Now, Lucinda. Just because a man has a reputation as a bit of a flirt, that's no reason to assume that he's been misbehaving." He wondered what the reaction would be if he told her, *And it wasn't in the music room.*

Lady Stone snorted. "A bit of a flirt? *You?* Thorne, you were a flirt the day you climbed out of your cradle. Since then, you've gone all the way through rake, and you're well on the path to libertine." She looked across the ballroom and said blandly, "Her name is Anne Keighley."

How the devil did Lucinda know who he'd been looking at?

His gaze returned to the dance floor, where his dark-haired debutante was dancing with—in the name of all that was holy—the most flagrant fortune hunter of the *ton*. Where the hell was her chaperone, if she was allowing her charge to have anything to do with Freddy Lassiter?

Except... now that he could see her more clearly, Anne Keighley did not seem to be a debutante after all. She moved with too much grace for a girl in her first season, smiled with too much assurance, and flirted—and there was no question in his mind she was flirting with Freddy Lassiter—with too much ease.

Even the dress that had looked so virginal in the dimness of the anteroom was nothing of the sort here; she must have chosen white not because it was proper but because it was so striking with her dark hair and vibrant coloring. Her figure—slender and small as she was—was definitely that of a woman, rather than a girl. And there was something in her eyes…

Yes, she was definitely older than this Season's crop of chicks.

Belatedly, the name clicked in his mind. "Anne Keighley," he said. "You mean Lady Keighley?"

"So you know who she is."

"She made her come-out some years ago. Her father married her off to old Keighley, and nobody heard of her again 'til he died the year before last."

Lady Stone nodded. "And now that she's finally out of black gloves, she has returned for another try." Her gaze slid over him and back to the dancers. "At least that's what they say."

*I want you to ruin me,* the dark beauty had said. That didn't sound much like a marriage-minded widow to Thorne. Unless she was playing a very deep game indeed.

"How old is she?"

Lady Stone shrugged. "Three and twenty, perhaps."

"She didn't seem it." He didn't realize until too late that he'd said it aloud.

"And here I thought that to a rake like you, all women were alike in a darkened room, Thorne!"

Thorne cursed his wayward tongue for letting that tidbit slip. Of course, Lucinda Stone wouldn't have missed it. She might even have noticed little Anne returning to the ballroom.

Still chortling, Lady Stone moved away to tend to her guests.

Thorne leaned against the pillar and pretended not to notice as Anne Keighley swept by him in the arms of Freddy Lassiter and flashed him the most brilliant of smiles.

&c

Anne picked up one of the silver baby rattles that the jeweler's assistant had laid out on a dark velvet cloth in front of her and shook it lightly, producing a gently musical tone. Just as she laid it down and picked up the other one, the clerk who was waiting on her bowed so deeply he was bent almost double. Obviously, she concluded, a customer far more important than mere Lady Keighley had just entered the shop.

As Anne looked over her shoulder, Lord Hawthorne came to stand beside her. "Doing a little shopping for the heir?" he asked. "But I must be mistaken—you have no heir, I believe."

She gave him her most haughty look. "I fear we have not been introduced, sir."

He smiled, teeth flashing. "Don't you recall? Lady Barnsley made us known to each other last night, Lady Keighley."

Oh, he *was* a quick one. *And what else did you expect?* "I have a lamentable memory, sir."

"I'm glad to know it's not personal." He picked up the rattle she'd already tested—and a frippery, too delicate thing it looked to her in his big, strong hand—and gave it a hard shake. The sound it made was harsh, discordant.

Anne wanted to cover her ears. "Not that one," she said to the jeweler's assistant. "I'll take the other for my friend's baby son. And then you may serve Lord Hawthorne."

"I'm in no hurry," Hawthorne said lightly. "I have no plans for the morning. No dragons to slay. No maidens to ravish."

"But then ravishing maidens has never been on your calendar," she said softly. "Far too risky, that territory. Married ladies are far more your style."

He acknowledged the hit with a slight bow. "You're out early for the morning after a ball."

"I'm generally an early riser. You might find it amusing, by the by, to know that Lady Barnsley offered to see me safely home last night. So kind of her to be concerned for my reputation when my sister-in-law took ill and my brother had to escort her home before the ball was over."

"Not that it would have been an inconvenience for her to convey you to your brother's house, since Braxton lives just a step from Lady Stone's."

So he knew where she lived as well. Lord Hawthorne was proving to be very well informed.

He turned to the jeweler's assistant. "I have a fancy for rubies today."

Anne couldn't help herself. "Oh, surely not. That would be the wrong coloring altogether for... a lady with reddish hair." *A carrot-topped tart like Charlotte Barnsley,* she wanted to say.

"Because, of course, in my entire life I have known *only* the one lady," he murmured. "Is that your maid waiting just outside the shop?"

"Not mine, actually. My sister-in-law's. Why? Is she craning her neck to see what's going on?"

He turned toward the door and lifted a hand lazily.

A moment later, Maria appeared in the doorway. "Did you summon me, my lady?"

Hawthorne held out a guinea. "Lady Keighley requires…" He paused, lifting an eyebrow at Anne.

She knew she should simply stay quiet. Instead, she said, "A lace-edged handkerchief from the shop across the way."

"A dozen of them," he corrected. "And she would like each one to be a different pattern. If you must search the length of Bond Street to find an appropriate variety, do so. Then return to her here." When the maid was gone, he said softly, "You disappoint me. You couldn't think of something more difficult to acquire than handkerchiefs?"

"I also have a lamentable streak of practicality," Anne said. "I can use a new handkerchief—or a dozen, for that matter. Most of mine still have black borders."

"Indeed. My apologies—and my condolences on your loss. If they're in order."

She darted a look up at him. What did he mean, *if* condolences were in order? She looked away. "Thank you, sir."

"Keighley was a great deal older than you." He glanced down at the ruby necklace the assistant had spread out before him and shook his head. "Not at all the thing. I prefer to look at the private stock, the jewels your master keeps in the back room. Would you care to assist me in my choice, Lady Keighley?" He waved a graceful hand toward a half-concealed door at the rear of the shop.

His voice was very smooth, with not a hint that what he was offering was racy, even scandalous...

*Oh, don't be a fool, Anne Keighley. He's hardly going to ravish you in the back room of a jeweler's shop. You offered him the perfect opportunity last night and he wasn't in the least interested, so why would he—*

Exactly. Why would he have changed his mind? What was different this morning?

Last night he'd thought she might be aiming to trap him into marriage. This morning, apparently, he was no longer concerned about that.

Her heartbeat had speeded up a little. "Since you've sent off my maid and I must wait for her return," she said demurely, "I may as well do all that's possible to make some lady happy with her gift." She stood up, dropping the silver rattle into her reticule. She could feel the blood pounding in her throat. "Send your account to me at Grosvenor Square, in care of Lord Braxton," she told the jeweler's assistant.

He bowed and showed them into the private back room. It was just large enough for two wing-backed chairs and a small velvet-draped table on which stood a single ornament—an exquisite enameled butterfly, the wings edged with tiny garnets and topaz. Hawthorne escorted her to a chair and took the second one himself.

"I think it's time you explain yourself," he said calmly.

"The jeweler…"

"…will not appear until he is summoned. You said last night that you wanted me to ruin you. What exactly did you mean, Lady Keighley?"

*This is what you wanted,* she told herself. "I should think it is quite clear."

"The result perhaps, but not the reason."

She bit her lip, but she didn't speak.

"Very well," he said. "I shall tell you what I know—or suspect—and you shall correct me where I'm wrong. You were married very young, not entirely by your own choice, to a man much older than yourself."

*Not entirely by your own choice…* that was one way of putting it. But there was no benefit in dwelling on history, so she settled for a nod.

"He left you reasonably well off but without children. Now you've taken the sensible next move, returning to London and society—with a larger fortune and more freedom than when you were a debutante—to choose a second husband."

"No!"

His expression remained impassive. "In that case, I deduce that in addition to being something of a hermit, Lord Keighley has left you with a distaste for men."

Anne wet her lips. "For husbands, at least."

"Your point is well taken. Yet you are not a wanton."

"Of course not. If I was, I'd hardly need to be ruined."

"That, you see, is where I seem to miss the point," he said pensively.

The silence lengthened. Any minute now, Maria might return. *Why didn't I ask for something much more complicated than handkerchiefs?*

"My husband was not only a hermit but a miser," Anne said. "I find myself possessed of a reasonable fortune."

"A heartbreaking handicap, indeed." There was the merest edge of irony in Hawthorne's voice.

"Yes," she flared, "for a woman, it is. I control my money only until such time as I marry, when it will pass into the hands of my husband."

"It is the law. But the answer is simple. Choose carefully who you marry."

"And hope that I have chosen a man who will cherish me as well as my fortune? No, thank you."

"You have no wish for a family? You could insist that your money be settled on your children."

She kept her voice steady, but that took effort. "Whether I would like to have children is beside the point. At any rate, what I definitely do not wish for is a husband. But the choice, I fear, is not entirely up to me."

"Your brother insists?"

"He has no power to compel me to wed. However, Braxton is something of a traditionalist. He frowns on the idea of me setting up my own establishment—yet he does not want me under his roof indefinitely."

"Ah. Perhaps Lady Braxton would prefer you to be… elsewhere?"

Anne doubted that Madeleine would admit that. Nevertheless, it might well be true—and Madeleine had ways of getting what she wanted without ever saying anything directly. "Lady Braxton and I get along well enough for a visit of a few weeks. But I fear that months or years in the same household would lead to great discomfort for both of us."

"It is a rare house indeed that can hold two ladies in comfort."

Anne couldn't help but wonder how he could possibly know. "I have been back in London just a week, and already my brother has given his permission to three different men to court me."

"And his approval gives credence to the idea that you are seeking a husband," Thorne mused. "However, I find it hard to believe you've done nothing yourself to encourage them. You were flirting with Freddy Lassiter last night, which is hardly the way to stifle his interest."

"I was not flirting... I was *dancing*. I could hardly refuse him a waltz. He told me he'd call on me this morning, so I assume he has also found favor in my brother's eyes. That makes four."

"Which leads one to wonder about Braxton's judgment, if he thinks the Honorable Freddy is a good match. He's a fortune hunter... but then, you said, you have a fortune."

"I think my brother gives more weight to the fact that the gentlemen in question are young and lively," Anne said thoughtfully.

"As Keighley certainly was not. I gather you slipped away this morning rather than listen to Freddy's proposal?"

"I pretended not to have heard him say he would come to call," Anne admitted. "At any rate, Freddy Lassiter's not the worst of them."

"We are veering from the point, Lady Keighley."

"I choose not to marry, but my brother refuses to believe that I am quite serious. Since he encourages men to think that they may find favor with me, I have no choice but to make it clear to the *ton* that I have no intention of marrying again."

"And you think taking a lover will accomplish that?"

"It will at least make plain that I will not allow myself to be compromised into marriage."

"Ah," he said. "Now we come to the nub of it."

"I thought that, as the target of many such plots yourself, you would understand," Anne said, almost plaintively. "I have already narrowly avoided several separate instances where I would have been alone with a man under questionable circumstances."

He ticked the possibilities off on his fingers. "Closed carriage. The darkest corner of a deserted terrace. A private room. Being out after dark…"

"None of those episodes would have particularly disturbed me," she said dryly, "had not each of the gentlemen involved reassured me—in their various ways—that if we were discovered, I could rely on them to preserve my reputation at any cost."

"Including marriage."

"I would say, *especially* marriage—even if I had no interest in marrying the gentleman in question."

"Yet you are alone with me," he pointed out.

"You, sir, have no desire to marry me. You have no interest in a permanent alliance and no need to add my fortune to your own."

"True enough."

"At any rate, once I make it clear to society that I

won't be embarrassed into marriage, I'll be left alone to live as I choose."

"Taking lovers." His voice was matter-of-fact.

"If I wish." Why the simple statement made her feel defensive she didn't know.

"Short-term alliances, purely for physical plea-sure—and, of course, to make sure no one ever forgets that you're ruined."

He didn't need to make it sound so calculating, she thought. "Perhaps for friendship, also. Fun. Conversation."

"All the things that were missing from your marriage?" he said shrewdly.

"I prefer not to discuss my marriage." She took a deep breath. "But like a gentleman's mistresses, my... friends... must understand the rules."

"You'd do better to start by using the proper names for things," he advised. "How many lovers do you think you will need to prove your point?"

"If *you're* the first," she said coolly, "not many."

He raised an eyebrow at her. "I assume you intend to take these lovers just one at a time?"

Anne felt herself flush at the suggestion. It was no wonder he'd struck back, of course; she *had* aimed a low blow at his reputation, pointing out that merely having her name associated with his in such a way would be enough to destroy her with most of the London matrons.

"I ask, you understand, because as a rake I do maintain certain standards when I take a lover," he went on smoothly.

Her breath froze. Surely he couldn't be agreeing! "I...

*Standards?* You *dare* to speak to me of *standards* when you were in that room last night with Charlotte Barnsley?"

"A tongue like a fishing gaff," he said softly, and rose. "You ride, of course."

Anne was taken aback. What did that have to do with anything? "Naturally I do."

"There's a coaching inn on the road to Islington called the Red Dragon. I'll meet you there tomorrow morning. Ask the innkeeper to show you to Mr. Wilde's private parlor."

She simply looked at him. "Mr. Wilde?"

"Shall we say eight o'clock? You did tell me, I believe, that you're an early riser," Hawthorne said blandly. "You should return to the shop now, before your maid finds you missing."

"Why? If I was discovered here with you—"

He smiled. "It would cause an uproar, true enough. But make no mistake, Lady Keighley. If you proceed with your plan, I do not intend to be merely a convenient shill. I will be your lover in fact. You were quite right last night—I am *not* a gentleman." He bowed. "Until tomorrow."

❧

It was just as well that men of his class didn't make bets on what ladies might do, Thorne thought the next morning as he turned his horse over to a groom at the Red Dragon well before eight o'clock. If he'd been offered a bet on whether Lady Keighley would turn up to keep their appointment this morning, he wouldn't have known which side of the proposition to put his money on.

She was a determined little thing; that was clear
enough. And even when she tried to keep herself
tamped down to a ladylike murmur, that unruly tongue
of hers occasionally got the better of her. One minute
she'd been all society polish, refusing even to say the
word *lover*. The next she'd flared up at him about his
supposed taste in women.

It could go either way, he thought as he lounged in
the private parlor he'd engaged. All in all, however, if
his life depended on betting correctly, he'd have to put
his money on her getting cold feet and leaving him in
the lurch.

Which would be a shame—for Lady Keighley
showed promise of being the most diverting mistress
he'd had in some time. That odd combination of
stylish lady and fishwife intrigued him. Even odder
was the contrast between the woman who calmly
stated her intention to take multiple lovers and the one
who kissed like a spinster governess.

Or a virgin.

Now there was a thought to make a man's heart
quake. But surely not... she'd been married for
several years. On the other hand, it *was* possible.
Keighley had been an old man. And there had been
no heir.

Thorne nursed a tankard of ale while he thought
about it and wondered if he'd ever find out for certain.
Doubtful, since it was well past eight of the clock,
with not a glimpse of her.

Just then the door opened, and the innkeeper
showed a lady into the room. She wore a dark-green
riding habit trimmed with big gold buttons down the

front, and her dashing hat sported a dark veil that half concealed her face.

A surge of relief swept over Thorne. Not because she'd actually kept the appointment, of course—but because today she was dressed like a woman and not like a schoolroom miss. If she'd turned up wearing something frilly and white…

*Like what?* He jeered at himself. *You told her to ride. Ladies don't ride horses while wearing white muslin and lace.*

"You're late," he said.

Her chin came up almost defiantly. "I could hardly ask directions. Not if it was to look to my groom as if I'd wandered here at random."

"And just what did you tell the unfortunate groom who will be kicking his heels in the stable while waiting for us?"

"That I thought my horse was going lame. I'm to have tea and rest while he walks the mare and checks out the problem."

"Then I shall order tea." He nodded at the innkeeper, who bowed and went away. "And I was not scolding you, merely commenting."

She seemed to hesitate and then walked across the room to warm herself at the fire. Thorne watched the sway of her hips with appreciation.

"There's no need for the tea," she said. "I'd really rather… get this over with."

"I'm flattered that you're so eager, my dear."

She obviously heard the irony in his voice. "Well, you did say—"

"That I intend to be your lover. With full

cooperation from you, I might add. I'm not particularly interested in a rigid sacrifice."

She bit her lip and turned pink.

A faint tap on the door heralded a maidservant with a laden tray containing a pot of tea as well as the delicacies Thorne had ordered earlier. He passed the maid a coin and waited until the door had closed once more. "Strawberries?" he asked politely.

She didn't answer.

"If you're having second thoughts," Thorne said, "I should point out that I have never taken a woman by force, and I don't expect to change my habits in the future. All you need do is walk away, call for your groom, and return to your home and the marriage-minded men who will attend you there. We will never speak of this again, and in fact, we will meet as strangers."

She stood stock still for a moment, then reached up and removed her hat. "No second thoughts."

"Then come here and have a strawberry." She came across the room to him. He held out the berry, grasping it by the hull—but when she reached for it, he shook his head. "You know what I want you to do."

Her eyes dilated, but she didn't protest. Instead, she simply opened her mouth obediently and bit into the plump pink flesh. When she licked juice off her lower lip, Thorne felt the temperature in the room shoot up.

"Come and sit next to me," he said softly. "I think a peach next, don't you? We'll share this one."

She shook her head. "I didn't come here to eat."

"You came to experience the delights of the flesh. All of them." He brushed the back of his hand down her cheek and delighted in the little shiver that ran through her. "Do you think perhaps you could take off your gloves, at least?"

He peeled the peach while she worked the tight-fitting gloves off her hands, and he almost cut his finger because he was watching her instead of paying attention to his task. She had worn white gloves at the ball and doeskin ones at the jeweler's shop. This was the first time he'd seen her hands, and they did not disappoint. She had long, tapering fingers with perfectly shaped nails. If her hands were as soft as they looked…

"If you're not hungry, then feed me," he suggested.

She sighed a little, but she picked up a slice of peach and jabbed it tentatively toward his mouth. Thorne caught her wrist and guided her hand, licking a drop of juice from her fingertip and letting his tongue linger over her skin. She caught her breath.

He picked up another slice of the peach, touched it to her lower lip, and then took the other end of the slice between his teeth. Now only the space of a breath remained between them, and—unwilling to wait another instant—he closed it, feeling the trembling of her lips under his.

This time she opened to him immediately. A fast learner, he thought. A willing pupil…

He eased her back against the cushions. He could taste the strawberry and the peach, their flavors intensified by the heat of her mouth against his. She kissed him inexpertly, awkwardly—and desire shot through him, making him light-headed. His fingers caressed the gold button at her throat, easing it free. Then the next… until the bodice of her riding habit gaped open and her breasts strained to be free.

He bent his head and licked, watching as the thin white fabric of her chemise turned wetly transparent over the rosy nipple. She arched against him as he suckled her, and he had to grab for self-control to keep from spilling her straight onto the carpet where he could stretch her out under him and bury himself deep within her.

He backed off a bit, cupping her breasts with his hands as he kissed her again, long and slowly and so deeply that he almost forgot to breathe. Then he found the edge of her skirt and slipped one hand under the hem to touch the silken skin just above the top of her stocking. She gasped and quivered, and he hushed her with his mouth against hers, letting his fingertips simply rest against her thigh until she grew accustomed. Then, when she had gentled to his touch, he moved on, teasing her legs apart until he could rest his palm over the moist heat at her core and touch the hidden silky folds with a gentle finger.

She bucked against him, and he used her own movement to slip a fingertip inside her. She was hot and slick, and his mouth went dry with need. Then she whimpered a little and resisted, and he regained his senses. How could he have forgotten that—virgin or not—she was definitely inexperienced?

"It's all right," he said against her lips. "I won't hurt you. I promise." *Not this time, anyway,* he told himself firmly. If she truly *was* a virgin… but he'd deal with that when the moment came.

She took a long breath, and he felt her force herself to relax. *One day soon, you'll give me this without resistance,* he thought. Slowly he began to stroke her, gently, patiently.

He felt her breath catch, and then all her muscles tightened and he knew she was at the brink. She gasped with fear; he caught the sound on his lips and increased the motion of his finger, sending her over the edge.

And as she clutched at him, he promised himself that next time she would give him that all-encompassing response with him inside her. Next time.

The sooner, the better.

※

If her body had actually broken into pieces, Anne couldn't have been more shaken. Her muscles spasmed, sending rivulets of sensation through her. When the shudders finally died down, he stroked once more with his finger, and she jerked as heat flared once more deep inside her. "So responsive," he whispered, and slowly—as though reluctantly—he withdrew his hand.

It was obvious what would happen next. She should be grateful that he had been so patient, that he had given her pleasure first to make things easier. She forced herself to focus. "You will want…" she began, but her voice didn't work right.

"I want to see that look on your face—to feel that sweet eagerness—as I bury myself within you," he said.

*Sweet eagerness?* That might be promising too much. But men had a way of thinking that whatever they wanted was not only the woman's duty but her pleasure. Anne braced herself. Any moment now, he would pull her skirt higher, spread her legs, invade her body…

"That is exactly what I want," he murmured. "And exactly what I will have. But not today."

She looked at him, feeling bleary. Could he possibly have said…

"I prefer my creature comforts, you see. A bed. A locked door."

The door hadn't even been locked? How had that not occurred to her before? Anne was horrified. Anyone could have walked in…

*And that was what you wanted, Anne Keighley,* she reminded herself. To be discovered in his arms in a private room, actually in the act of making love… the word would have been all over London by nightfall, and her aim would have been accomplished.

But that hadn't happened, and so they weren't finished. Not until he was satisfied—and he had told her exactly what he intended to have.

"Besides, anticipation is an even better aphrodisiac than oysters," he went on. "Your groom—and your horse—must be getting restive by now. I'll send you word of our next meeting. In the meantime…"

His kiss was long and slow, like a drug stealing through her, robbing her of the ability to move. His hands skimmed over her body, caressing her skin as though the heavy wool of her riding habit was the sheerest silk. "Every whisper of the senses that you feel will be like me touching you again," he murmured, "until the next time we meet."

✖

*No question about it,* Thorne told himself. *I am an idiot.*

With a whole inn full of bedrooms just up a flight of stairs, with a woman in his arms who at the merest word would have welcomed him, with his body aching and screaming to possess her... he had sent her home instead.

But not for long. Not only would he have her—and soon—but the having would be far sweeter because of letting her have a day or two of anticipation. Why settle for a single morning's tumble in the Red Dragon's best bedchamber? If he played his hand right, Lady Keighley would be his for precisely as long as he chose.

So much for her plan to take multiple lovers. He would keep her so busy she wouldn't have time to look for his replacement and so sated that she wouldn't be able to think at all.

So he'd sent her home before the groom got curious and before her brother had reason to ask where she'd gone on such a long ride. And then he began planning their next assignation.

✖

"The mare's fine now, my lady," the groom said. "I don't know what could have been wrong, that you thought she was going lame."

"Better to be safe." Anne took the reins. "She's my favorite—it would be such a shame if she was injured." She gestured, and the groom lifted her into the sidesaddle. He climbed onto his horse as Anne settled her skirts. "No more exploring, I'm afraid—we must go straight home."

The groom looked at her as if she'd lost her wits.
Perhaps she had, Anne thought. Being in a hurry now
didn't make much sense after she had come so far and
dawdled for an hour over her supposed tea… which
she'd never even sipped.

*Every whisper of the senses you feel will be like me
touching you again,* Hawthorne had said. He was right.
The breeze on her face, even the brush of the fragile
veil against her cheek as she rode across London, sent
ripples of sensation through her.

She dismounted at the front door of her brother's
town house and let the groom take her horse round to
the mews. The butler let her in, bowing slightly as he
opened the door. "Lady Braxton has been asking for
you," he said loftily.

"Thank you, Digby. Where is she?"

From the morning room, Anne heard her sister-in-
law's voice. "Anne? Is that you? Come here, dear."

Anne grimaced but went to the door. Madeleine
was reclining on a chaise, looking quite fetching in
a morning gown of warm yellow. It reminded Anne
of peaches.

"My apologies, Maddy. I'd better not get too
close; I must smell of horse." And quite possibly other
things, she thought. Peaches and strawberries… and
Lord Hawthorne and lust…

"You must hurry and change. We could have
morning callers at any moment."

Freddy and the other men her brother was encour-
aging, no doubt. "I'll be as quick as I can." Anne ran
up the stairs.

She had ordered a bath before she left the house

that morning, and the tub stood ready in her bedroom. As Anne entered, the upstairs maid was pouring in the last brass can of steaming water. "I'm sorry for being delayed, Polly. How did you manage to have the water just right?"

"One of the footmen saw you coming around the corner, my lady, and slipped up to tell me," Polly said.

That was another potential hazard to keep in mind, Anne thought—footmen who saw everything that happened on the street… Really, this carrying on an intrigue was most complex.

Polly was watching her warily. "He ought not to have talked to me, I expect, my lady. If Mr. Digby finds out…"

"I'm not going to tell, Polly. Only—which footman is it? And is he courting you or just currying favor? Or has he tried to take liberties with you?"

Polly turned pink. "Only flirting, my lady, I'm sure. Nothing more than that. A footman and an upstairs maid…" Her tone was pensive.

There was no future for them; Anne could almost hear her say it. And Polly was right—junior servants couldn't afford to marry, even if their positions had allowed them to do so. Well, perhaps if Anne managed to set up her own household someday soon, she could do something about Polly and her suitor…

"If you don't mind helping me, Polly, I won't wait for Maria."

Polly shook her head and smiled. "I'd be happy to help. Miss Maria's gone to take care of Lady Braxton's wardrobe, anyway."

"Ah. She grew tired of waiting for me?" Anne was

relieved. Right now, she would just as soon not take the chance of Maria observing something that she might confide to her mistress. "I'm going to need a maid of my own, Polly. Maria doesn't have time to wait on two ladies now that the Season is in full swing. If you'd like the post…"

Polly's eyes grew round. "Oh, my lady—I'd be that pleased!"

"Then I'll take it up with Lady Braxton and the housekeeper." Anne was unfastening the gold buttons of her habit as she spoke, trying not to think of Hawthorne's hands toying with each fastener, spreading the bodice, and touching her breasts. At the mere memory, her nipples tightened. She slid into the water and tried to wash away his caresses…

No, that wasn't fair. During the four years of her marriage, she had sometimes tried to scrub her body free of her husband's touch, but if she was honest, Hawthorne's had been anything but unpleasant.

Why hadn't he pushed to finish what they had started? Lack of desire wasn't the reason—she was certain of that, for his voice had held an edge that she recognized. It was the sound of lust, lurking just beneath the civilized surface. What she didn't quite understand was why he had restrained himself.

*Anticipation is an even better aphrodisiac than oysters,* he had said. Well, perhaps for him it was. Hadn't he said something similar to Charlotte Barnsley that evening when Anne had been eavesdropping? For herself, however, Anne wanted things settled. The sooner, the better.

The warm water lapped over her skin, sending

rivers of sensation through her, and she could almost hear his voice. *Every whisper of the senses that you feel…*

From miles away, he had invaded her bath—just as he had said he would. She lay there for a moment, once more feeling his hands on her skin, as smooth and warm as the lavender-scented water… Anne sighed and reached for the towel Polly held out.

⟡

Anne turned down the red gown Polly offered, choosing instead a royal blue one with a high neckline and trimmed in cream-colored lace. She had barely reached the morning room where Madeleine was holding court with a couple of young matrons when Digby appeared and announced Freddy Lassiter.

Anne pasted a smile on her face and held out a hand to greet him.

Freddy thrust at her a bunch of deep red roses that were already wilting from the heat of his hands. "Don't know what's the matter with these," he said stiffly.

"They need water, the poor things," Anne said. "Digby, if you would bring a vase…"

"Why not take them into the breakfast room where you can arrange them easily?" Madeleine asked. "I'm sure Freddy will keep you company."

With the door closed tightly, no doubt, Anne thought. "I would not wish to miss out on the conversation, Maddy." She sorted through the flowers, wondering if any of them could be revived.

Freddy hovered over her. "I've talked to your brother. He's given his permission for me to pay my addresses to you. I tried to call on you yesterday to tell you, but you were not at home." His voice was not quite accusing.

"I had an errand to run. A dear friend down in Somerset has a new baby, and I was shopping for a christening gift." Digby brought her a vase full of water and a pair of secateurs, and Anne began pruning stems.

Freddy didn't seem to be listening. "Now that Braxton's said it's all right for me to court you—"

"Braxton may have said that," Anne pointed out, "but I have not."

"Oh, that's just missishness. I'm bound to be the favorite, Braxton says. I'm the youngest of your suitors and the most up to snuff."

*Then perhaps Braxton will want to marry you himself,* Anne thought tartly.

Digby reappeared. "Lady Braxton, Lord Hawthorne has called and wishes to know if the ladies are at home."

The roses slipped from Anne's suddenly nerveless hands and scattered across the carpet.

One of the matrons let out a squeak. "You're never going to let *him* in, Maddy!"

The other chimed, "You could say you're not receiving."

"Told him myself you'd be at home today," Freddy offered. "Met him on my way over here."

Anne bit her lip to keep from giggling at the glare Madeleine gave him. Braxton might think Freddy the favorite, but Lady Braxton's opinion of him had obviously suffered an abrupt change.

Madeleine frowned. "Hawthorne is on visiting terms with Braxton. And since he knows I'm receiving this morning…" She glowered at Freddy again. "I can hardly refuse him admittance. Show him in, Digby."

A strained silence dropped over the morning room. Even Freddy seemed to belatedly recognize his gaffe, and he bent to pick up the roses Anne had dropped—perhaps to stay out of Madeleine's sight.

Hawthorne had changed from riding clothes into morning garb. Until she saw him again, Anne didn't realize that she'd paid attention earlier to how elegantly his riding coat had fitted, how well cut and spotless his buckskins had been. Now he was simply gorgeous in a deep blue coat with a sapphire nestled in the folds of his cravat.

He bowed low over Madeleine's hand and begged pardon for intruding. "I hope I find you well, Lady Braxton. I come because I have been entrusted with a message for your sister."

His gaze came to rest on Anne, and she felt herself go warm all over. The nerve of the man! *I'll send you word of our next meeting,* he had said. Anne hadn't given much thought as to what form the message might take—she supposed she had expected a secret note tucked in a posy. Instead, here he was in person, looking unbearably handsome and aggravatingly at ease while making an assignation with his mistress under the very noses of three matrons who would be horrified if they knew what was really going on.

"You are looking very well this morning, Lady Keighley," he murmured. "London agrees with you?"

"As well as can be expected," Anne managed to say. The brush of his lips against her hand made her vibrate from head to toe.

"What beautiful roses," he said. "Just the color of ripe strawberries. It seems we have a friend in common," he went on, before she could do more than think about kicking him. "You remember Mrs. Wilde?"

*I'll never forget* Mr. *Wilde,* she almost said. *But I'd be amazed to hear he had a wife!*

His eyes—which turned out to be almost the same midnight blue as his coat—sparkled as if he'd read her thoughts. "I believe you met her some years ago when she was visiting her cousins near Keighley Park."

"I…" Anne said. Try as she might to read his expression, she could see nothing but polite inquiry in his eyes—as if he really didn't care whether she followed his lead or not. "I believe I do recall her. A very small lady."

She noticed that Madeleine was watching her intently and improvised. "A dear soul. Rather round, I recall. Quite interested in…" She fumbled madly for something that would sound feasible and remembered the ornament in the jeweler's shop. "Butterflies. She was very lively—for her age."

"And for her condition," Hawthorne agreed solemnly. "She seemed pleased to discover that we are slightly acquainted and to hear that you are now residing in London. She begged me to ask you to visit her at her home at Number 5 Upper Seymour Street. Tomorrow, if possible—at three."

Madeleine said, "I don't believe I could accompany you then, Anne. Another day, perhaps."

"Your pardon, Lady Braxton," Hawthorne said. "Mrs. Wilde lives very quietly. Her health often prevents her from rising from her bed at all, and even when she is able to be up, she is never able to receive more than a single visitor at a time."

As the double meanings mounted up, Anne wanted to roll her eyes.

"May she count on you, Lady Keighley?" Now there was no doubt about the challenging glint in his eyes. Did he actually doubt that she'd go through with it?

"Of course," she said.

Freddy offered, "I'll take you."

Her gaze tangled for an instant with Hawthorne's, and Anne thought they were both going to burst out laughing. Then he said, sounding only slightly strangled, "I will take my leave of you and convey the message. Thank you for allowing me to intrude, Lady Braxton." He bowed beautifully and departed.

"Well," said one of the matrons. "*I've* never heard of a Mrs. Wilde."

"Why didn't she just send a note if she wanted Anne to visit her?" said the other.

"Her health," Anne said. Her lips felt stiff. "It's… not possible for her to use her hands."

"More likely she can't write at all," the matron sniffed. "If Hawthorne knows her, she must be a dodgy sort."

"But why is he willing to be her errand boy?" the first one asked.

"She must be a neighbor," the other put in. "Upper Seymour Street is right around the corner from Hawthorne's town house on Portman Square."

Madeleine said nothing at all. She was staring at Anne, with a little wrinkle cutting between her very elegant eyebrows.

Anne rescued the few roses that had survived Freddy's grip and began arranging them in the vase. So she was going to see Hawthorne again tomorrow.

Tomorrow. It seemed a long way away…

Visiting Mrs. Wilde, indeed!

❧

Thorne managed to hold out until he was well away from Braxton's house before he gave in to a bellow of laughter that startled his horses and made his groom look at him with concern.

If not for Freddy's ingenuous offer to deliver Anne to him tomorrow, he'd have enjoyed staying another half hour to torment her. But it was just as well he'd had to leave. It was much too soon to be dropping the sort of hints that would lead Lady Braxton to ask uncomfortable questions.

He could wait until tomorrow… barely.

In fact, however, he did not have to wait till the morrow, for he saw Lady Keighley again that evening.

Thorne was standing at the edge of the ballroom floor as she finished the figures of a country dance, and he thought that she almost forgot her steps when she caught sight of him. As she left the floor, he smiled and bowed slightly and then turned back to Hastings, who was telling him in interminable detail about yet another horse. Thorne was far too experienced at stalking prey to rush the hunt—and he was not naive enough to think that this particular quarry was yet guaranteed to be his.

So he half listened, and when Hastings finally wandered off to the card room, Thorne flicked a glance across the ballroom—not that he needed to; he could have told within three feet where Lady Keighley was—and then took a meandering path through the watchers to where she stood.

With Lady Stone beside her. Well, that couldn't be helped—though he'd rather not be carrying on his intrigues directly under Lucinda's eagle eye, especially when she'd come so close to shopping him at her own ball just two nights since.

Lady Keighley's quick little inrush of breath told him that she was just as much on edge as he could have wished, and that sent heat surging through him. "I came to beg for this waltz, Lady Keighley, if you have it free."

"I don't, my lord," she said.

He reached for the little dance card dangling from her wrist and looked down the list of names. Freddy Lassiter's scrawl was there twice. The fellow was beginning to be a serious annoyance.

"I see you managed to cadge an introduction, Thorne," Lady Stone said. "Do take the man off and dance with him, Anne, or he'll stand here and bore me with all his conquests. I'll tell Freddy you had a better offer."

Thorne gave Lady Keighley the space of a breath to deal with her warring emotions. He could almost see her thinking about which would be the greater risk, taking the floor with him or dancing with Freddy Lassiter. After a moment, the first notes of the waltz sounded, and he took her hand and escorted her onto the floor.

"Do you?" she asked abruptly. "Tell Lady Stone about all your conquests, I mean."

"Certainly not—no matter how much she begs for the details. And thank you for the compliment." She frowned, obviously puzzled, and he went on, "I find it quite flattering that you assume Lady Stone would not be bored to hear of my exploits."

"Oh. That wasn't intended as a compliment."

"I was afraid not. But I shall take it that way nevertheless." He swept her around the room, delighting in the ever-so-slight tremor of her fingers as they lay in his and the way that her body responded to the smallest pressure of his hand against the small of her back. "Will you come for a drive with me tomorrow?"

She looked up at him in utter astonishment. "What of Mrs…" She swallowed the name.

"Mrs. Wilde? I could deliver you to her door."

"You just don't want me to take Freddy up on his offer. Don't fret… I will not do so. But I hardly need your escort."

"As you wish. Though a turn in the park beforehand would certainly make tongues wag nicely."

She looked at him in consternation—as if she'd forgotten the entire point of their agreement for a few moments, but now it had come crashing in on her again. "And this waltz won't?"

"It's a step," he admitted.

"You could sweep me off to a little alcove. Don't even try to tell me you don't know where to find one."

"Of course I do. But there's no challenge there. No creative spark to the idea. And I'll do nothing to put tomorrow in jeopardy."

Her eyes had gone wide and dark.

How, he wondered, could she not recognize the

passion in herself when he could see it so clearly? How was it possible for her to talk glibly and sensibly about taking lovers when the barest touch banished all rational thought from her head?

The fact was that he would be doing Lady Keighley a great favor by teaching her the game of love—before she fell in with some jackanapes who would use her passion to manipulate her.

The thought of her being used was an unpleasant one. To banish it, he pulled her just a little closer and swept her once more around the floor.

"Is there really a Mrs. Wilde?" she asked.

"You'll find that out tomorrow," he murmured as the music ended. *Along with a great many other things, my dear...*

When he returned her to Lady Stone, Freddy Lassiter was standing there, fists clenched. "I should call you out, Hawthorne."

"By all means," Thorne said sweetly, "if you wish to make a cake of yourself. You were not here when the music started... I was. The alternative was for Lady Keighley to miss out on the waltz." He let his gaze rest on her face. "Something she would have very much regretted."

"Don't be a fool, Freddy," Lady Stone said sharply. "The man pilfered a dance, that's all. I'm sure someday you can return the favor. Or do you truly wish to commit suicide by meeting Hawthorne with pistols at dawn?"

Freddy backed down.

"Idiot," Lady Stone said. "Freddy, take Lady Keighley off and get her a cool drink before she wilts."

Thorne watched as the pair moved away. He

was not surprised—but he was pleased—when Lady Keighley looked back over her shoulder and colored deliciously when she caught his eye.

Lady Stone rapped his knuckles with her fan. "Come, Thorne. Stop gawking at the girl and promenade with me—to atone for your many sins. What are you up to this time, pray tell?"

"Atoning," he said.

She sniffed. "I'll bet."

&#x223D;

The house at Number 5 Upper Seymour Street was small and neat and very quiet. The entrance was tucked farther back from the street than the other houses along the way, and every window was discreetly curtained. The front was well kept, with the step scrubbed clean and the door freshly painted in a rich, shiny black.

The absence of a knocker made Anne pause for an instant. It was the universal signal that the residents were not at home or that callers were not welcome.

But, of course, that was no surprise, Anne thought. Any woman Thorne had in keeping would not be encouraged to entertain anyone other than him—and he, no doubt, carried a key.

The footman who had helped her out of Madeleine's carriage looked around for a knocker and then gave her a quizzical glance. *Now what?* Anne wondered. She had tried to discourage him from walking her to the door, but he had insisted. Or rather, she suspected, Madeleine had ordered him to insist.

Before she could gather her thoughts, the door

swung open and she found herself facing an elderly and very correct butler.

"I'm... I was asked to call on Mrs. Wilde," she said.

"Come in, my lady." He looked down his nose at the footman. "The carriage need not wait. Mrs. Wilde will arrange to convey her guest home."

The footman sputtered a bit, but the butler stepped back into the hallway. Anne hesitated for the merest instant. Then she crossed the threshold, and the door closed behind her.

The butler did not pause. "This way, my lady." He started up the stairs.

Anne's breath caught in her throat. But she was committed now. There was no backing out.

At the top of the second flight, he tapped on a door, opened it, and closed it behind her without a word.

She had expected a bedroom. Instead, she found herself in a small jewel of a sitting room that looked as if it had never been used. She noted cream silk walls, heavy velvet drapes, delicate furniture and—standing near the fireplace—a very tall man who turned with a smile to greet her.

"I hardly think you're Mrs. Wilde," she said calmly.

"I'll be happy to entertain you in her stead." Hawthorne's lips lingered on her hand.

"Is there really a Mrs. Wilde?"

"Such a curious lady you are. Ask her servants, and they will assure you they serve her."

"I'm not asking the servants. I'm asking you."

"Then I am forced to admit that Mrs. Wilde is a figment of my imagination—unless you choose to step into the role."

"It appears I've already done so. I'm here—and the butler sent my carriage away."

"Yes," he said thoughtfully. "Mrs. Wilde has a very nice one that you may use at any time."

He had actually set up not only a house but a *stable* for his flirts? *How very convenient*, Anne thought. No wonder he'd said at the Red Dragon that he preferred his creature comforts... he had so many of them! She must be nothing more than one in a long series of women he had brought here...

Which she had known all along; that was, after all, the reason she had approached him in the first place. Still, the thought was oddly depressing. She tried to stifle it as she took off her hat and stripped away her gloves. "Shall we get down to it?"

"Certainly. You seem to be in a hurry."

"I see no need to play games." She nodded toward a connecting door. "I assume that's the bedroom? I'll just go get ready, then."

He waved a hand in a sort of dismissal. As she crossed the room, he moved toward a tray she hadn't seen before, nestled on a stand near a comfortable settee, and pulled the stopper from a crystal decanter.

Anne paused. "Is that brandy?"

"Would you care to join me?" He splashed the rich liquid into a glass.

"No. I..." *It doesn't matter,* she told herself.

"What is it, my dear?"

"It's just... I don't care for the smell of brandy. Or... the taste." Her voice was very small; she could barely hear herself.

His eyes narrowed.

THE MISTRESS' HOUSE

What a stupid, *stupid* thing to say. Gentlemen and brandy were a natural combination—and even more so when a woman tried to get between them. He'd probably have an extra glass just because of what she'd said...

She fled through the door and closed it behind her, leaning against it as she fought back tears. This was weakness, and she would *not* be weak! But her fingers shook too much to unfasten her dress.

She tried to inventory the room to distract herself from the image in her mind of him drinking deeply before he came to her. But all she could see was the enormous bed, under a green-velvet canopy trimmed in gold, with white silk side curtains held back with gold tassels, the coverlet turned down, and the pillows plumped.

She wondered how many women he had brought to this room. The deep green and gold would be perfect colors for Charlotte Barnsley, with her red hair... though the white silk hangings would be less friendly to her complexion...

*It's not my business who else he has brought here,* she reminded herself. *That wasn't part of our arrangement.*

The door opened and Hawthorne came in. He looked grim, and Anne closed her eyes and berated herself once more. Why had she been so stupid? Why hadn't she just stayed quiet?

"That's why you froze up when I kissed you at Lucinda's ball that night. I'd been drinking brandy."

She darted a glance at him and looked quickly away. "I'm sorry. I should not have said..."

"Keighley drowned himself in brandy and came to

your bed sotted with it. That's where you learned to dislike the taste."

Since it wasn't a question, she didn't bother to answer.

He swore under his breath. "It's a good thing for him that he's dead, or I'd be sorely tempted to kill him. My dear..." He cupped her chin in his hand, raised her face to his, and kissed her, slowly and far more gently than she had expected.

She was trembling when he raised his head. "You didn't drink it after all. You did that for me?"

"A man does not need brandy when he can drink his fill of you," he whispered, and she was lost.

He undressed her with more care than any lady's maid who had ever attended her, caressing each square inch of skin as he uncovered it. He kissed the bend of her elbow, stroked the nape of her neck, and nuzzled the edge of her shoulder blade. He released her hair from its knot and used the long black strands of silk to tease and caress. By the time he'd disposed of the last of her clothing, she was writhing in his arms, trying in vain to drive him as far beyond reason as he'd sent her, and when he scooped her up in his arms and laid her on the bed, she tried to pull him down to her.

"Don't you want me to take my clothes off, too?" he murmured, and freed himself.

She lay against the pillows and watched him take off his shirt, admiring the breadth of his shoulders, the dusting of dark hair across his chest, the strength apparent in his arms. Then he shed his trousers, and her breath caught. The size of him...

She looked away, but he seemed to read her

thoughts. "He hurt you, didn't he?" he said. "I won't. I promise."

"I know you don't mean to." She didn't understand why she was so certain of that, but she knew it none-theless—any pain he caused would not be intentional. Still... how could he help it?

For a long moment, he simply looked at her, as if feasting on the sight. Then the mattress shifted as he stretched out beside her, leaning over her and propped on one elbow. She moved a little, turning onto her back and spreading her knees, and he gave her a preda-tory smile.

"Oh, no, my dear. You might be in a hurry, but I'm not. I've waited too long to rush through our pleasure now."

"It's only been two days," she protested—and wondered herself how they could possibly have trav-eled so far in so little time.

"It feels as if I've wanted you forever." His fingertips skimmed along her body, from knee to throat. His touch was light, but Anne felt as if she'd been branded, claimed in some primitive ritual. Then he kissed her breast, and she gave up thinking altogether.

He caressed her slowly and thoroughly, moving gradually down her body until she was whimpering. Each feather-light touch of his fingertips sent shivers over her, and each caress made her skin ache for the next. His tongue teased against her nipple and then released her—and the warmth of his mouth, followed by the touch of the cool air, sent a dart of awareness straight through her.

When he gently spread her legs and moved over

her, she sighed a little in regret. She'd liked it so much, the way he had touched her—and she didn't want him to stop. It was too bad, really, that the touching and the gentleness couldn't last forever—but very soon, she knew, she would feel the pressure and the discomfort as he entered her, the out-of-control lunging, the weight of his body as he gained release...

But he didn't roll on top of her. She opened her eyes just as he bent his head to the moist curls over her most private area. "You can't!" she protested.

"But I can." He breathed gently on her, and his warm breath sent her straight over the edge.

After that she wasn't sure what he did—only that he didn't stop. With each new touch, before she could gather herself and get a breath, he swept her on to the next and even stronger sensation. His tongue brushed a sensitive little spot that she'd never known she had, and Anne shrieked and surged up off the mattress.

"I gather you like that?" he whispered, and the vibration of his voice sent her into a spiraling cloud of sensation. But instead of satisfying, his touch now made the hollowness inside her ache. She had never felt anything like it—this intense emptiness, the fierce need to be filled...

She was aghast at her own reactions but at the same time too frenzied to stop her body from demanding more. If she'd been able to think clearly, she would have been amused by the contradiction. She was shocked at the very idea of wanting him to possess her in that way, while at the same instant she was frantic to pull him inside her and reach satisfaction...

She rocked her hips, trying to urge him closer, and clutched at his shoulders, trying to pull him toward her.

And then quite suddenly he was simply gone from her. No more tormenting touch between her legs, no more big, warm body looming over her, promising— and delivering—delight…

She wanted to scream, to pull him back, to demand—she wasn't sure what. "Please," she managed to say.

"A moment's patience, my sweet," he said. His voice had a rough edge to it. "I'm protecting you— that's all. I couldn't stop now, no matter what."

There were no more contradictions in her mind. The instant when she thought he had abandoned her had been too awful to bear. She didn't know exactly what she waited for, but she knew she must have it—she must have *him*—or the frustration would kill her.

When he came back to her, she wrapped her legs around him and buried her hands in his hair, deter- mined not to release him until he'd given her what she wanted. Then, finally, he slid slowly inside her, filling her hollowness with heat and power.

He had been telling the truth, she thought in awe. It *didn't* hurt. In fact, it felt so incredibly right that tears stung her eyelids, and she tried to blink them away.

"Look at me," he demanded, and she could do nothing but obey.

She felt his body tense against her, and then he brushed a hot tear from her temple. "I'm sorry," he whispered. "I've hurt you after all."

She shook her head, and he kissed her eyelids and very slowly started to pull away.

He would do that? Interrupt his own pleasure because he thought he'd hurt her? He'd said a moment earlier that he couldn't stop, no matter what... but he *would* stop nevertheless?

"No," she said. "No—it's fine. I want..." She couldn't find the words. She didn't know the words. Instead she tightened her legs around him, slid her hands down his back, and pulled him more deeply inside her.

She hadn't thought it could get better—and yet the more of him she possessed, the more she wanted.

She gasped with the pleasure of it and whispered, "Make love to me."

He stayed still for an instant, as if he didn't trust that she was telling the truth.

Instinct told her what to do; she raised her hips slightly, allowing him to penetrate further yet, and she felt his body jolt with the realization that she meant it. His eyes locked with hers, and he began moving. Each long, slow thrust lifted her toward an unseen, unknown goal; each withdrawal made her fear she could never reach it...

She was staring into his eyes when she could bear no more, when she screamed and shattered. He held himself still as her muscles clenched around him, and then he thrust hard and deep, gave a groan, and collapsed against her.

They lay tangled together, breathless. Every muscle in her body was still quivering, totally out of control. Her release at the Red Dragon had been a surprise;

this had been a revelation. She was still trying to sort out what had happened to her—exactly how he had made her world shift—when he said, "I hurt you, didn't I? At first, I mean." He sounded frustrated, angry.

For a moment Anne's mind withdrew, afraid of what might come next—and then she realized he wasn't angry at her but at himself. "No. You didn't."

"You were crying." He touched her temple with a gentle fingertip, as if retracing the path of the tear he had brushed away.

"Because it was so beautiful. Because I've never felt that way before. Because you are very..." *Skilled? Wonderful? Thoughtful? Romantic? Stop blathering this instant,* Anne told herself, *before you say something that makes him think you've forgotten this is only a brief affair!*

He looked intrigued. "I'm... what? Please do go on, my lady."

"*Arrogant*, to think that I might wish to flatter you!"

He laughed. "Then it *was* something good you were going to say about me—if you think I have cause to be arrogant over it. I shall treasure your compliment forever."

"You're quite certain of yourself, aren't you?"

"It seems I have reason to be," he pointed out. "You do not appear to be disappointed." His lips grazed her jawline and moved slowly down her throat, and his tongue flicked playfully against the hollow at the base.

Her senses stirred once more. "No wonder people take lovers," she admitted, trying to sound casual. "I've never felt so... relaxed."

His eyebrow quirked in obvious disbelief. "Are you certain *relaxed* is the word you want? If it is, I've obviously done something wrong."

*No,* she thought. *You did everything just right.*

She was looking for a way to say so without adding fuel to the man's already immense self-confidence when he shifted his weight and freed himself from her arms.

"No," she whispered. "Don't go."

"Not in such a hurry anymore?" he teased.

She sat up a little and watched with curiosity as he took off a little silken-looking pouch and put it aside. "I knew, of course, that there are ways... things a man can use..."

"To prevent a pregnancy. Yes."

"But that isn't necessary. Not with me."

He stood very still. "You sound quite certain."

She shrugged. "After four years of marriage and no child, the doctors said..." *It's a* good *thing,* she reminded herself. *Especially now.* She had no reason to be feeling an inexplicable sadness.

He came back to the bed, gathering her closely into his arms—skin to skin, warmth to warmth. She saw desire flare once more in his eyes and felt it in the pressure of his body against hers. "You can't," she said uncertainly. "Not *already.*"

"But I can, my glorious Mrs. Wilde," he whispered against her lips. "And so can you."

This time was different because she knew what to expect. She knew what he would do and how he would bring her to satisfaction. At least she thought she did—but though anticipation certainly built her own arousal to a feverish pitch, she soon found she could not, after all, predict how he would touch her or what he would do next.

He seemed to be on an expedition to discover which sections of her body were most exquisitely sensitive. She hadn't known that her elbow was one of them until he kissed it, sending shafts of heat through her. But once she was aware... "I'll never again be able to walk along a street with a gentleman holding my arm," she gasped.

He raised his head. "Oh, no. You've nothing to fret about. It only works when the arm's bare." He flicked his tongue against the delicate skin inside her elbow, just over the vein. "Unless," he added thoughtfully, "you're with me, of course. Then it won't matter how many layers you're wearing. The moment I put my hand on you here..." He cupped her elbow with his palm, big and warm and sensuous, and smiled as she nearly jolted off the mattress.

"Or for that matter here... or here..." He brushed her hand, her wrist, her waist—all the spots where a gentleman might touch a lady even when they were in the most public place—and she knew that the next time they danced together, he would be seducing her even as they spun around the floor, for each touch would remind her of this.

She writhed in his arms, and he seemed to take pity on her, filling her once more. But then he was still, holding himself deeply inside her while he nibbled her throat and toyed with her hair, until she learned how to stroke him in return with her inner muscles. Then he laughed and began to move.

His thrusts were long and slow and languorous,

as though he was caressing her—or tormenting her, Anne thought. She urged him deeper, arching to meet each thrust with one of her own, until she was rewarded when his breath grew harsh and uneven, his thrusts jerky. Her own climax was even more explosive this time, and a moment later, he gave a hoarse cry and shuddered against her, burying his face in her hair as he came.

❧

When the small, elegant, unmarked carriage delivered her home, Digby admitted her with a bow. "Lord and Lady Braxton are at tea, my lady."

Anne took a deep breath and waited for the butler to open the drawing-room door for her. It required immense effort not to brush a hand over her hair, trying to reassure herself that it would pass inspection. She reminded herself that the neat little maid who had come to help her dress—Mary, her name was—had been very skilled, as well as surprisingly respectful.

*But then she probably takes care of all the mistresses,* Anne thought, and wondered again exactly how many of them had paraded through that bedroom.

Madeleine set the teapot down on the low table in front of the fire and looked directly at Anne. "Digby tells me you sent the carriage home while you paid your call."

"It seemed foolish to keep it waiting about for hours when you might need it."

"But how did you know your call would require hours?" Madeleine asked softly.

*Watch your step, Anne.* "I assumed we would have

much to talk of. If my visit had been shorter, Mrs. Wilde would still have sent me safely home."

"*Much to talk of?* An elderly woman you met once at Keighley Park and barely remembered? And don't you find it odd that a woman who never goes out keeps a carriage?"

Braxton bit into a cream cake. "Now, Maddy. Maybe it makes it easier for her friends to come and visit."

Madeleine opened her mouth and then obviously thought better of it.

"Anyway," Braxton went on, "it seems to me that Anne was being thoughtful. You were saying last week we needed to add another carriage, now that she's with us." He finished off the pastry and inspected the cake stand. "But I must say I think your time would be better spent in society, Anne, rather than dancing attendance on an invalid. I saw Freddy at the club today. He was looking downcast because you wouldn't go driving with him this afternoon."

"He knew perfectly well I had a previous appointment and could not break it. Braxton, why are you so set on me spending time with Freddy Lassiter?"

"Not Freddy necessarily." Braxton shrugged. "But how you can decide on a husband if you don't even look around is beyond me."

"I've told you—I don't care to choose a husband."

"Don't be silly. You just need some liveliness in a man after old Keighley."

"Freddy's certainly lively," Anne murmured. She wondered if Thorne was right and Freddy was seeking a fortune. Or did Thorne merely think the worst of him?

*Because he's jealous, I suppose? Don't be a fool.*

"Indeed," Braxton said, "Freddy knows how to have fun. You could learn a lot from him, whether you want to marry him or not. I told him you'd drive with him tomorrow. It will be good for you to get out and to be seen in the park, not just in the ballrooms."

Digby came in, carrying a small, brightly wrapped package. "This was just delivered for you, Lady Keighley."

Anne accepted it warily. But she could think of no option except to open the parcel—no possible excuse for delaying until she was alone. The only marking was her name, but her heart told her who must have sent it.

*You asked to be ruined,* she reminded herself, *and this just might do it.*

And what if it did? At least then Braxton would stop throwing men at her, and Madeleine would stop asking uncomfortable questions—indeed, would probably stop speaking to her at all—and Anne would no longer have to watch every word, every look, every thought…

She pulled on the cord and loosened the wrapping paper. Inside the small box was the exquisite enameled butterfly, its wings edged with tiny garnets and topaz, that she'd seen in the jewelry shop.

She opened the card. *The jewel of the collection,* it said. *With the compliments of Mrs. Wilde. May she expect the pleasure of your company again tomorrow?*

Anne was mortally certain Hawthorne hadn't been thinking about butterflies, or small enameled ornaments, when he'd composed that note. He'd been thinking of her—the jewel of *his* collection. At least, she supposed, the current jewel.

*Tomorrow…* a delicious little curl of anticipation tickled her from head to toe. Tomorrow they would once again explore…

Madeline was looking over her shoulder at the note. "What a pity it is you can't go." Insincerity dripped from her voice.

"Why can't I?" Anne asked absently.

"Because you have a previous engagement—with Freddy. And you've just finished telling us how strongly you feel about not changing your plans once they've been arranged." She picked up her cup. "Have you not, dearest Anne?"

❧

The last place Thorne would have chosen to spend an evening was at the opera. But that, his sources told him, was where Lady Keighley would be—so that was where he would go as well.

Ordinarily, after the sort of afternoon they'd shared, he would have sent a gift and then let a few days—perhaps even a week—go by before issuing another invitation. It wasn't wise to let a lady think that he had nothing better to do than dance attendance on her.

But in this case, wisdom seemed to have nothing to do with it. Who was he trying to fool? Not himself, that was certain. He hadn't been able to get enough of her—and far too soon, the time had come when he had had no choice but to summon the carriage and send her home.

So he had dispatched a footman with the jeweled butterfly, including that suggestive little note, and then he'd sat back with a glass of wine to relive the afternoon. What a fascinating mix she was—part lady and part... *not,* he thought with a smile.

He was still in the little sitting room on Upper Seymour Street, planning their encounter for the following day, when the footman returned with her reply.

It was brief and to the point, advising him that she could not call on the morrow and had no idea when she would once more be free.

He shouldn't have been surprised, of course: A lady could scarcely disappear from society for two afternoons in a row without causing comment. He should have known better than to suggest it.

But that was exactly the sort of comment she'd said she wanted, he reminded himself. Though perhaps it was not the sort he wished to invite. Not yet, at any rate—for once society knew of their affair, a great deal of the intrigue would vanish, and with it the fun, the challenge, the fascination.

No, he wasn't ready for Lady Keighley to be known as his newest mistress. Not now, and perhaps not for a long while to come. At least, not as long as afternoons with his glorious Mrs. Wilde were as satisfying as today had been.

Still, that note of hers hadn't simply been a refusal. It had been stiff, curt, almost cold—and he wasn't about to let her dismiss him like that.

He dined at his house on Portman Square, looked in at his club, and arrived at the opera just before intermission. Lady Stone spotted him and waved from her box; Thorne bowed in acknowledgment and made his way across the crowd to join her.

"You're looking well fed," she greeted him. "And not on roast beef, I'll wager."

He kissed her hand and pretended not to hear the remark.

She gave him a beady look. "What's this I hear about a new fancy of yours? A Mrs. Wilde?"

"Hardly a fancy. A neighbor, rather." Thorne's gaze roved the boxes and found Lady Keighley, wearing a dress of deep garnet red that left her remarkable shoulders nearly bare. Freddy was right next to her, of course—probably looking down her cleavage—but there were others as well. The entire collection of suitors must be there. She'd mentioned four serious candidates—but, of course, that had been a couple of days ago. By now, Braxton might have given his permission to another half dozen. One thing about the man, he didn't seem to play favorites.

"A busy place tonight, Braxton's box," Lady Stone said. "Ah—here comes Charlotte Barnsley. I haven't seen her since the night of my ball."

Thorne wanted to groan. Instead he did the pretty by bowing over Charlotte's hand when she fluttered into Lady Stone's box, her escort trailing behind. "What a lovely surprise to see you here, Thorne," Charlotte cooed and then dropped her voice. "I've been packing everything I—we—could possibly need for the house party."

Oh, yes. Arabella Winchester's house party—the one he wouldn't have been caught dead at, even before Lady Keighley had caught his eye... Surely he hadn't forgotten to send Charlotte a note to say he would not be going? It was true that his mind had been preoccupied with other matters ever since Lady Stone's ball… But no, he remembered telling Perkins exactly what to say—it had taken quite a little effort to get the phrasing just right.

Damnation. He'd looked away from the Braxton box for one brief instant, and Lady Keighley had vanished. No, there she was; she'd just been hidden behind the considerable bulk of one of her suitors.

"Whatever are you looking at?" Charlotte asked. She darted a glance at her escort and lowered her voice. "Perhaps we could travel to the Winchesters' estate together. When will you be going?"

Thorne suppressed a shudder at the idea of a full day in a closed carriage with Charlotte Barnsley. "I'm not."

Charlotte's eyes narrowed. "You told me you were going."

"I told you I'd been invited," he corrected as gently as he could. "But I'm staying in town instead. Did you not receive my note?"

"Well, of course I did," she said impatiently. "But I didn't think you *meant* it—only that you wanted it to appear to be happenstance when we met at the Winchesters' after all. I even showed it to Barnsley so he wouldn't be suspicious."

Thorne felt his jaw going slack and was grateful that he'd expended so much effort on that little missive. There was nothing that Barnsley could possibly object to, was there? Surely Perkins wouldn't have taken it upon himself to add a flourish or two of his own… No, not straitlaced, reliable Perkins. "I had no such Machiavellian motives, Lady Barnsley—I have business that requires my presence in town."

"Yes, that's what your note said. *Business!*" Her tone made the word sound like a curse. But she seemed to think better of it, for she reined in her temper with an effort that made her face go red—a shade that did not go at all well with her hair. "I don't suppose you'd really be staying because of someone named Mrs. Wilde, instead?"

"Do you know her?" Thorne kept his tone casual. "How interesting."

"I do not. Perhaps you can introduce me."

It was amazing, he thought, that Charlotte could talk at all with her teeth clenched so tightly. "She doesn't go out in society," he said.

"But I understand she receives callers."

"I will ask if she would like you to visit her," he said politely, "when she's well enough to again receive me."

Charlotte turned her back on him and flounced out. Her escort shrugged, bowed to Lady Stone, and followed.

"Yes," Lady Stone said meditatively, "she really *is* as thick as she seems. You know, dear boy, I was quite beginning to think you'd lost your touch—letting Charlotte Barnsley reel you in. Such a relief it is to know better."

Thorne barely heard her. He was once again eyeing the Braxton box, looking for Lady Keighley. But this time there was truly nothing to see.

The box was empty. She was gone.

❧

Anne was floating on a sea of white silk, her body aflame as he caressed her, when suddenly an anxious little voice interfered. "My lady? Oh, do wake up, my lady."

She blinked. "Polly?" Her voice felt rough, and her body ached with desire—the more so because this afternoon, instead of lying once more in his arms, she would be driving out with Freddy.

*This will never do,* she thought. If Hawthorne could invade her dreams... How he would enjoy knowing that!

"There's a message for you."

Anne sat up, puzzled, and reached for the much-folded slip of paper Polly held out. "What time is it, anyway?"

"Not yet eight. But James..." Polly colored a bit. "He told me the man who gave it to him said it was important you get it right away."

"James being your tame footman, I presume?" Anne pressed the paper flat.

*My dearest early riser: Join me this morning? I shall wait for you.*

It was not signed, of course. Hawthorne wouldn't have taken that much of a risk, in case one of the servants had an attack of conscience or the slip of paper went astray. But there was no question who the note had come from or what it meant.

She toyed with the paper for a moment, delaying. "And where did James come by this interesting missive?"

"From a groom he knows. I don't know who he works for, but James said it's one of the grand houses on a big square."

She shouldn't go, of course. She should burn the note, send Polly away, pull the coverlet over her head, and return to her dreams...

*Why, when you can have the reality instead?*

It was almost as if Hawthorne himself stood there, asking the question. Anne found herself pushing back the blankets, helpless to resist.

"We're going shopping," she told Polly. "At least, *you're* going shopping, and so far as anyone else knows, I'll have been just a step or two away in the next shop the entire time you're going up and down Oxford Street."

Polly chewed her lip doubtfully.

Inspiration struck. "We'll take James with us to carry all the bundles," Anne added. "Which means— as long as you manage to collect a convincing number of bundles to prove how busily we've shopped—I don't care a rap what the two of you do with the rest of the morning."

Polly's face started to glow. "Oh, my lady! I'm sure James will have some ideas of what we might do."

Anne didn't doubt it a bit.

*And who are you to talk, my lady?* she scolded herself.

Half an hour later, they set off in a little parade— Anne wrapped in her best dark purple cloak, Polly following two steps behind, and James bringing up the rear. As soon as they crossed Oxford Street and left the shops behind, Anne pulled her hood closer and walked a little faster.

She paused in front of Number 5 Upper Seymour Street, and when the door didn't immediately open, she wondered for the first time if she might have made a mistake. He had not, after all, actually specified where to meet—or when. He might have reminded her of being an early riser because he wanted her to come to the Red Dragon…

No, surely not. He liked his creature comforts; he'd said so himself. And she was certain he would no longer be satisfied with a romp in the private parlor of an inn—not after their last tryst.

She looked across the street to where Polly and James hovered, wondering if she should summon them to escort her home.

The door swung open as before, but this time the butler wasn't the one who stood in the shadowed foyer. It was Hawthorne. She stepped across the threshold into warmth—and pleasure—in his arms.

❦

She was cold. Thorne could see it in her face and feel it in the brush of her wool cloak against his hands. Clearly, she had not so much as hesitated; the moment she received his message, she had hurried to him… Something primitive stirred deep inside him— something he didn't want to think about. "You're freezing," he said, and swept her up in his arms. "I've had a fire lit upstairs."

"Without waiting for me?" she murmured.

He smiled at the playful tone. "It's a poor substitute compared to the one we'll kindle together, Mrs. Wilde." He didn't stop in the sitting room but carried her straight into the bedroom, which was warm with firelight and fragrant with beeswax candles everywhere.

She was just as impatient as she had been the day before, he sensed—but from a different, far more delightful cause. Today, she knew the pleasure that awaited her… or at least she thought she did. He still had a few surprises in mind.

Her eagerness fed his own, and he undressed her quickly and, without a word, joined her in the bed.

She whispered, "I dreamed of you last night, my lord."

"Did you?" He kissed her, long and slowly. "Perhaps you should tell me what we did in your dream. It might be more fun when you're awake, and we can share."

She turned a shade of pink so delicious that he wanted to start with her eyebrows and lick every inch of her all the way to her toes. "I can't... say those things," she whispered. "Not out loud."

Thorne swallowed hard. Twice. It didn't help much.

Her fantasies might be innocent ones—or not—but just imagining what she might have seen in her dreams was enough to make him dizzy. "Then perhaps I shall experiment," he said. "I trust you'll let me know when I achieve the desired effect?"

He nuzzled her neck and let his tongue trail softly along the fullness of her lower lip, tracing the outline of her mouth. She tasted like chocolate. He had never before understood how some people could be so fond of the flavor, but suddenly Thorne saw the attraction. Chocolate and Anne's lips—now that was a potent combination. One he'd like to sip every morning...

*At least for a while,* he told himself. Days, absolutely. Weeks, yes. Months...?

Why this sudden obsession with time? he asked himself. Now was all that counted—and right now, she was *here*—in his arms, with the taste of her morning chocolate still on her lips...

She arched against him as he nibbled the corner of her mouth. "My lord," she said softly.

He raised an eyebrow. "Though you refuse to tell me of your fantasies, I'll share mine. I want to hear you say my name."

"You mean…" She stretched a little. Her breasts brushed his chest, and desire slammed through him. "…Mr. Wilde?"

"My friends call me Thorne."

Her eyes sparkled. "Not rose? Or stem?"

"Minx." He held her face between his hands. "Say it."

When she finally did, his name was no more than a sensual whisper on her lips, caressing his skin like the silken strands of her hair. Any hope he might have had of maintaining control slipped out of his grasp. He pulled her under him and, with one strong thrust, buried himself deep within her. She was ready for him, hot and slick, and their joining was as quick and breathless as though they had both been starving.

Afterward, he nestled her close and toyed with her for a while—caressing and teasing. He let his fingertips wander across her stomach, and when she asked what he was doing, he said, "I'm writing my name on your skin, Mrs. Wilde—so you will never forget."

She frowned just a little, as if he'd sounded odd. He thought it was quite likely. What had made him say something so possessive, so demanding—and so supremely foolish? Of course she would never forget him, just as he would never forget her. He had never felt quite this way with any other mistress, but then none of them had been the odd combination Anne was—part lady, part fishwife, a seductress so shy she had no idea of her own power…

But he didn't want to think of that just now. He wanted to make love to her while there was still time—before she had to leave him and return to the ordinary world. He didn't want her to leave…

So he started all over again to seduce her, distracting her—and himself—until there was no more room in either of their minds for rational thought.

❦

The morning had been gray; the afternoon was dismal and positively chilly. When Freddy arrived, Anne suggested that they give up the notion of a drive in the park. "We could sit by the fire and chat," she suggested brightly, and tried not to think of what she'd rather be doing instead.

Not chatting, that was sure.

*You're insatiable, Anne Keighley. You were just with your lover this morning…*

Though when she thought it over, they had actually talked in the intervals between making love. It had been mostly nonsense, of course…

*"What are you doing?"*

*"I'm writing my name on your skin, Mrs. Wilde—so you will never forget."*

But Freddy just shook his head at the idea. "New team. Prime high-steppers. Can't keep them just walking up and down the street while I sit by the fire, you know."

And she really couldn't tell him that the reason she knew it was too cold to be comfortable while driving in the park was because she'd walked to Upper Seymour Street that morning…

So, reluctantly, Anne changed into a wool carriage dress with a matching cloak and joined Freddy in his curricle to drive through Hyde Park. On the way, as they left Grosvenor Square, she caught a glimpse of a baggage wagon being loaded in front of Charlotte Barnsley's house.

Multiple trunks meant that Charlotte was going much farther than Upper Seymour Street. Oh, yes—Arabella Winchester's house party. Perhaps, Anne thought, that was why Hawthorne had been so eager to see her again today; he'd wanted to fit in another tryst with one mistress before he left town to join another. Perhaps that was why he'd looked at her so strangely this morning—because he had intended to break the news that he was going away but then decided not to tell her after all.

Freddy tooled his horses through the gates of the park and slowed them to a walk. Despite the chill, society was out in force, and the roadways were crowded. It took half an hour to make one round, and by then the horses were restive. "I'll just let them have a bit of a run," Freddy said.

"Would you mind taking me home first, Freddy? I'm very cold."

"Wrong side of the park," Freddy said earnestly. "We'll go the long way around. It'll be faster than going back through that crowd."

*Perhaps I could still be at Upper Seymour Street by three.*

A treacherous thought, that. And a foolish one, as well. Since Hawthorne wasn't expecting her to return, he might have made different plans. She might find anything going on inside that neat little house—though more likely his well-trained butler would have been instructed to simply close the door in her face. Whether now or later, that was bound to happen sometime. Then she would be just one in a long line of ex-mistresses.

"*I'm writing my name on your skin, Mrs. Wilde…*"

He had been making sure that no matter how many lovers she might take in her life, she would never forget him. But had he already been preparing to move on?

As the horses picked up speed, the breeze grew stronger, threatening to snatch her hat and pulling a wisp of hair loose. She brushed it out of her eyes and looked around. "Freddy, I don't see the park any more. Where are we?"

"Going the long way around," he said.

But something in his voice didn't sound truthful, and she sensed that they had come a long way from the park while she'd been lost in her memories. "Freddy, I'm freezing. Please take me home."

He didn't take his eyes off the road. "No. But I'll take you somewhere warm, very soon, if you'll promise to be good."

She was not reassured. "Sir, what are your intentions?"

"Sooner or later, you're going to marry me—but after seeing that crowd of men fawning over you at the opera last night, I figured I'd better make it sooner, just in case. If you behave yourself and promise not to make a scene, I'll take you to an inn. If you don't, we'll just keep on going north—headed for Gretna."

"You'll have to stop to change horses."

"Not until there's no chance of getting back tonight. When word gets out that we spent the night together, you'll have no choice but to marry me."

"I really don't care about my reputation, Freddy."

"Braxton does. He'll make sure of it."

There was no reasoning with the man. Anne tried to still her throbbing nerves long enough to consider her options. Trying to escape would be suicide; the curricle was moving far too fast for her to jump, and trying to grasp the reins of a fresh and unknown team would probably send the horses into panic and flight. Better to bargain, stay as close to London as possible, and hope to find an opportunity she could seize.

"All right," she said, doing her best to sound disgruntled. "I'm far too cold to go on."

Freddy grinned. "Just in time, too," he said lightly, and turned the horses at speed. The curricle rocked onto its offside wheels, and Anne clutched her hat with one hand and the edge of the seat with the other.

He pulled the team to a halt in an inn yard. "This is a nice little inn, I'm told. The landlord is very friendly and helpful. And discreet."

Anne pushed her hat back into place and looked up at the sign. Of all places, he had brought her to the Red Dragon…

For an instant, she was relieved. Then reality set in. Merely recognizing the inn would do her little good. She didn't know her way around, since she'd only been in the entrance hall and the private parlor Hawthorne had engaged. And the innkeeper wouldn't recognize her; he had only seen her veiled. In any case, a friendly, helpful, and discreet innkeeper was one that kept his mouth shut, no matter what went on in his private rooms.

An ostler ran up to take charge of the horses, and Freddy leaped down and lifted Anne from the curricle. She tried her best not to shudder at his touch.

The innkeeper showed them to a private parlor. Thankfully, Anne thought, it was not the same one Mr. Wilde had engaged.

Freddy tossed his driving coat aside and strode across to the fire. "Glad you showed sense. I'm frozen solid. Knew I should have worn my heavy greatcoat— only it would have been a bit of a giveaway that I had a trip planned. Take your cloak off, and come here to get warm."

Anne didn't move. "I won't marry you, no matter how much you try to compromise me."

"Oh, I think you will. There'll be a chance of a child, you know, by the time I'm done. Braxton will have something to say about that."

Her insides convulsed, but she kept her voice steady. "Don't pin your hopes on it, Freddy. I was married for four years."

"That's the beauty of it. I don't need an heir—but I'll enjoy trying to get one." He turned. "I said, come here." It was unmistakably an order, and when she didn't move, his face hardened. He strode across the room to her. "No use pretending you don't know the game." He ran a hand down over her breast.

"I won't be embarrassed into marriage. Once Braxton knows I've—" She caught herself, too late.

"Knows you've what? That you've already got a lover? That's no surprise. You're no virgin, so one lover more or less makes no odds. Who is it, anyway?" Freddy's gaze turned cunning. "Hawthorne, I'll bet. Now there's a good joke. Who'd have guessed I'd take Hawthorne's mistress away from him?" He rubbed his hands together. "Oh, yes, I'm going to enjoy this."

Her heart sank. How could she have miscalculated so badly? She should have realized that taking a lover wouldn't keep her safe at all. Instead, she had only made herself an attractive form of ammunition in a quarrel between men.

The door opened, and a maid came in carrying a loaded tray. Tea, Anne saw. Well, perhaps the pot was hot enough to serve as a weapon. And the maid... Though she'd barely noticed the servants on her previous visit, surely this was the same maid who had brought the strawberries and peaches. If Anne could make her understand what was going on...

Freddy swore. "Get that swill out of here," he ordered. "And bring two bottles of your best claret instead. My lady will drink with me."

The maid bobbed a curtsey and picked up the tray. As she turned toward the door, she caught Anne's eye and winked.

"The wine will warm your blood," Freddy said. "Or not. I don't much care which, because the result will be the same."

The momentary sense of relief Anne had felt faded, like a dream at the moment of awakening. The maid meant well, that much was apparent—but what on earth could she do? Anne was on her own.

❧

The Braxtons' butler showed no signs of budging from the threshold. "He will want to see me," Thorne repeated.

Finally the man stepped aside. "I will inquire if his lordship is at home," he said grandly, and left Thorne pacing the entrance hall while he made his way up to the drawing room at a glacial pace.

A moment later, Braxton himself came to the landing. "Come on up for tea, Thorne."

Thorne made his bow to Lady Braxton and accepted a cup of tea with bread and butter. "Is Lady Keighley not at home?"

"One might almost think you have a partiality for her," Lady Braxton said. "How is it you met, by the way? I do not recall making an introduction."

Braxton shook his head and smiled. "Now, Maddy. Everybody knows Thorne. Anne's out with Freddy Lassiter today, in his curricle. They must have got into a crush in the park."

Prickles ran down Thorne's spine. "In this weather? How long have they been gone?"

Braxton shrugged. "Or perhaps they stopped to visit a friend, and they're having tea there. He'll look after her. He's got a *tendre* for the girl, after all."

*You have no right to ask questions,* Thorne reminded himself. *Not yet, at any rate.*

"So what can I do for you, Thorne?" Braxton asked expansively.

"I'd hoped for a private word."

"You, too?" Braxton said with a grin. "Well, whatever you like. You'll excuse us, Maddy, m'dear? We'll just step down to the library for a bit."

Braxton led the way. From the top of the stairs, Thorne saw a scuffle at the door as a thin, wiry man in the garb of a groom pushed past the butler. Once inside, the groom skidded to a halt on the marble floor and looked around wildly, as if he had no idea what to do next.

"Jenkins?" Thorne said. "What is it?"

"A message, my lord. For you."

"I assume you left the messenger holding my horses?"

Braxton stopped dead in the center of the staircase. "What is the meaning of this? Your servant assaults my butler, pushes his way into my house…"

Thorne brushed Braxton aside and ran lightly down the stairs.

Jenkins ducked his head. "Sorry, my lord. But he wouldn't let me in." He glared at the butler. "There's a groom outside from the Red Dragon. Says he's been looking for you for hours, sir."

Thorne was already at the door. When he came back just a minute later, Braxton was standing in the middle of the hall. "You—and your servants," he began, "are no longer welcome in—"

"Stubble it, Braxton. Freddy Lassiter has eloped with Lady Keighley."

"What? Don't be ridiculous, man. They'll be at a friend's—"

"Does he have friends who live at a coaching inn on the road to Islington? And since it has taken two hours for the man to find me, we have no time to lose—so stop your blathering and order your horses, man."

Braxton gestured imperiously at a footman. "Why did they come to find you and not me?"

"Because they know me at the Red Dragon. But it's an excellent question. Remind me to have a word with you, Braxton, about how you look after your sister. *After* I have her safe."

The butler came forward with Braxton's coat, and his lordship scrambled into it. "Exactly why did the people at the Red Dragon think *you* would have an interest in what happens to my sister, Hawthorne?"

Thorne's patience had been eroded to the vanishing point. "Because I had an assignation with her there on Tuesday," he said crisply, "and it would have been quite clear to anyone with a head that I'd not be in favor of any other man sharing her favors. *That's* why."

If the situation had been less desperate, he'd have enjoyed watching Braxton's eyes bug out.

❧

The maid brought the wine, and a little later she came back to say that Cook wanted to know if they wished a meal.

"No," Freddy said.

"Oh, for heaven's sake, Freddy," Anne argued, "you don't want me to faint from hunger. Or you, either, come to that. Yes, we'll have dinner."

Besides, it would mean the maid could come in and out a half dozen times, laying the table and bringing the food—and as long as Freddy knew the door might open at any moment, he couldn't do anything too awful. At least, Anne hoped not. And surely she could drag out the meal until…

It was the *until* that was worrying her. Freddy had

finished the first bottle of wine and made serious inroads in the second one. Maybe she should encourage him to keep drinking… or would that only make him forget inhibitions like a servant walking in?

"Please bring another bottle," she told the maid, and the girl bobbed another curtsey and went out.

"I'll share," Freddy said, and waved the bottle he was holding in her direction.

"I'd prefer to have one all to myself." And if the opportunity came to crack him over the head with it…

Freddy started to laugh. "So he taught you to nip a little, did he, old Keighley?"

The door opened again, and for an instant Anne couldn't believe what she was seeing.

Braxton stood in the opening, the capes of his coat still swirling. "What's going on here, Freddy?" he said sternly. "Why do I find my sister with you in compromising circumstances? How dare you put her good name at risk?"

Anne's heart, which had soared at the sight of him, sank again. Freddy had been absolutely correct in his assessment. So long as Braxton was thinking only of her reputation, he would take the shortest path to preserving it—and that path led directly to the altar.

Then she saw who had followed Braxton into the room, and misery swept over her in a wave. When Braxton picked up her cloak and swept it around her, she didn't even protest.

Freddy was standing in the middle of the room, weaving slightly, a bottle in his hand. Lord Hawthorne strolled up to him and, without a word, planted his fist against Freddy's nose. The impact sounded like a melon smashing. The nose gushed red. Freddy rocked back on his heels and fell as heavily as a rotten tree.

Hawthorne stood over the fallen man, rubbing his knuckles. He hadn't even looked at her.

"Come," Braxton said curtly. Anne let him usher her out of the room.

❧

Anne stared at herself in the dressing mirror. "I don't want to go to a ball tonight."

Madeleine glared at her. "You don't have a choice, Anne. The story's bound to get out. We accepted the invitation, so you have to make an appearance at the ball or people will ask questions about why you're not there."

"I have a headache."

"You *are* a headache, Anne! You have to be seen tonight. You have to look perfectly normal, happy, unconcerned—so people won't give credence to the story and your reputation won't end up in tatters."

"I don't care about my reputation." But the words felt hollow on Anne's tongue. Now that it was too late, she realized she did care. She'd blithely convinced herself she could avoid marriage by having an affair—but she hadn't given thought to everything else she would lose along with her good name. Friends, family, her position in society... Now that those things were at risk, she realized how much they meant to her. Somehow, she'd convinced herself she could continue just as she had, only in her own household instead of her brother's...

Or perhaps there was a huge difference between

ruining herself with Hawthorne and ruining herself with Freddy Lassiter.

She didn't want to think about that. Not just now.

Madeleine put her hands on her hips. "Anne, Braxton says…"

"I don't care what he says or does," Anne said dully. "I'm not going to marry Freddy."

Madeleine sighed. "Then you *must* go to the ball. If you don't quell the gossip before it starts, you'll have to marry somebody—and since Freddy's the one you ran off with…"

"I didn't run off with him," Anne pointed out. "He ran off with me. It's an entirely different thing."

"I know it is, Anne. But you have to think about how it looks!"

"Fine. If I pull it off and my reputation isn't in tatters by the end of the evening, then there's not the least need for me to marry."

Madeleine hesitated. "Well…"

"If you promise me I won't have to marry anyone, I'll do it."

"It's not for me to say. I'll leave that to Braxton."

"Oh, Maddy…"

"Anne, please. Let Polly finish your hair. Put on your ball gown, and let's go. It's the best thing for you—getting out among people, taking your mind off what happened. An hour—just a few dances—and *I'll* plead a headache and beg you to come home with me, I promise. Heaven knows I'll be telling the truth."

Anne sighed. "I'm sorry, Maddy."

"And so am I. I never thought Freddy would do anything so utterly mad."

Neither had Anne, when it came right down to it. *Freddy Lassiter's not the worst of them,* she had told Thorne… and she'd meant it. She'd thought him harmless. A nuisance. A bit silly. But never threatening.

Odd, she thought, that the man all of society thought was the dangerous one had treated her with nothing but care and gentleness, while the fribble who everyone found amusing had almost destroyed her life.

Only… why hadn't Thorne even looked at her? Why hadn't he been the one to bring her home? Why hadn't he comforted her?

Did he blame her for what had happened? He'd told her once that she'd encouraged Freddy, if only by dancing with him. But surely Thorne didn't believe that a woman who loved him could ever go off willingly with another man…

*Loved?*

The mere word cut her as sharply as the edge of a sword, but Anne could not deny it. She had intended merely to take a lover. Instead, she had fallen in love.

❧

Perhaps Madeleine had been right, Anne thought. After an interminable hour at the ball, she stopped feeling numb. She stopped merely going through the motions, and she actually managed to smile and almost mean it—except when she spotted Thorne across the ballroom and he didn't come to ask her for a dance.

She was sitting in the corner of the ballroom with Madeleine—who was indeed looking pale and as if her head hurt—when Lady Stone swept up to them. "Have you heard what happened to Freddy Lassiter today?"

Anne got to her feet out of respect for the older woman, her hand clenched tightly on her silver filigree nosegay holder, while Madeleine sat up a little straighter, almost as if tensing herself against an expected blow.

Lady Stone plumped down into Anne's chair. "They say he got drunk and fell out of his curricle. Broke his nose."

"It's a wonder he didn't break his neck instead," Thorne added, coming up behind her. "Lady Keighley, may I have this dance?"

"No," Anne said, automatically.

He arched his eyebrows at her and reached for her dance card. "There is no name written opposite this dance," he pointed out. "In fact, there are no names for the rest of the evening. Are you planning to make an early night of it?"

"Anne, take the man away before he becomes annoying," Lady Stone ordered. "There's no place for you to sit, anyway. I'll stay and coze with Madeleine while you dance."

How very rude of him to leave her entirely alone for most of the evening and then demand a dance! And of course he couldn't have chosen one of the stately country dances, where she wouldn't have to talk to him, Anne thought resentfully. No, it would have to be a waltz, where she was required to circle the room clasped in his arms, reminded with every step of a very different sort of dance they had

shared in the bedroom on Upper Seymour Street…
reminded of the way his warm hands had felt against
her bare skin…

He led her onto the floor, and his hand on the
small of her back seemed to burn her, even through
his glove and the fabric of her moss-green dress.
They made a stately circle of the ballroom without
a word, and she began to hope they might finish the
dance in silence.

Except it felt even worse to be in his arms and
share no teasing double meanings, no wickedly funny
remarks, no whispered reminders of what they had
been to each other, no suggestive smiles.

Without even an angry accusation…

She began to hope that he'd rip up at her for being a
fool because she'd ended up in Freddy's clutches. Unfair
as it would be if he said such things, it would prove that
he cared—at least a little—what she did. Because right
now he didn't seem to care at all. Was he only dancing
with her now because—having paid attention to her for
days—there would be talk if he didn't?

*It's all over,* she thought wearily. *I'm in love with
him—but he's already moved on.*

"Are you all right?" he asked finally.

She looked up at him, intending to give him her
brightest smile, her most reassuring sparkle—and felt
instead the prickle of tears.

He said something under his breath that she didn't
catch, and a moment later they were gliding off the
edge of the dance floor and out of the ballroom, across
a deserted hallway and into a small reception room
where a few candles glowed and a fire had burned

down to embers. The door creaked as he closed it, but then there was no sound.

"Come now, Mrs. Wilde," he said.

Anne bit her lip. "Don't torment me. I can't stand it."

He took out a handkerchief and used the edge of it to blot her lashes.

She forced a smile. "I just need a moment to gather myself. Go back to the ballroom, please."

"A rake returning without the lady he has just escorted from the room? My reputation would never recover."

"You dare mention reputations to me?" she flared. "Why didn't you tell me how silly I was being to think that taking a lover would solve my problems?"

For a moment, she thought he wasn't going to answer. "Because it fitted very well into my plans."

"Your... plans?"

"Did you think it was mere chance that we met at the jeweler's shop that morning, Anne?"

"It was not?"

"No. It took me rather a lot of effort to discover where I could find you, but eventually my groom made connections with one of Braxton's footmen, who had overheard you... Oh, my dear girl. You seriously thought that a dalliance with me would make you unmarriageable? My heart, you could have seven illegitimate children and still men would want you. I would want you."

It was a shame, she thought sadly, that there couldn't be a child. Then, at least, she would have a reminder of him always.

"Look at me, Anne." His voice was gentle, but

his hand under her chin was insistent. "Will you marry me?"

The world rocked underneath her. Had her ears failed? Was she—somehow—dreaming? She stole a look up at him. He seemed perfectly normal… except that he wasn't smiling. His eyes were darker than she'd ever seen them, and there was a tightness about his mouth…

"*What?*" she burst out. "You told me you had no desire to marry me!"

"If I recall the conversation correctly," he said pensively, "you told me what my intentions—or lack of them—were."

"But you *agreed*!"

He smiled, faintly. "Yes—at the time. You have changed my mind."

She could barely get her breath. "It's Braxton, isn't it? He's desperate to save my reputation. Even Braxton can't bring himself to marry me off to Freddy—"

"Of course not. Freddy will be making a long stay on the Continent, by the way, as soon as his nose and the other injuries he sustained from his… fall… have healed enough for him to travel."

"That's good news, I suppose," she said absently. "But Braxton's obviously still determined to marry me off, so if he can find someone else instead of Freddy…"

"Me, you mean? I don't act because someone like Braxton attempts to compel me, Anne. In any case, he didn't. This is entirely my own idea."

She stared at him. He sounded quite serious. And yet—the most confirmed rake in London proposing marriage… to *her*?

"Oh, dear," he said. "Well, that confirms it—you're standing there with your mouth hanging open, and I still think you're the most beautiful creature on earth."

"You don't want to marry," she protested.

"I never have before. But there has never been a woman I couldn't live without, before."

She wanted to believe, but she couldn't. "You're only saying you want to marry me because of what Freddy did."

"On the contrary, my dear. Freddy's not going to talk—or come back anytime soon, either."

There was a thread of steel in his voice. Anne couldn't decide whether to be glad her brother had taken her out of the Red Dragon before Freddy had come back to his senses after that first blow or to regret that she'd missed seeing what had happened next. How much persuasion had Freddy required before he'd decided that a lengthy repairing lease on the Continent would be just the ticket? She wondered exactly how badly Thorne's knuckles were grazed and if that was why he hadn't removed his gloves tonight…

"In any case," he went on, "my decision was made before Freddy acted. I had just sought your brother out this afternoon to tell him I intended to marry you when I got the message from the Red Dragon."

"But… but why marriage? It's so… so…"

"Final? Permanent? Exclusive? Am I getting close?" She nodded, sadly.

"But that's exactly the reason, Anne. If you were to remain my mistress, I would have you only in scattered moments, whenever you could break away from your other obligations. I want you all the time. I want the joy of protecting you and the pride of claiming you as my wife. And…" his voice dropped. "I need you."

She swallowed hard. He had made his proposal; she had given him every opportunity to withdraw it… Or had she? "No," she whispered. "No. I can't marry you."

He smiled at her.

Anne's heart dropped to her toes. Was he relieved that she had refused him, in no uncertain terms? He could no longer be held responsible…

"*Yes*," he said. "If you wish a formal courtship, I will call on you tomorrow to renew my question, and the day after, and the day after that, for as long as it takes until you can no longer deny that I mean what I say."

Hope fluttered inside her.

His voice was almost somber. "Keighley was an old, sick, selfish man. I know he gave you a distaste for marriage, Anne—but I beg you to take your chances with me. I love you. Please say you'll have me."

Her head was telling her she should continue to resist, but her heart was skipping madly. *He loves me… He loves me!* Then she remembered something else, and the flutter of hope died. "I can't give you an heir."

"Then I will live happily without one. But I think there's a very good chance you may be carrying the next Lord Hawthorne right now."

She was trembling. "No. That's not possible."

"I assure you it is. I didn't make certain you were safe from a pregnancy, my dear—not after the first time we made love. I made a deliberate choice not to, and I would make the same choice again. You were so sad then, when you told me that you could never have children, that I wanted you to have a child. *My* child. That was when I began to know—though I didn't want to admit it—that having you as my mistress would not be enough."

"But it's not fair to you if I can't have a child. And you can't expect… It was four years, Thorne!"

"We shall see, in due time. And until then, we shall have a lot of fun testing which of us is correct." Somehow he'd gotten his arms around her, and he was kissing her throat.

She tried—but only halfheartedly—to break free. "Wait a minute. You said you went looking for Braxton to tell him you intended to marry me. Not to ask his permission?"

"Not at all. If he had tried to withhold his approval, I'd have made you an offer anyway. However…" He paused. "You need to know that in a moment of fear this afternoon, I told your brother what we have been to each other. If you don't marry me, he will certainly call me out, Anne. And I'd have to let him shoot me, you know, because of what I've done. "

"You told him?" Anne was stunned. Not by the idea that Braxton knew she had taken a lover, though that was certainly problem enough. Her rake—the man who had never played a card wrong in the game of love—had been so frightened for her that he'd lost control of what he said?

The little flutter of hope had expanded, shifting into a bubble of joy so strong it threatened to lift her off her feet. The sheer wonder of it—that Thorne loved her—was making her dizzy.

"Save my life, darling. Marry me." He kissed her temple. "We haven't had much time for conversation," he said softly. "But there has been fun and, I believe, the foundation of friendship."

Did the man remember everything she had ever said to him? She tried to make her voice severe. "You've left me no option, my lord."

"I do hope not." A silvery gleam was suddenly dancing in his eyes again. "Because if you happen to think of another one, I'll have to set about destroying it, as well—even though I'd much rather be kissing you." He demonstrated.

The door creaked open, and light from the hallway poured in and captured them—Anne with her head thrown back, Thorne nuzzling the top of her breast, and not enough space between them to fit a sheet of paper—just as Charlotte Barnsley burst into the room.

Thorne stopped nuzzling, but he didn't release Anne. "I do hope you meant that as a yes, my darling," he murmured, "because I really must leave off being a rake. I've lost my touch. Charlotte, if you're planning to expose us…"

Charlotte's eyes flashed. "Oh, no! I'm not going to do anything that would make it easier for her to capture you! Just because this trollop—"

Thorne's tone was chilly. "Be watchful what you say, Lady Barnsley. An apology is in order."

"—likes to masquerade as the nonexistent Mrs. Wilde—"

A tart voice from the door interrupted her tirade. "*The nonexistent Mrs. Wilde?*" Lady Stone said. "Oh, dear. My good friend Mrs. Wilde will be quite unhappy to hear she doesn't exist. A small lady. Elderly. Quite round. Very fond of butterflies…"

Charlotte looked as if she'd been slapped. "There really *is* a Mrs. Wilde?" She stamped her foot and stormed off.

"…And strawberries," Lady Stone said blandly. "You owe me, dear hearts. I'm going to demand every detail—later. But now that Charlotte has been routed, I suggest you follow me back to the ballroom, before every last one of the people who are holding their breaths to see what you're about faints in unison." She left the door wide open when she departed.

Anne looked up at Thorne in puzzlement. "Charlotte doesn't know about Mrs. Wilde? But she was…"

"Charlotte was never my mistress. Really, Anne— give me leave to have some taste. In any case, there has never been another Mrs. Wilde. Only you."

"Oh, really? You expect me to believe you have never before used that oh-so-convenient little house as a trysting spot?"

"Why do you think I didn't take you there instead of to the Red Dragon the first time we met? Because it wasn't ready. Oh, I had some such idea when I bought it last autumn—a nice quiet little house, so conveniently located just around the corner from my own. But I hadn't got round to fixing it up. It wasn't until I wanted to take you there that I had the workmen start. Did you actually not notice that the furnishings were the perfect shade to complement your coloring?"

She hadn't. She'd been too busy thinking of how

Charlotte Barnsley's red hair would look against the rich emerald bed curtains…

"You have no idea how difficult it is to redecorate in just two days."

"You did that for me?"

"I wanted everything to be lovely for you. Not sordid."

"You've lied to me, you know," she said softly. "You *are* a gentleman. Even when I was only your lover—"

"My dear, you could never be *only* a lover. I'll give you the house, if you like—so long as I may come and visit Mrs. Wilde from time to time."

"Whenever you wish—Mr. Wilde."

"Though now that I think about it…" He paused to kiss her so thoroughly that Anne almost forgot what he was talking about. "*Not* Mrs. Wilde," he said finally. "You shall be Lady Hawthorne all the time, of course. But now and then, will you be my Lady Wilde?"

She whispered her answer… and he smiled.

# Three

## The Countess Receives a Letter

ANNE, LADY HAWTHORNE, ROSE LATE AND LOOKED over her letters as she breakfasted on a slice of dry toast and a cup of tea sweetened with honey. The Season would be coming to an end in a few weeks, and then London would be quiet as the *ton* retreated to resorts, to the seaside, or to their country estates—but she needed to respond to a considerable number of invitations in the meantime.

The invitations were forgotten, however, as she unearthed a letter at the bottom of the pile, broke the wafer, and spread the page. The letter was short, the lines uncrossed, the handwriting firm and deliberate and clear.

> *My dear Anne—What wonderful news! I cannot tell you how happy I am for you or how touched that you have invited me to visit you. You have reminded me that though I still miss my father very much, it is long past time to put off my black—and that means a visit to London. So I shall look forward to calling on you in Portman Square within the next week.*

*However, I cannot think your husband would like
to have your old school friend actually in residence for
any length of time, and I fear I would be a burden
to you. I prefer not to go into society, and I would
not have you give up your own plans to keep me
company. In any case, once established in London,
I may decide to stay for a while, replenishing my
bookshelves as well as my wardrobe and enjoying all
the culture that the capital offers.*

*Perhaps Lord Hawthorne's man of business—I
assume he has one?—could be prevailed upon to
assist me in finding a small house that I could lease
for a few months. If such a house exists, perhaps
he would go ahead and make the arrangements in
my name so that I might finalize them immediately
upon my arrival.*

*With greatest sincerity I remain,*
*Your devoted friend,*
*Felicity*

Anne had not seen Felicity Mercer for years, but
obviously the girl she had known hadn't changed as she
had grown into womanhood. Felicity had been—and
evidently still was—always thoughtful of others, always
reluctant to call attention to herself, and always afraid
she might accidentally create trouble for someone.

Anne knew better than to try to convince Felicity
to stay in Portman Square. She hadn't missed her
friend's painful little phrase about preferring not to
go into society. It was nonsense, of course—despite
Felicity's origins, she was better educated and more
well mannered than the average lady of the *ton*.

Anne refolded the letter and rang for the butler to tell Perkins she needed to see him. Poor Perkins would have his hands full trying to find a house for Felicity at this time of year. In another month such a search would be easy, as families began to leave town. But now, with the Season still ongoing…

However, if Felicity wanted a house, then a house she would have.

"My lady?" Perkins stood at the door of the morning room. "You wished to speak with me?"

"I appreciate you coming so promptly, Perkins. Come and sit down. Would you like tea?"

He looked uneasy at the notion of sitting at table with the lady of the house, much less partaking of refreshment in her company—even though, in his position of responsibility, he was hardly a servant.

Or perhaps, Anne thought with wry humor, he was feeling uneasy over what she might be building up to ask. Not that she could blame him.

"No, thank you, my lady. Was there something you needed?"

"A house." Anne picked up the letter. "A small house for a friend of mine to lease for a few months, starting next week."

She thought Perkins smothered a sigh. "Yes, my lady. I shall do my best. Although…"

"I know it won't be easy at this time of year. But I have great faith in your powers, Perkins. His lordship often says that you work miracles."

He cleared his throat. "My lady, there *is*… No, I beg your pardon—I should not have spoken of it."

"Please, Perkins. What were you going to say?"

He swallowed hard. "I was just going to mention that Number 5 Upper Seymour Street is… Now that his lordship is no longer… I mean…" He turned fiercely red and looked terrified.

Anne surveyed him thoughtfully. "Now that his lordship no longer needs it?" she asked sweetly.

Perkins looked as if he were swaying on the edge of a precipice and a deep breath would send him over the edge.

Now why hadn't she thought of that herself? Upper Seymour Street would be perfect for Felicity—a quiet house in an out-of-the-way location, already staffed with very good and very discreet servants.

Of course, Anne would need to make sure Thorne didn't mind her loaning out the house for a few months. But if she asked him tonight—while he was making his daily meticulous and very sensual inspection to see whether her stomach had started to round out yet and precisely how much her pregnancy had enlarged her breasts—he probably wouldn't mind.

To tell the truth, no matter what she said in the middle of his daily inspection, Thorne wouldn't mind. He probably wouldn't even *notice*.

She sat back in her chair and smiled at Perkins. "That is an absolutely brilliant solution." Mischief made her add, "I'm certain when you tell Lord Hawthorne the plan, he'll instruct you to go ahead."

Perkins choked and turned purple.

"No, no," she said hastily, afraid he was going to collapse. Poor man—it wasn't his fault that he was so much fun to torment; she really *must* be more careful in the future. "I was only funning. You don't have to consult his lordship—I'll see to that. But if you'll instruct Mrs. Mason to make certain everything at Number 5 is in order for Miss Mercer's arrival within the week…"

"Your servant, my lady," Perkins stammered, and hurried out.

He was probably fleeing for his life before she could ask him for anything else, Anne thought.

Yes, Felicity could borrow Number 5 Upper Seymour Street with the Countess of Hawthorne's good wishes. Anne wasn't going to be needing it for a while.

# Four

## My Lady Desire

THE JOURNEY SOUTH ACROSS ENGLAND HAD BEEN A long one, and by the time the post chaise drew up in Portman Square, Felicity was exhausted. The steps of Lord Hawthorne's town house seemed to rock under her feet as she climbed to the front door, and she actually dozed for a moment in the little reception room before the butler returned to take her to Anne's morning room.

"Lady Hawthorne," Felicity said formally, and curtseyed.

"Oh, Fliss, stop it." Anne Hawthorne rose from a low chair and came to hug Felicity. "I won't put up with you standing on formality."

Felicity looked her over closely. "It suits you, Anne. The title—and marriage. You're positively blooming. It's going well, then?"

"Once I get past the first hour of the morning, yes," Anne said with a little laugh.

"And… he's good to you?" But there was no need to ask; her friend's glowing face told the story.

"Yes, my dear. You'll see at dinner."

"I wasn't planning to... Anne, I would really prefer not to go into society. Lord Hawthorne..."

"You can't mean that you choose not even to meet my husband? Felicity, what's this nonsense about avoiding society? What has happened to you?"

For the barest moment, Felicity considered telling her. But nothing would be gained from asking for pity. "Merely maturity and understanding of the way the world operates. The prejudices held against a schoolgirl because of her father's birth and his occupation grow even stronger when she reaches marriageable age."

"Only by people who have more hair than wit. You're better educated and more of a lady than most of the females in the *ton*—and trust me, I've encountered all of them. If you will let yourself observe, you'll soon see a gentleman who will overlook..."

Pain shot through Felicity. She held up one hand in a jerky warning gesture, and Anne stopped uncertainly. "But that's my very point, Anne." Her voice felt almost hoarse. "How condescending it would be of him to *overlook* the fact that my father worked in a mill and to *accept* the flaws in my heritage!"

"Your father owned the mill, Fliss."

"Not at first. And it's not much different, really, in the eyes of the world—owning it or simply working there. If I brought a vast enough fortune to the altar, a gentleman might be induced to take me, I suppose—but still, every time he looked at me, he would be reminded that he had married far beneath himself. He would feel superior to me in every way, and every word and gesture would make his feelings clear. I choose not to put myself in that position."

"Not all gentlemen are alike."

"Can you really believe that it wouldn't matter? Not at all? I see the truth in your eyes, Anne. You know better." Felicity forced herself to smile. "Perhaps in the end I am fortunate to be left with a competence rather than wealth so I am not tempted to believe that money could ever balance out birth."

"A competence? But I thought the mill—"

"It's doing well, my manager says—but the expenses are heavy and sales have not been as strong as in past years. I can afford my stay in London and my comforts. But I've arranged to sell the house in York."

"Your *home*?"

Felicity suppressed a shiver at the reminder of the big, dark old house where she had never felt really warm. "Please don't think it a sacrifice. It was far too large for one person. When I return, I'll find a smaller one—something more to my taste."

"For *one* person." Anne sounded disgruntled.

"Just because you're now happily paired off... As schoolgirls, we were very fond of fairy tales, Anne. But now that we're grown up, we must acknowledge that not every woman finds a mate."

"If you're telling me that you kissed a frog and he didn't change into a prince," Anne said, sounding a little acerbic, "I should point out that neither did the first frog I tried."

Felicity was stricken. "Oh, Anne, I do beg your pardon. I should not have reminded you of Lord Keighley."

"There's nothing to be sorry for. Come, let's have tea and a good long talk. Then I'm sending you up to rest— because you *are* coming down to dinner. If you don't,"

Anne threatened lightly, "I'll... I'll instruct Perkins not to show you the house we've arranged for you."

Felicity's heart soared. "You've arranged it already? Anne, what a good friend you are!"

She would have a house—a place that would be entirely hers, even if only for a few months. A place with no memories, no sadness lurking in the corners. A place to think, to plan, to decide... to heal.

She could hardly wait. A formal dinner was a small price to pay.

⁂

Felicity's best dinner gown was gray, of course—a remnant of her year's mourning for her father. She looked at it hanging on the door of the wardrobe and then told her maid to get out the only colored dress she had brought instead. It was a shade of gold so dark it was almost brown, trimmed with matching bows—and it was seriously out of date.

She didn't realize exactly how unstylish it was, however, until she saw Anne's dress—elegantly cut and the deep, rich shade of garnets—when they met in the drawing room just before the dinner hour.

Shopping for clothes would definitely have to take priority over the many other things Felicity wished to do in the capital, if she was to look anything other than a dowd.

Not that she was trying to impress. She didn't care what the *ton* thought of her; she would encounter the ladies and gentlemen of society only by chance—at a museum perhaps or while picking up a book at Hookham's. They would not pay any mind to her, and she would take no note of them. It might even be better if she did not draw attention to herself by having a fashionable wardrobe.

She sighed inwardly. She could try all she wanted to talk herself out of caring about pretty clothes, but she doubted she would succeed. "You said you have a favorite modiste, Anne?"

"Indeed I do, and I've sent word to her to expect us in the morning. We'll start with the basics—walking dresses and perhaps a riding habit—and then…"

The drawing-room door opened, and two gentlemen came in. They were both in dinner clothes, their black coats perfectly fitted, their linen snowy. Both were tall and straight—commanding men. But Felicity's gaze came to rest on the second one, and she could not look away. The resemblance, she thought, was really quite extraordinary.

He was very fair, with brilliant blue eyes. His slightly curly golden hair caught the candlelight, and for a moment he seemed to be surrounded by a halo.

But, of course, it was fitting for this man to look like an angel—as long as the angel in question was Lucifer.

One of the men—not the one Felicity was trying her best not to stare at—spoke. "Of course you remember Colford, my dear? I told him he must come and do the pretty to excuse me being late."

"Certainly I remember," Anne said. "If you would care to take dinner with us, my lord, you would be most welcome."

The second man smiled—a beautiful, winning smile—as he bowed over Anne's hand, and again Felicity thought of fallen angels. "I should be honored to take my pot luck at your table, my lady. But I could not intrude, and indeed I am expected elsewhere. I came only to pay my respects, to make Thorne's peace with you, and to beg pardon for keeping him overlong about business."

"It is just now gone eight—it is no trouble at all. Let me make you known... Felicity, this is Lord Colford... my good friend Miss Mercer."

So much for not having anything to do with society. But of course Anne could have done nothing else; not to have introduced one of her guests to another would be an unforgivable slight.

Felicity fought the coldness that had settled over her and forced herself to extend her hand. Colford bowed over it; she stared directly into his eyes and felt rewarded when uncertainty—perhaps even a hint of dismay—flickered in his gaze. From the corner of her eye, she saw Anne's eyebrows arch, as if she felt the sizzling hostility in the air.

Felicity forced the corners of her mouth to turn up. "A pleasure, my lord." Her voice was lower than normal, almost husky.

Anne stepped into the silence that followed. "How is Lady Colford?"

"As well as can be expected." His voice was grave. "She's not seeing anyone just now."

"I shall call on her when she is receiving again."

And then he was gone—but Felicity's heart was still thrumming wildly as they went in to dinner.

What were the odds that of all the gentlemen in London society, Lord Colford would be the one to appear on her very first night in the city?

*Colford*... of all people!

She shot a look at Anne. Could she have arranged this? Brought him here on purpose? After all that talk about going into society...

But the Countess could not possibly have known. No one had known, except Felicity's father—and even he hadn't suspected the whole. Felicity's own guilt had colored her reactions.

And no one, Felicity told herself, must *ever* know what a fool she had made of herself.

❧

Felicity had hoped that Anne—or, rather, the earl's man of business—would be able to find her an adequate house. Her expectations were not high; she'd have been content with a cottage. But when Perkins took her around to Number 5 Upper Seymour Street, she was delighted. The house was a mansion, in Felicity's eyes—big, elegant, and quiet despite its location next to the entrance to Berkeley Mews. The fact that only a few steps through the gardens would take her to the side door of Anne's house was an unexpected benefit.

"It's beautiful," she told Perkins. "Only—it's so big! And in such a prime location... I don't know whether I can afford it or the servants to run it."

Perkins fixed his gaze on a point somewhere past her shoulder and said, "The house is owned by his lordship, who is... er... not in need of it at the present time."

The tone of his voice said it all. His lordship didn't need it *at the present time*? So her new house had been a trysting site, Felicity thought.

She felt a bit hollow—upset for Anne's sake. But what had she expected? Lord Hawthorne was apparently a gentleman in true London style—with an adoring but pregnant wife at home and a mistress tucked away just around a handy corner...

But the whole point, she reminded herself, was that Lord Hawthorne *didn't* have a mistress just now. Or perhaps the empty house meant only that he'd opted to be a bit more discreet than usual for a while and keep his mistress at a greater distance. If Felicity had been a gaming sort of woman, she'd have laid her bets on the latter.

Perkins cleared his throat. "The staff is all in place, as well. If you wish to make changes among the servants, please consult me so that I may arrange matters."

*Because his lordship will not want to dismiss the people who have been entrusted with his secrets...* "Of course." She was glad that she'd made the decision she had— not to have anything to do with London society. It was far too complicated with all its rules and standards... or lack of them.

She looked up at the quiet front of Number 5. It was classic, unassuming, clean, bright... But what had she expected? A sign on the door proclaiming its use?

Then she walked through the shiny, black front door, and the house reached out to her. It was richly furnished, and full of light and air. The moment she stepped inside, Felicity loosed a long sigh and felt herself at home.

Mason, the butler, was very old, and—Felicity suspected—a bit deaf. How perfectly convenient for his lordship, she thought.

Perkins introduced her to the housekeeper, who was brisk and efficient despite being nearly as old as her husband, the butler. Mrs. Mason conducted her through the house. Felicity inspected the library, the reception rooms, the dining room, the drawing room. She looked through all the bedrooms, ultimately choosing one that looked out over the garden at the back of the house.

"You don't want to use the main bedroom?" the housekeeper asked in surprise.

Felicity suppressed a shudder. "It's too big and too grand. All that emerald green velvet would smother me." It was true, though hardly the entire truth. She couldn't sleep where Lord Hawthorne had entertained his mistresses; she'd never be able to close her eyes. "This one is homey. Comfortable."

Mrs. Mason went away to tell Cook to send up a tea tray. Felicity set her maid to unpacking the few things she had brought with her and then sat down by the window to look over the garden and the stables beyond.

During the following week, she ordered clothes; she visited the bookstores; she took out a membership in the lending library; she toured the British Museum.

And she thought about Colford. The way his hair had gleamed in the candlelight. The way his long, curly lashes had drooped as he'd bent his head over her hand. The look of uncertainty and dismay in his brilliant blue eyes as he had faced her...

She wondered what he had been thinking just then.

❧

Since Anne had found it was advisable not to be too active when she first rose from her bed, Felicity soon got in the habit of crossing the garden to the Hawthorne town house early each morning to visit her, and they sat quietly sewing and chatting for an hour.

One morning, Felicity glanced from the tablecloth she was rehemming to the dainty baby gown in Anne's lap. "That border you're stitching is really lovely."

"And tedious. The motif is taken from the Hawthorne crest, and why I ever thought *that* was a good idea—"

"Because Lord Hawthorne expects a son?"

"I don't think he cares whether it's a girl or a boy," Anne said absently. She stroked the soft fabric and then took up her needle again.

"Of course, he cares. A son to inherit, to carry on the name and the title…"

Anne looked up in surprise. "What has made you sound so bitter on the subject, Fliss? I really want to know. You've changed from the woman I remember."

"You mean, the *girl* you remember."

"I'm beginning to think he wasn't a frog at all," Anne said somberly, "but a *toad*—the man who made you like this."

Felicity felt the sting of tears. "It's nothing, really. Certainly not like what you suffered with Keighley." *Not at all the same,* she told herself. *Equally painful, perhaps—but different.*

"That's beside the point. What was it, darling? Obviously he was someone who wasn't worthy of you—or he'd have married you despite what society sees as differences."

"He was," Felicity said. "Worthy of me, I mean.

But his family didn't think I was worthy of him. And that's the end of it. What a darling little dress that is... What fun it will be to have a baby of your own."

Anne was opening her mouth—intending to return to the attack, Felicity was certain—when the butler appeared in the doorway. "Lady Stone has called, ma'am. Are you at home?"

"Yes, Carson—thank you." The butler bowed and retreated, and Anne made a little moue at Felicity. "I have to be at home to Lady Stone—she's one of Thorne's favorite people."

Felicity felt that horrid empty feeling once more. Was she about to meet Lord Hawthorne's mistress—the woman who had used Number 5 Upper Seymour Street?

"Mine as well, of course," Anne went on. "And I think you'll like her, too—for she's even more outspoken than you are. But I realize that you choose to visit at this unfashionable hour every day just so I can't press you to come again later and meet my other callers."

Before Felicity could answer, the butler had returned with a tall, thin old woman with a craggy face, a beaky nose, and brilliant black eyes. She looked at least twice Hawthorne's age, and Felicity had to smile at her own mistaken assumptions.

"Anne, my dear," Lady Stone said. "Tell this fellow of yours that one of the privileges of age is drinking port instead of tea at whatever hour I wish. And since I know quite well Thorne's got a cellar full of it, there's not a reason in the world for me not to partake."

Anne waved a hand at the butler, who bowed and

retreated, and then greeted her visitor with a hug. "Lucinda, what brings you out at this hour?"

"Sheer cussedness," Lady Stone said promptly. "And a desire to meet your friend." She advanced on Felicity, hand outstretched. "Anne tells me you think yourself too good for London society."

"I did *not*," Anne protested. "I haven't talked about you, Fliss. At least—only a little."

Felicity curtseyed. "It is an honor to meet you, Lady Stone."

Lady Stone's beady black gaze ran over her from head to foot, and slid past her to the sizable stack of sewing Felicity had abandoned to rise in greeting. "What's that you're doing?"

Felicity felt herself color a bit. "Mending household linens," she admitted.

"Practical sort, aren't you?"

"Well, I have no need for any additional mono-grammed handkerchiefs." Her tone was crisp, and the words were out before Felicity stopped to think.

Lady Stone laughed, and Felicity relaxed. "Anne told me you were an original, but I hardly dared think it possible. I'm just surprised she hasn't got you embroidering for the heir. She even tried to drag me in to do that job—but my eyes won't stand that nonsense anymore." She sat down and sampled the port the butler had quietly brought in, with evident satisfaction. "Come to think of it, I never could abide doing fancywork. I was far more interested in gardening."

"That calls for equal patience," Felicity observed. "Just a different sort." She picked up the tablecloth again, but her hand trembled a little at the suggestion that she might help to sew clothes for Anne's baby. It hadn't even occurred to her to offer—and Anne hadn't asked…

For the rest of the visit, Felicity kept her voice cheerful and never left a pause in the conversation. But underneath, she was wondering exactly *why* Anne hadn't asked. Had some instinct made Anne realize how painful it would be for Felicity to take up a needle and a baby gown?

A bit later, she caught a name in Lady Stone's rapid-fire conversation. "Have you called on Lady Colford yet, Anne?" the older woman asked.

"No. Lord Colford said she's not receiving anyone. I can't like the woman, but—"

Lady Stone snorted. "*That's* quite the nicest thing I've ever heard anyone say about Blanche, Anne."

"Lucinda, really. This can't be easy for her."

"No—but just because she's weary of being in mourning is no excuse for making Richard's life a living hell when he's grieving for his brother."

*Grieving for his brother…* Well, Felicity told herself stoutly, she knew what that felt like. And perhaps Lord Colford had extra reason to grieve for his brother. Feeling guilty had that effect, sometimes…

When Lady Stone had finished her port and excused herself, Felicity went back to Number 5 Upper Seymour Street, where she stood in the window of her bedroom for a long time, thinking. Then she sat down at her desk and wrote a letter.

❧

Three days passed before the Earl of Colford came to call on her. Felicity had almost concluded that he meant to ignore her completely, and she had begun to contemplate her next move by the time her butler came into the drawing room and announced that she had a caller.

Felicity's hand clenched the stem of a rose she was inserting into a tall vase, causing her to stab her finger with a thorn. "Show him in," she said calmly.

A moment later, Colford checked on the threshold and looked around the room. "Your chaperone is not present, Miss Mercer?"

"I have no need of a chaperone. I am three and twenty, and well on the shelf."

"Not everyone would agree with that assessment."

"I am not a simpering society miss, my lord. I asked you to call in order that we might have a private discussion. You are in no danger from me." *Not just yet, at any rate.*

"I cannot think what we would need to discuss, Miss Mercer."

"No?" Felicity said sweetly. "Yet… you are here." She inspected the vase, shifted a rose, and set the arrangement on the table where it showed to best advantage. "If you believe we have nothing to talk about, why did you come?"

"It is good manners for a gentleman to respond to a lady's request."

"A *lady*?" Her voice was brittle. "That was certainly not how the Colford family perceived my station when your brother wished to marry me."

"I… beg your pardon?"

"Tell me, my lord—had you forgotten my name? Or did you never bother to find it out? Your brother, Roger... Surely you do remember *him*? You have very much the look of him, and you must be reminded by your mirror every morning."

He didn't answer, but the flash of pain in his eyes gave her pause. "What do you want, Miss Mercer?"

Felicity steeled her resolve. *This is your one chance,* she told herself. "I want what your brother should have given me. I want a child."

❧

Though she looked perfectly normal—or better than normal, actually—the woman was totally mad. No question about it.

Richard, Lord Colford, knew that the worst thing to do when confronted by an insane person was to challenge her beliefs, for that would almost certainly push her into violence. But what the devil *was* he to do with her?

He cursed himself for letting his curiosity get the better of him, for coming to see what she wanted of him. When he had met her the week before at Thorne's house, she had intrigued him. She was beautiful, vibrant, and exotic—with green eyes that slanted just a bit and fair hair wound into a coronet worthy of a princess. It was an old-fashioned style, but it had suited her. Her dress had been out of date as well—yet somehow it had made her look timeless, rather than dowdy.

Then he had made his bow over her hand, and the chill in her face had frozen him to the core. Such immediate and strong dislike had puzzled him. He wasn't used to that reaction from women; he'd always been a favorite with them, and not because of his rank.

He had racked his brain to think whether he could have met her before—if he might have slighted her somehow—and concluded that they had never met. He couldn't have forgotten that bright gold hair, those almond-shaped eyes.

So he told himself that she simply didn't like him—it was nothing more nor less than that. She had a right to her feelings, and not everyone thought he was wonderful. Blanche certainly didn't. In fact, Blanche and Miss Mercer might have a grand time together cataloguing his faults…

So he had put Miss Mercer out of his mind.

At least, he had tried.

When her letter—a stiff, polite little request for him to call on her, containing no hint of what she might really want—had arrived, he decided to ignore it. He had even pitched the letter into the fireplace but then scrambled to pull it out just as the edge of the paper began to smolder, crushing the scorched corner between his fingers.

He couldn't forget her message. Couldn't stop debating why she wanted to see him. Couldn't keep from thinking about the chill in her face and wondering what he could possibly have done to cause it. And—if he was honest—questioning what he might do to turn that coldness into warmth.

So here he was, three days later—confronting a woman who had just calmly announced that she wanted to bear the child of a man who'd been dead for well over half a year.

Yes, her carriage had definitely lost a wheel. Maybe even two of them.

Unless… was it possible she didn't realize Roger was dead? He didn't see how she could be unaware of that fact. On the other hand, lunatics weren't known for their reasoning powers. But if she really didn't know, and he just announced the fact out of the blue…

Obviously the only way to handle her was to appear to take her seriously—and then, just as soon as he could make his escape, to go warn Thorne that his wife's bosom friend belonged in Bedlam, not in Upper Seymour Street.

He pulled himself back to the drawing room with an effort. "Why don't you tell me about it?" he said easily.

As her eyes narrowed, they seemed to slant even more, and they darkened to a sultry deep green. Under other circumstances, he'd be trying to get even closer, testing to see if passion would darken them even further…

"You already know what happened."

"Not the details," he pointed out. "And not your side of it. Perhaps we could talk about it over…" He hesitated. Not wine, he thought; the only thing worse than dealing with a madwoman would be dealing with a tipsy madwoman. "Tea?"

And perhaps, he thought, he could signal the butler to call for help. He hadn't seen a single footman since he'd arrived, so no aid could be found there. But Thorne's grooms were close by in the mews…

Not that he needed assistance. Miss Mercer was a small thing and slight—there should be no reason he couldn't easily overpower her by himself. But he'd heard that the insane could sometimes display the strength of several people. If he tried to subdue her by himself and she fought him… He wouldn't want to have to injure her.

Her voice dripped irony. "Whatever you wish, my lord." She rang the bell, and when the butler responded, she said, "Lord Colford would like tea. And perhaps Cook has some of her poppy-seed cakes today, as well."

Poppy-seed cakes would choke him—but one excuse was as good as another. Richard tried to catch the butler's eye, without success. He cleared his throat, but the butler turned away.

Miss Mercer was watching him closely. "Mason is quite deaf, you know," she said finally. "Especially when it suits him to be. I assure you, my lord, I am not a danger to you."

Richard wasn't so certain—and the perceptiveness she showed worried him. "Tell me, Miss Mercer, how did you meet Roger? And what made you think he wanted to…" He couldn't bring himself to say it.

"To marry me? Let me think. It *might* have been when he said, *Felicity, will you marry me?*"

His jaw dropped. "Roger said that?"

"Not quite," she admitted.

Richard didn't relax—he was much too alert to let down his guard entirely—but some of the tension went out of his body at the confirmation that he'd been correct.

"He said he wanted to marry me, but he feared that his family wouldn't allow him to do so. And he was right," she said bitterly. "If there had only been more money, I might have made a palatable bride, if not exactly a welcome one. But there wasn't. So the son of an earl could not throw himself away on the daughter of a mill owner."

"He told you this?" Richard didn't believe a word of it. Yes, their father had been a stiff-necked old goat, but since when had Roger listened to anything the earl had said, much less actually obeyed an order? "When was this?"

"More than a year ago—at the beginning of spring last year. Roger was recalled from York to London, and I never heard from or about him again, until word filtered back through his friends that he had taken a chill—and died of it."

So at least she did know that much—but Richard wasn't sure whether to be relieved or even more upset. Not many people had known about Roger's stay in York, so how had this chit heard of it? And yes, she was right that it had been more than a year ago, just as winter had given way to spring, that Roger had returned to London. Richard remembered it well, because his brother had complained so much about how cold it had been in York…

The details were coming back to him now. Roger had been on a sort of rusticating lease for a few months, lying low with some of his less-reputable friends, waiting until the earl had gotten over being furious at him. Richard had never heard the details of why their father had been so angry; he only knew it was because of something Roger had done around Christmastime. Richard himself had been too caught up in his own duties to pay attention to the details. It was nothing unusual, after all, for the earl and his son to be at loggerheads, so this time had seemed no different.

But then, instead of calming down and summoning Roger home as expected, the earl had quite suddenly died... and *everything* was different.

So it was possible—even if just barely possible—that Miss Mercer was telling the truth. That Roger, in his boredom, had wooed and won a wench in York. And if the earl, already furious with his son, had heard that Roger had taken up with the daughter of a mill owner...

But why hadn't Richard heard about it—about her—then? It wasn't the sort of thing that the old Earl would have handled with finesse; he'd have bellowed like a bull...

Richard's attention had slipped away from Miss Mercer for a moment, and when he looked back at her, he realized that she was unbuttoning her dress. The neckline gaped open, and he could see the swell of her breasts peeking out beyond the pale blue of her gown. Was it his imagination, or was her creamy skin really giving off heat in waves?

"Oh, no you don't," he said, and sprang toward her. He seized her bodice just as she jerked back, and the dainty, pale-blue lawn tore in his hands. The sound of it ripping seemed to echo, just as the butler backed into the room with the tea tray.

Richard froze, his hands still clenched on Miss Mercer's dress, his knuckles grazing her breasts. Her skin *was* hot—for he was feeling extraordinarily warm just now...

The butler looked past them as if he saw nothing, set the tray on the table, and went out again soft-footed.

"Oh, do close your mouth," Miss Mercer snapped. "It's very unattractive, letting it hang open that way. Don't be any more of an idiot than you must, my lord. He's seen this sort of behavior before."

"You mean you—" He stopped himself, but it was already far too late.

The gold darts in her big green eyes should have slain him where he stood. "Do I regularly entertain men, do you mean? No—not in front of the butler, nor in any other circumstances!"

"I profoundly beg your pardon, Miss Mercer."

"I should think you would. In the small chance that you did not already realize it, this house is Lord Hawthorne's private bordello."

He almost choked. Not at the idea that Thorne had a trysting place set up—though why he'd locate it right under his countess's nose was another question—but that this chit could speak of it so calmly. Was *she*...?

She had gone straight on. "All the servants are well trained to see nothing, hear nothing, and say nothing. And before you ask—no, I am *not* Lord Hawthorne's mistress."

"I did not suggest—"

"You were wondering." She pulled a thin gold chain out from inside her dress. "Before you made fools of both of us, I was merely reaching for this to show you."

At the end of the chain dangled a ring. Roger's ring—an engraved gold signet that his brother had worn for years. Richard would have recognized it anywhere.

He'd never realized it was missing. He wondered how long she'd had it—and where she had come by it. He had no idea how long it had been since he'd seen the ring; could it have been missing for a full year without him noticing? That was possible, he concluded, since Roger would have put it away when their father died, anyway…

He closed his hand around the ring, and only then did he realize how close he was still standing to her. They were linked by the fine chain that had suspended the ring between her breasts. The gold signet was so warm that it almost burned his hand, and his fingertips tingled as if he—and not just the ring—had caressed the shadowed crevice of her cleavage.

"You're saying he gave you this?" Richard asked. His voice felt hoarse.

"Do you think I would confess that I stole it from him?" she asked sharply. "*Yes,* he gave it to me! Why is that so difficult for you to believe? He would have married me… I *know* he would have married me, if his father hadn't been furious and his mother outraged at the very idea…" For the first time, her voice broke.

Richard fought the impulse to draw her close, to comfort her. He believed her now—or, more accurately, he believed that she was convinced she told the truth. But she hadn't known Roger as well as he had. Roger no doubt had given her the ring—but he doubted that his brother had meant it as a token of betrothal.

He let the ring drop to the end of the chain and stepped away from her to a safer distance. "What is it you want, Miss Mercer?"

"I told you. I want a child."

"Why not the usual way? Find a husband, and in due course…"

Her mouth tightened to a hard line. "That is not possible."

Richard considered the possibilities and the tautness of her face, and took a deep breath. "Did my brother bed you?"

She nodded, finally. "I am an unmarried woman who is no longer a virgin. I am the daughter of a tradesman, and though I have enough money to support myself in comfort, I have it on the best authority—that of your prestigious family—that I am not wealthy enough for a gentleman to overlook my handicaps. When I lost Roger, I thought for a while that at least I would have his child. But that was not to be." She stood even straighter, if that were possible. "I want what I should have had then. I want a child who bears his blood."

Chills ran up Richard's spine. "But my brother is dead, Miss Mercer."

"I know. That is why I want *you* to give me a child."

❧

As the silence stretched out, Felicity thought that perhaps she was being a little unfair. After all, Colford had only had a few minutes to take in what she was saying. She'd been thinking of this for a week—or maybe even longer than that.

She hadn't planned this exactly, but perhaps this scheme was what had been lurking in the back of her mind from the moment she'd received Anne's letter and began to make her plans to come to London. For

where else would Lord Colford be found during the
Season but in London? It was expected of a peer of
the realm.

If she *had* been plotting this, the thoughts had
been so deeply buried that she hadn't even realized it
herself—until she had actually met him and recognized
the opportunity, and then the plan had seemed to
spring full-fledged into her head.

She had known, of course, that Roger had a
brother—for her lover had told her enough about
him. Richard had been the satisfactory son, Roger
had said one day when he was feeling particularly
annoyed at having been banished to the far reaches
of the country. Richard was the one who saw eye to
eye with their father. The one who followed the old
Earl's orders and carried out his wishes. The one who
exceeded every expectation and never, *ever* quarreled
with their sire...

Yes, she knew a great deal about Richard... far
more, she thought, than Roger had realized he was
telling her. And now she intended to use the fact that
Richard was the traditional one, the one to whom
reputation and family mattered above all.

Lord Colford wasn't necessarily slow in understanding what she had asked, she reminded herself;
he simply hadn't had time to absorb it all, as she had.
He didn't seem to be stupid or simple—but perhaps he
just couldn't grasp the magnitude of her longing. Or
perhaps she hadn't told him clearly enough.

She was drawing a breath to try again when he spoke.

"There are other men you could marry, Miss
Mercer. Tradesmen like your father."

"I have no wish to marry anyone, Lord Colford. I learned the hard way what to expect from gentlemen—I am not foolish enough to expect a better result now that I am soiled goods. As for the men of my own class, they too put a premium on virginity. In addition, they seldom welcome the idea of a wife who has been educated beyond her station—or theirs."

He looked away, obviously unable to meet her eyes.

*Good,* Felicity thought. At least he understood the immensity of her problem.

"In any case," she went on crisply, "I will not beg or bargain with a man to convince him that I am of value. I have faced the truth. Marriage is not possible for me—nor would I want it, even if it were somehow to come within my reach." She paused. "What I want—*all* I want—is a child. I will devote my life to being a good mother."

He nodded, as if he understood. Or perhaps, she thought darkly, as if she had confirmed some hidden conviction.

She looked directly at him. "My lord, will you give me what I ask?"

"And leave myself open to blackmail for the rest of my life? I think not."

She let a smile play across her lips. "I could blackmail you anyway, you know. There are other men who would indulge me. Then if I were to visit Lady Colford in a few months and tell her that the child I carry is yours…"

The only hint of emotion he displayed was the slightest lift of his eyebrows. He was getting better at concealing his feelings, Felicity admitted. Or perhaps he was simply adjusting to being around her.

She went on, lightly, "It might be… amusing… to see what she did then."

"*You* might be amused," he said calmly. "Blanche would not. But neither would she be particularly upset."

His cool assessment of Lady Colford sent chills down Felicity's spine. She wasn't certain which bothered her more—a wife whom he portrayed as a block of ice or a husband who was so clearly undisturbed by the fact. But, of course, theirs wouldn't be the first society marriage made because of connections and bloodlines and money, rather than fondness—much less love. Most society couples made their separate ways through life—taking lovers, living apart, agreeing on nothing more than the need for discretion. That was one of many reasons that Felicity wanted no part of the *ton*.

"And what faith could I put in your promise of secrecy, if I were to do as you wish?" His voice was low, soft, and very sensual.

Felicity's breath caught. Was he going to take her request seriously? "I give you the word of a lady," she said.

He smiled and said softly, "But my dear, you've just told me that you're *not* a lady."

෴

Instantly, Richard regretted saying it. True though it might be that she had not been born a lady, he had uttered an insult of enormous consequence. He waited, breath held, to see how she would react.

If she had burst into tears—as Blanche could so capably do whenever she felt herself slighted—he would not have been startled, but he would have remained unmoved. Feminine tears, he had learned the hard way, were too often nothing more than a tool for manipulation.

If she had flared up at him, screaming abuse in return—something else Blanche was quite good at doing—he would not have been surprised. He would have bowed politely and walked away. One shrewish woman in his life was quite enough; he was not about to acquire another.

Instead, Miss Mercer took a short, sharp breath—in very much the same way as men on the battlefield did, he had noticed, in the instant they absorbed a mortal blow. Her eyes filmed over, but she blinked the tears away, squared her shoulders, and said, "Thank you for hearing me out, my lord. Good day." Her voice was low and full of pain and dignity and sheer raw sensuality.

"I am sorry," he said. "I should not have said... what I did. Not only was it rude and unthinkably offensive, but it is not true. You are far more a lady than many who can claim the title from birth."

"Thank you for that much, my lord." She turned away, her hand outstretched for the bellpull. "And for hearing me out before you refused my request."

It was done. Over. All he had to do was bow and walk away.

Instead, Richard caught her wrist, preventing her from summoning the butler. Her bones felt fragile in his grasp, yet he was startled to realize that a power within her held him just as tightly as he was holding her. "But I have not refused."

She looked up at him, and he watched as her eyes widened. A man could drown himself in those eyes, he thought, and never even think about coming up for air.

"If this is truly what you want, Miss Mercer…"

"It is," she whispered, and the tip of her tongue flicked against her lower lip.

A primal urge slammed through him. Desire, pure and simple—the automatic reaction of a male to a female who had shown herself eager for his attentions. And he had no doubt of that; he could smell the sensuality that seeped from her. At this moment, her entire being was passion at its most primitive, its most needy—even though wrapped in the trappings of a lady. The combination was oddly erotic, and one that sent lust surging through his veins.

Richard knew with dreadful clarity that no matter what it might cost him, he could not simply walk away.

She looked at him directly—her chin held high. "You see," she whispered, "I loved him."

For a moment, reminded of his brother, he almost let her go. *Almost.* But the lust was too strong, the need too overwhelming. He would satisfy her fantasy, fulfill her desire—and at the same time, slake his own urges.

"I loved him, too," he said hoarsely. But though that was true enough, it was not the reason he would grant her request.

For a moment, they stood there as Richard quivered on the brink—trying to regain his senses, even though he knew it was too late. Then he said, "As you wish, Miss Mercer. Shall we begin?"

He did not touch her or even offer his arm, but Felicity was so aware of him just behind her on the stairway that her skin prickled and her knees trembled. She was astounded that she could walk at all.

She paused at the top of the stairs, wondering for an instant what to do next. She had never thought this far into her plan; she supposed she had never truly believed that he would grant her request.

She shuddered at the idea of taking him to her own room, for it was her haven, her most treasured spot. If she'd had any idea that he'd actually agree, she would have ordered a fire in the main bedroom—the green-velvet one that had so obviously been intended for seduction—to take the chill off the unused room. But now there wasn't a servant to be seen. They really were *very* well trained, she thought a little irritably. She had caught no more than the glimpse of an apron whisking out of view around a corner as she and Richard climbed the stairs.

Perhaps she should simply ask him to come back another time? Tomorrow would do as well…

But instantly she dismissed the notion. She *must* seize the moment—for once he left her, he might never return. She couldn't blame him if, once he gained some distance from the emotion of this encounter, he had second thoughts. She was having a few herself… but only a few.

No. This afternoon, this moment in time, was all she would have—all she would dare to ask for. She must make it count.

She pushed open the door of the sitting room that

lay next to the green-velvet bedroom, and stopped short. The apron-clad maid she had spotted rounding the corner must have been in this room—for a fire was burning merrily in the grate and candles stood ready, with one already alight.

Lord Hawthorne's servants were indeed worth whatever he paid them, she thought—for they had read not only the situation but her mind as well.

"Miss Mercer?" Lord Colford asked.

"Through here." She led the way into the bedroom, where she was not surprised to find the velvet hangings pushed back invitingly and the coverlet already turned down. Here, too, a fire had been lit and candles glowed. The chill had already left the room.

She turned to face him and caught an intense look in his eyes. Suddenly realization of the magnitude of what she was about to do—of what she was asking—flooded over her. "I shall be a good mother, my lord. My child will never want for love—or for anything else."

He reached out to put his hands on her shoulders and gently pulled her close, tipping up her face to his. "I believe you," he said, and brushed his lips across hers.

The kiss was not even remotely sexual. It was a salute, a gesture of honor, a pledge—all wrapped into one.

She stayed quiescent in his arms, and when he released her, she quietly went about undressing. Doing her best to pretend he wasn't watching her, she folded her dress across the back of a chair and sat on the edge of the bed, still wearing her chemise as she lifted up the sheet.

"Take it off," he said softly.

"Why? It's not…" She felt herself flush. "It's not necessary."

"Then why bother to take your dress off when you could have just lifted your skirt? Why bother to bring me to a bedroom? The drawing-room floor would have done as well for the purpose."

Her voice caught. "You needn't be crude."

"Have the goodness to at least pretend that what we are doing is different from a stallion with a mare, Miss Mercer."

She bit her lip. Then she slowly took off her chemise and laid it aside. She started to slip beneath the sheet, but he caught her hand and stopped her and then pulled the sheet back to the end of the bed so she was fully exposed.

He didn't take his gaze off her as he disrobed. Felicity had never felt as naked as she did lying there on the bed while he looked his fill. She tried not to look at him, but it was impossible not to notice the broad shoulders and the dusting of golden hair that formed a triangle on his chest and drew her gaze slowly downward as he took off his smalls.

"Oh," she said—half in admiration, half in dismay.

The mattress shifted as he lay down beside her. He brushed a hand lightly over her breast, and her skin quivered.

"You needn't do anything except..." Her voice cracked.

"Except the main event? If you're telling me you don't want me to touch you, Miss Mercer, then it may be a little difficult to achieve your purpose."

"Of course not. I just meant... if you need to do... anything... to get ready... then, of course, do so. But you needn't concern yourself with..."

"With your comfort? Very well." He gently pushed her legs apart, settled himself there, and nudged his erection against her core. Then he stilled, letting her feel his weight and the heat of his penis. "Brace yourself."

Felicity twitched a little, her muscles tightening. He was so big… surely he was going to hurt her.

"That's what I thought." He rolled, taking her with him, until he was lying on his side but still nestled between her legs. He cupped her breast with one hand, toying with it, stimulating her nipple with his thumb, and insinuated his other hand between her legs.

"What are you doing?" she whispered.

"Every farmer knows that soil is more fertile when it has been properly prepared." This time his lips were hot against hers, his tongue tracing her mouth until she opened for him. His fingertip slipped through the curls between her legs and found the little nub of sensitive flesh there. The rhythm of the stroking of both places—slow and intense—began to build inside her. All the heat in her body seemed to follow, pooling around his touch. She quivered and strained toward him. "Patience," he whispered. "Give yourself time."

The emptiness inside her ached. She tugged at him, and finally he rolled her onto her back and entered her, moving slowly and carefully. She felt herself stretching to accommodate him, but she was no longer afraid that he might hurt her. He was just the right size—and she welcomed him, inch by inch, until he was fully inside her.

Slowly he began to thrust, sliding deeply within

her, only to pull almost entirely away before once more advancing. His touch was gentle and firm at the same time, sure and deliberate, as he stroked her over and over until she thought the heat and friction of his rhythm would set her ablaze.

She wrapped her legs around him, pulling him closer. When she tried to catch his rhythm to bring him even deeper within her, he shifted suddenly to quick, shallow strokes, and suddenly sparks danced across her vision and her body clenched in a long, slow, shuddering release. He held himself still for a moment as she convulsed around him, and then he once more plunged fully inside her.

Felicity's eyes wouldn't focus. Her thoughts were a hodgepodge. Her senses were aflame.

"Roger," she whispered.

He stilled for an instant. Then, very slowly, he began to move once more, and before she had even regained her breath, he had once more driven her over the brink. This time, as she climaxed, she shrieked. He caught her wordless cry with his lips, and with a hoarse groan, he released his seed.

It took a while before Felicity's breath stopped rasping and came easily once more. She opened her eyes and realized he was watching her, his gaze sober and thoughtful. His face was only an inch from hers, so close that she could count his individual eyelashes, long and golden and curly.

*Now what?* she asked herself. Embarrassment flooded through her. They were still intimately entwined, tangled together just as they'd collapsed. She supposed that lovers would take advantage of this time to caress and kiss and whisper soft words. But they weren't lovers... not in anything but the raw physical fact. So what were they supposed to do now?

She'd never thought about the practical aspects of this whole situation—like exactly how, after the deed was done, to go about disentangling herself from him. How to get her clothes back on. How to get him to the door. How to say good-bye...

"You should not rise for at least a few minutes," he said. "I shall call on you tomorrow."

She was startled. "I hardly think that will be necessary."

"Only time will show whether it is or not." His voice was level. "To have the best chance of success, it would seem a practical move to... repeat the process."

"Oh." Felicity's face was hot with shame. "Of course."

"Then I will see myself out. Until tomorrow." Efficiently, but without hurry, he gathered his clothing, dressed, and was gone.

❧

He had done exactly what she had asked of him. The matter should have been finished. Perhaps this one encounter would be enough to result in the child she said she craved. Richard had certainly done his part; he could not recall having had such a powerful reaction to any other woman, ever.

He should have been pleased to be finished, eager to be gone, content to leave the matter to chance.

Instead, he had made an assignation for the morrow. Why?

Because, in the midst of her passion, she had called out his brother's name? That wasn't a surprise, exactly—considering that she had only settled for his seed because Roger was gone. But it pricked his pride.

Roger had been the favorite son; even from his earliest childhood Richard had known that. It was simply a fact, and he had always accepted it as such. Even when the old Earl had been outraged by Roger's behavior, he had always shown a tinge of pride in the spirited defiance Roger showed and the way he managed to push aside obstacles to get his way.

Richard, meanwhile, had been the dutiful son—the quiet one who watched over the family estates, who tended to the tenants' needs, who listened to the steward's ideas and put them into action, who never once rebelled. He was the farmer who knew how to make the soil most fertile…

He had not resented Roger for always having first choice of whatever he wanted. Not until now, at least. For Felicity Mercer had been no different to Roger than the toys they had shared in childhood. Roger had seen her, wanted her, taken her… and discarded her.

Richard was certain that she had never before experienced anything like the pleasure he had given her today. Roger might have bedded her, but he had not made love to her; Richard was the one who had initiated her into the joy of lovemaking.

Yet she had called out Roger's name.

*Next time, it will be mine.* The thought was fierce, steely, primitive.

Only then would he be done with her—after he had planted himself so deeply within her body, and within her memories, that she could never again pretend that Roger was the one who had made her soar.

Anne's modiste had hurried to produce a few morning dresses and walking gowns for Felicity, but the remainder of the wardrobe she had ordered was still to be completed. Anne went with her for fittings the next morning, and they were poked and pinned in unison, each with a team of seamstresses working over her.

"The current fashion is quite a good thing for a woman in my circumstances," Anne said lightly as the modiste pinned her into a royal blue gown with a very high waist. "As long as the seamstresses leave enough room in all the seams for my maid to let them out a bit, I'll be able to wear these for months. And a good thing that will be, too—since in a few weeks we'll be going home to Surrey. I won't get a glimpse of London again 'til after the baby comes."

"And by the time the Season starts next spring and the new fashions take hold, you'll have regained your shape. You couldn't have timed it more perfectly. That's a really wonderful color for you, Anne. I wish I looked as good in those dark, rich shades as you do."

"I thought perhaps you'd wear that light blue lawn today," Anne said as she stepped out of the royal blue dress. "It seemed to be your favorite of all the things you chose."

Indeed it had been, Felicity thought ruefully, until Lord Colford had ripped it yesterday. She had considered bringing it back for expert repair—until she realized that Anne would certainly ask questions about how Felicity had managed to tear a brand-new dress in such an unusual way. "I wore it yesterday," she said. "That's a lovely dressing gown."

The gown Anne had donned was truly beautiful—a deep, rich scarlet velvet that made Anne's black hair and pale skin even more dramatic. "It feels lovely, too," Anne said. "You should get one, Fliss."

"Too rich a color for me."

"Oh, not red, of course. On you, the blue of a robin's egg would look better. Or purple—yes, that's it." She glanced around for the modiste. "Do you have a light, clear purple velvet for Miss Mercer to look at?"

The modiste nodded and hurried off, coming back a few minutes later with an armful of fabric the color of lilac blossoms. She draped it around Felicity, who had to admit that the sheen and the feel of the cloth was incredibly sensuous, and the color was the perfect foil for her golden hair and fair skin.

"A dressing gown," Anne decreed. "Made with a neckline that can be drawn up close around the throat for warmth or spread enticingly wide to show off your elegant shoulders..."

Felicity felt herself turning pink. She could picture herself in a purple dressing gown so loosely wrapped around her body that it had slid off one entirely bare shoulder... and she could see Lord Colford stooping to kiss the exposed hollow just under her collarbone...

"An unmarried woman does not need a thing like that," Felicity managed to say.

"Oh, nonsense. Every woman needs to feel beautiful in her boudoir—even when she's alone." Anne turned slowly, studying her own red robe in the mirror. "Just a half-inch shorter, I think. I won't be wearing shoes with it."

Felicity's heart was still skipping madly at the mental

picture she had created. How had Lord Colford invaded her daydreams?

"She'll take the velvet dressing gown," Anne told the modiste. "And if she doesn't, I'll make it a gift—so it ends up being the same thing."

Felicity drew in a deep breath to refuse—and found herself nodding instead. It was almost wrenching to let the modiste take away the velvet, for the whisper of the fabric against her skin had felt so comforting, so secure, so right. It had caressed her in much the same way that Lord Colford had done yesterday...

And that, she told herself, was quite enough of *that*.

Still, each time they brought out another gown to be fitted, she found herself touching the fabrics, testing each one for its sensual potential in a way she had never thought to do before.

Finally, however, they were finished and once more dressed for the street. As they left the modiste's and settled into the carriage, Anne gave a sigh of satisfaction. "You won't mind stopping at Hookham's, I suppose?" The question was careless, as if the answer was never in doubt. "It's just down the street, and I really want the next volume of Miss Austen's *Mansfield Park*. If I don't hurry, I won't finish reading it before we leave London."

Felicity checked the small watch pinned to her pelisse and sighed in relief. "Yes, I have time before—" She stopped too suddenly and felt herself coloring.

"Before what? I didn't realize that you had become so very busy, Fliss. What wonderful things have you planned for this afternoon?" Anne's gentle tone and the interest in her gaze were just a little too sweet to be truly innocent.

Felicity could have bitten off her wayward tongue. As the carriage lurched to a stop outside the lending library, she ran rapidly through a list of possible excuses. *A friend is coming to call…* No, that wouldn't work, for Anne knew everyone Felicity did in the whole of London, and she'd be hurt if she wasn't invited to join them.

*I have an appointment…* No, for Anne would likely ask what kind and with whom, and Felicity had no answer. *I have to sort the linen…* No, for Anne must know that Mrs. Mason had the whole of Number 5 Upper Seymour Street firmly in hand, and there was simply nothing left for Felicity to do in running the house.

Inspiration struck. "I'm expecting the manager of my mill to call on me with a report," Felicity said. "He thought that he'd be in the city sometime this week." Surely, she thought, the Countess of Hawthorne would not be interested in a report on the workings of a Yorkshire manufacturer—and the excuse had the advantage of being somewhere near the truth. Her manager *had* said he'd be making a trip to London sometime during her stay, and of course whenever he arrived, he would call on her to make a report.

"I see," Anne murmured, and allowed the footman to assist her from the carriage. "How very… interesting… that will be."

Relief flooded through Felicity, for the tone of Anne's voice indicated that she expected the report to be anything but interesting—and therefore she wouldn't give it another thought, much less wonder what her friend was really up to. "There's Lady Stone," Felicity said, pleased to spot another potential distraction. "I wonder if she's going to Hookham's, too."

"No doubt," Anne said, and waved at Lady Stone. "Lucinda—may I presume on your friendship to bear me company to Hookham's? Miss Mercer wishes to return to Upper Seymour Street to await a caller."

That, Felicity thought, would be the perfect solution. She really needed to go home right now... even though Lord Colford hadn't said exactly when he'd arrive, just that he would call in the afternoon. Still, a bit of preparation seemed to be in order. After all that dressing and undressing at the modiste's, she felt the need of some serious grooming.

"What's his name?" Anne asked.

Felicity gulped and sputtered. Lady Stone's beady black eyes fixed on her with interest, and Anne was watching her with fascination.

Finally Felicity remembered the excuse she'd given. The mill manager—*that* was who Anne was asking about. It was a sensible, logical question that had absolutely nothing to do with Lord Colford; her own guilty conscience had nearly tripped her up.

"Mr. Rivers," she said.

"Well, have a good time with him," Anne murmured. She gave an order to the footman to see Felicity home immediately and then return to Hookham's to pick her up. Then she linked her arm into Lady Stone's, and the two of them disappeared into the lending library as Felicity, feeling very warm and rumpled and absolutely coated with embarrassment, let the footman assist her in climbing back into the carriage.

Really, she thought. This business of carrying on an intrigue was *most* complicated!

❦

Before the next hour had passed, however, Felicity
was wishing that she'd stayed at Hookham's and
looked at books. It wasn't that she was dreading
Lord Colford's arrival, for she wasn't. If she was
honest, she was already anticipating his lovemaking.
The most uncomfortable little shivers kept running
through her, making her ever so aware of her body.
Her skin seemed to remember the way he had
stroked her; her tongue had developed a distressing
habit of running slowly along her lip in the same
way that his had done yesterday; and as for her most
secret places… well, if he happened to be in a hurry
today for what he had called "the main event," she
wouldn't mind at all, for she already felt warm and
embarrassingly moist.

No, distaste for what they would do together was
not what was making her uncomfortable. She knew
what would happen in her bed, and she was not only
ready but eager.

The problem was that she had no idea what to do in
the meantime. Should she wait for him in the drawing
room, as though he were an ordinary caller? Or now
that she was his mistress, would he expect her to act
the part?

Perhaps she should tell the butler to bring him
directly up to the main bedroom… but she shuddered
at the idea of *that* conversation.

Oddly, however, she didn't shudder at the idea of
actually waiting for him in bed. Undressing in front
of him, under that intense and brilliant blue glaze,
would be no easier than it had been the day before. Of

course, if he didn't arrive at all, she'd feel a prize fool lying there waiting all afternoon…

But if she received him in the drawing room like any ordinary caller come to share tea and conversation, and he expected that she'd be already in bed… well, that would be equally awkward.

The very idea of tea and conversation reminded her that yesterday she'd ordered a tea tray that neither of them had even touched. Felicity didn't want to think about what the servants had made of that fact. Though, considering they were Lord Hawthorne's servants and no doubt used to that sort of thing…

This was all *far* too confusing.

In the end, she said nothing to the butler and retreated to the small sitting room next to the main bedroom. She sat there for what seemed hours, toying with a bit of needlepoint until finally the tangled yarns defeated her.

She had just tossed it aside when the butler came in. "Lord Colford has inquired whether you are at home to him."

She took a deep breath. "Yes. Show him up, please, Mason."

The butler seemed to take forever to descend the two flights of stairs and return with her caller. In the meantime, Felicity—suddenly breathless with nerves—looked around the perfect little room and straightened a pillow, twisted a vase round half an inch, pushed a china shepherdess just a fraction closer to the shepherd figurine on the mantel, and then put her back precisely where she had been.

The door opened, and she could feel him standing

there behind her. Her very skin knew he was in the room and that they were alone.

His voice was soft and deep. "I regret that I've kept you waiting. I was unavoidably detained."

Had he found it difficult to get away from his wife today? A tinge of guilt seeped through Felicity. Then she told herself firmly, *I'm not taking anything from her. It's just this once...*

*Well—all right. Twice.*

But it wasn't as if Felicity was going to continue to be in Colford's life or to be the sort of mistress who would demand his time and attention. After today, they would likely never see each other again. Blanche would never know, so this interlude would make no difference in the Colfords' marriage—such as it was.

What was it Lady Stone had said about Blanche making his life a living hell? Felicity decided she didn't want to know the details—not that a gentleman would share them with his mistress anyway.

"It is no matter," she said. "I realize you have other obligations. If you're expected elsewhere..."

He stopped halfway across the room, looking at her thoughtfully with his head tipped to one side. "Are you having second thoughts?"

"No," Felicity whispered.

He smiled, and she felt a rush of warmth between her legs. It almost made her knees weak.

"No tea today?" he asked lightly.

Good manners kicked in. "If you would like..."

"What I would like isn't to be found on a tea tray." He tipped her face up to his and kissed her.

Only their lips were touching, but sensation

swept over Felicity in waves as every inch of her body reacted to that isolated but all-encompassing caress. She swayed toward him, and without breaking the kiss, he picked her up and carried her into the bedroom, pushing the door open with the toe of his boot and finally setting her on her feet beside the bed.

Her hands trembling with anticipation, Felicity began to unfasten her dress—but he stopped her. "Allow me," he said, and with infinite caution he dealt with buttons and ties. "I am reminded that I owe you a dress." He released her breasts and bent his head to nuzzle first one and then the other.

Felicity was barely thinking. She only knew that he was taking too long—far too long—so she started to unbutton his shirt, seeking to get past the cool linen so that her skin could touch his.

He smiled at her eagerness, and with quiet efficiency he removed her chemise and then turned her away from him. Startled, she looked over her shoulder just as he began to remove the pins and clips from her hair.

"My lord," she said. "There's no need…"

"In a hurry, my sweet? I suggest you curb your impatience, for despite our late start, I've no intention of cutting our afternoon short."

He released her coronet and unwound each braid, slowly and patiently. By the time he was done, she was vibrating as if each strand of hair was the string of a violin and he was the concertmaster, fine-tuning her body like a rare instrument. He scooped up the golden tresses and kissed them, and his mere touch made her thrum with desire.

Only then did he finish undressing himself. She watched and, with the experience of the day before, was quietly satisfied. He might speak of patience, but his body said otherwise. So she was not surprised when he immediately spread her legs and brushed her curls with his thumbs.

"I am ready, my lord," she murmured.

He smiled, and humor as well as desire sparkled in his eyes. "That's what you think." He kissed her navel, flicking his tongue into the little depression. Then, instead of mounting her as she'd expected, he slowly worked his way down.

※

His fingertips gently parted her curls, exposing her secret places. She cried out incoherently, and Richard raised his head and said politely, "Yes? You were saying, Miss Mercer?"

"But that's… it's…"

He settled back between her knees, holding her open with gentle ruthlessness. His tongue flicked against her nub, and she gasped and stopped talking. He felt her shudder run all the way through him as well, roiling his senses.

*Forbidden? Distasteful?* He wondered what she had intended to say. Not that he cared much about the reasons for her objections, for by the time he was done with her this afternoon, she would have forgotten them. Demonstration was so much more effective than argument in these matters. But exercising his intellectual curiosity also helped him rein in passion—and a good thing, too, for as hot and wet as she already was, his self-control was eroding quickly. Only his determination that today she would give him every reaction a lover could want was allowing him to maintain the façade of cool control.

Though perhaps it would actually be a good idea to take her fast and hard the first time. Then, with his most urgent hunger slaked, he could truly focus on giving her pleasure and on wringing from her the admission that she never had, and never would, find such satisfaction with any other man...

But the urge to satisfy himself first was selfishness talking—and he was determined that she would have not the faintest reason to regret the bargain she had made. Almost lazily, he licked—and when she gave a little groan and bucked against him, sending a surge of heat to his groin, he had to grit his teeth for a moment to restrain himself.

He was bent on making certain that, if her wish was granted, she would never be able to look at the fruits of their lovemaking without remembering exactly how that child had come into being. Furthermore, he was intent on providing every possible opportunity for her wish to be granted...

Which was why when Thorne's man of business had kept prosing on to the two of them this afternoon about that bloody canal he was so certain would make them both even more wealthy, Richard had excused himself—saying something vague about pressing business, if he recalled correctly.

But why was he thinking about canals when he had so many more interesting things to think about—like the way she was panting in short, sharp, almost painful breaths… or the way his own breath kept catching in his throat…

On the other hand, thinking about canals would at least keep him from embarrassing himself.

Maybe.

He nibbled gently, and she came apart.

He watched almost in awe as waves of sensation flooded over her, engulfing him as well. He'd never been with a woman who was so responsive. It was all he could do not to act on his pressing business right then and *press* Miss Mercer between himself and the mattress.

Then she whimpered, and his self-control broke. He held her while she trembled, and while she was still quaking from the force of her climax, he slid inside her with one long, powerful thrust, a hot brand intended to mark her as his property, and felt as if he was coming home.

She was incredibly, supremely tight—cupping him closely with taut muscles still quivering from her own satisfaction—and yet she was hot and slick and eager. His mind reeled, and all he could do was thrust again and again, his goal tantalizingly near… Just one more… *one* more… and he exploded deep inside her, just as she called out his name and clenched tightly around him.

He sagged against her, their bodies slick with sweat, his lips pressed against her temple.

"Richard…" she breathed. Then he felt her body tighten under him. "I beg your pardon, my lord." Her voice sounded hoarse. He was so closely pressed against her that the breath she drew rocked him as gently as a cradle.

He shifted enough to relieve her of his weight but

took advantage of the opportunity to seat himself even more firmly inside her. "For presuming intimacy by using my name? Under the circumstances, I think it would be foolish to stand on ceremony. *Richard* will do… Felicity."

※

Her name sounded different on his lips. She'd never particularly liked it—it was a silly name for a human being, she thought; who could possibly live up to being called *the quality of happiness*?—but he made it sound prettier. More sensuous. More appealing.

His voice was slow and soft and lazy, as if for the first time since they had met he was truly relaxed. She felt a rush of tenderness toward him. It was nonsense, perhaps, Felicity thought. But if she could help him forget his situation for a little while—give him some ease from Blanche and the living hell she was said to be making of his life—in return for all he was doing for her…

Definitely he was relaxed, she realized. His eyes were closed, his muscles slack. Surely he hadn't actually dozed off… but if he had, how long was he likely to sleep?

"My lord," she said softly, and nudged his shoulder. "Are you asleep?"

"Yes." He didn't open his eyes. "I thought we agreed on first names."

"If we're finished…"

"Why? Do you have other plans for the rest of the afternoon?" He opened his eyes then and began toying with her hair, using a lock of it to trace her cheekbone, her jaw, her throat, and the valley between her breasts.

"No," she admitted.

"Then there's no hurry. All in good time."

Somehow that reminded her of something he'd said the previous day, and before she thought twice she asked, "Are you a farmer?"

That brought him fully alert. "I beg your pardon?"

"Yesterday you said…" She felt herself turning pink. "Something about… preparing soil."

He didn't laugh at her, and she was profoundly grateful. "I have farmland on my estate, of course."

"What's it called? The estate."

"Collinswood. It's in Surrey."

"That's where the Hawthornes live. Is it close to them?"

"Twenty miles or so. It's a big county."

"What do you grow there?"

"A little of everything. I've always been interested in the land—managing it, making the estate self-sustaining, finding new methods to increase yields."

She was feeling the most interesting sensation… without moving, he seemed to be stirring inside her and filling her once more. It seemed yields weren't the only thing that he was interested in increasing… and suddenly Felicity lost her fascination for an estate called Collinswood as once more he took her to the heights.

A while after that, he left her for a couple of minutes to light the candles, and then they made love yet again in the soft glow. But eventually he kissed her gently and said, "I must go. Remind me to bring a picnic basket next time."

*Next time…* Despite being pleasantly relaxed, her senses went on high alert once more. "I could ask Cook…"

He laughed. "No, my dear—Cook wouldn't be nearly as skilled at sating my hunger as you are. And in any case, I must keep my engagement for dinner."

"With Lady Colford?" She was quite proud; her tone was perfectly casual, careless.

His hands stilled on the buttons of his shirt. "Yes, as a matter of fact."

"Will I see you tomorrow?" *Twice,* she had promised herself, in her guilt over Blanche; she had sworn they would only meet these two times, and then she would let him go. But the question slipped out despite herself.

"I'll come if I can. I'll send you word in the morning."

"I'll wait for your message." She sat on the bed and watched him dress. "Richard," she said finally.

"Yes, my dear?"

"I would like sometime to talk to you of… Roger." The name felt awkward on her lips—but somehow it helped to assuage her guilt by reminding herself that this was, after all, about her lost love.

He paused in the midst of arranging his neckcloth. "What about him?"

"What he was like as a child… what games he played… where he grew up." She shrugged. "You could tell me anything, really, and I'd love listening to it. How he felt about being a younger son… how he died."

"Of course," he said politely. "At your convenience."

"And about you, of course," she added. "Roger told me you were always the good son—the one who was more like your father."

He looked at her inquisitively. "How very odd of him."

A moment later he was gone, leaving Felicity feeling that somehow, unexpectedly, things had gone sadly wrong—though she wasn't quite certain how.

❧

It was childish of him, Richard knew, to want to kick the nearest piece of furniture. After an entire afternoon spent in his arms, and a bit of the evening, as well, his oblivious little golden beauty had wanted to talk about his brother. His *brother*! The man who had bedded her but not bothered to show her the joys of love. The man who could have married her... but hadn't.

*You could tell me anything, really, and I'd love listening to it. How he felt about being a younger son... how he died.*

She'd planted him a facer with that one, and no doubt about it. But she'd puzzled him as well. It was past time for him to find out what Roger had really been doing in York two years ago and why he had lied to Felicity Mercer. Richard thought he knew who might be able to tell him.

But he would have to rush a bit to be on time for dinner at Colford House.

❧

Rather than joining Anne for their usual morning coze, Felicity sent a maid to deliver her regrets and settled into her own drawing room with a book to wait for a note from Richard. But after she'd read the same page a half-dozen times without registering a single word, she put the book aside and sat in the window that looked out over Upper Seymour Street.

For the first time, she found herself regretting her

decision not to even attempt to go into society. She certainly couldn't ask Anne about Lord Colford; inviting Anne's curiosity would be disastrous. But if Felicity had begun to develop a separate circle of acquaintances in the city, she could have asked leading questions and listened to chatter. She couldn't have aspired to the heights of the *ton*, but surely she could have found some friends who, like herself, occupied the fringes. They would have heard—and shared—the gossip. She might have been able to find out all kinds of things about Lord Colford.

She told herself briskly that she was being foolish—acting like a schoolgirl in love…

The idea seemed to echo in her head.

*A schoolgirl in love.*

She was long past being a schoolgirl, that was sure—but apparently she was not too old to behave like one. In fact, she realized with a sudden sinking feeling, she was every bit as foolish as any schoolgirl she'd ever known—for she had fallen headlong into love with a man she could never have. A man who was so incredibly wrong for her that there weren't even words to express how foolish she had been…

Her stomach felt jittery, her chest tight. How had this happened? How could she have been so shortsighted?

Was it possible she was just feeling a sort of infatuation, born of Richard's kindness and the undeniable, exotic joy of his lovemaking? If that was the case, then perhaps she would forget him if their paths didn't cross in the future…

Pain lanced through her at the very idea of never seeing him again. She clenched her fists against it until her nails dug into her palms, but it didn't go away.

No, she would never be able to forget. This was different. This was… overwhelming.

More than a year ago, she had realized, even as she'd let herself fall in love with Roger, that they were too far different in station to actually marry. Though she had been heartbroken when he left her, she had not—in a way—been surprised.

But if a love match between the daughter of a mill owner and the younger son of an earl was almost unthinkable, how very much more ridiculous the idea was when it concerned the daughter of a mill owner and the earl himself.

Not that she had ever thought of marriage where Richard was concerned. But perhaps simply knowing how impossible it would be had made her let down her guard. Because Felicity had felt herself safe, she had been in even greater danger of losing her heart to this charming, dangerous man…

She heard the knocker fall against the front door, and she had to force herself to sit quietly rather than rush out to see if the sound heralded the message she was waiting for. In that moment—as she sat like a proper lady in her drawing room, wanting with every fiber of her being to run to the door, to seize the paper from the footman's hand, to find out whether he would be coming to her today or if she would have to wait—she admitted the truth.

She had never intended to know Richard well enough to actually care about him. He was supposed to be a fleeting encounter, a convenient replacement—a pale substitute for the man she had lost.

What she hadn't realized until far too late was

that Richard wasn't a pale substitute for anyone or anything. And so the inevitable had happened.

Only this time, she suspected, the pain would be even worse than what she had felt when she'd lost Roger—because this time the situation was so clearly her own fault. She should have known better...

Mason came in just then to tell her that Lady Hawthorne was calling.

In fact, Anne was just a step behind him. "I'm presuming on our friendship," she announced, "and being very rude indeed to burst in on you like this without waiting for Mason to ask if you'll receive me. But when you sent a message this morning instead of coming, I was worried. Are you all right, Fliss? Did you get bad news?"

*The worst,* Felicity thought. How had she let this happen? After having her heart broken by Roger, how could she have been so naive as to think she could walk away from his brother unscathed? She had intended to use Richard to get what she wanted... but instead, she was the one who had been caught up in her own desire. She was the one who would pay the price.

"Oh, my dear," Anne said. "Is it very bad? Is the mill in trouble?"

"The mill?" Felicity couldn't focus. "What do you mean, the mill?"

"Your manager. You said Mr. Rivers was coming to speak with you. I thought perhaps he'd brought bad news and you couldn't bear to see anyone. Felicity, look at me." She seized Felicity's arm and shook her.

Felicity dragged her mind back to the drawing

room and to her friend. "No, not at all. Mr. Rivers hasn't been here."

"Then you haven't... Oh, my goodness. I'm so sorry—rushing over here because I'd jumped to conclusions that you were suddenly impoverished. How silly of me! But why didn't you come to sit with me this morning? Are you ill?"

"No—I just... Anne, should you be walking around so early in the day? You've had such trouble in the mornings."

"Not for a few days now. I seem to be over the worst—now that the first few months are past. I really was afraid for a while that I was going to be ill every morning until Christmas!"

Christmas... it would be a special one for Anne, for they had calculated her baby would be born in December. And as for Felicity's...

With any luck at all, Felicity's child would be just a couple of months younger. And if they lived close enough to each other... *Our children can play together,* she thought idly.

Then she stopped herself cold as the harsh truth struck home. Her child would not grow up anywhere near where Anne lived—certainly not at his father's home at Collinswood. Her child would have no claim to the estate or to the family. He could not be acknowledged by his father.

Her child would be the son or daughter of an earl; yet without a father's name, that child would not—*could not*—be a suitable playmate for Anne's child. Even Anne, who was Felicity's dearest friend, would not lightly flout society's rules on that head. And in any case, Felicity would be going back to York, far from Surrey and Collinswood…

Far from Richard.

Her child would never know its father.

*What have I done?* Felicity asked herself.

Being the child of a mill owner was a serious social handicap, as Felicity had learned the hard way when she went off to the boarding school where she had met Anne. Not every girl at the school had been as willing as Anne to overlook Felicity's origins; some of them had been downright cruel.

But the social stigma Felicity had faced paled in comparison to what she had so carelessly done to her own child. Yet being illegitimate wasn't the worst burden she had placed on her baby—there were ways around that, stories that could be told. She could make up a husband who had conveniently died…

But that would mean lying to her child—denying him the truth and the right to know his father…

*I must stop this now,* she told herself. *And I must hope and pray that it isn't already too late, that we haven't already made a child…*

Her body rebelled against the idea of never touching Richard again… but perhaps even worse, against the idea that she might not, after all, carry his child.

She had dreamed long ago of having Roger's baby—and she had mourned when that obviously was not to be. But that was nothing compared to the twin griefs she felt now. She wasn't even sure which grief she felt more deeply—the idea that she might bear a child who would eventually blame her, perhaps even hate her, for not giving him or her a father… or the idea that she might *not* have Richard's child to love and cherish forever.

The butler came in. "This was just delivered, Miss Mercer. The servant is waiting for a reply."

Felicity took the folded paper with stiff fingers. How could she take the chance of opening Richard's message in front of Anne? But she couldn't ignore it, for the footman who had delivered it was waiting to take back her answer.

She unfolded the message, but it took her a couple of minutes to register what it said. It wasn't from Richard at all but from Jason Rivers, the manager of her mill. He was in London and would call on her that afternoon, if it was convenient.

"So he's here at last," Anne said. "Of course you were concerned because you didn't hear from him yesterday—and no wonder you wanted to be at home today, to be certain not to miss Mr. Rivers' message. And Mr. Rivers." She looked quite pleased with her deduction. "Tell me—is he nice? Will I like him?"

Felicity could imagine no circumstances in which the elegant Countess of Hawthorne and the rough-edged Mr. Rivers would be in the same room, much less that they would ever get to know each other. "He's very attentive to the business," she said. "But I hardly think that I could introduce him to…"

"Oh, Fliss, if he's important to you, of course I want to meet him."

And that, Felicity thought hollowly, was truly the death knell for her silly, girlish dreams. If even her dear friend Anne thought that the manager of her mill was an appropriate match for Felicity Mercer…

How utterly foolish she had been. She supposed next she'd catch herself wishing that someday Lord Colford would stop *making* love to her long enough to realize that he was *in* love with her!

But even if that could happen—and it couldn't, for she must stop this madness now—there could be no hope of a future.

Anne's head was tipped inquisitively to one side.

"It's not like that," Felicity said.

"Well, something—or *someone*—has rattled you so completely that you can't finish a sentence. If it isn't Jason Rivers, who in heaven's name is it?" Fortunately Anne didn't wait for an answer. "Now that I know you're all right, I'll leave you, so you can get ready to receive him."

❧

Richard lingered at his club, pretending to read the newspapers and half listening as Hastings, the old rattlepate, told anyone within range about the team of sweet goers he'd bought the previous week at the Newmarket horse fair.

He had sent word to Felicity that he would call on her this afternoon, but as the hour approached, he found himself hesitating. It was not that he didn't want to go to her, for visions of himself entwined with Felicity had kept him awake the night before as he contemplated what he would do with her the next time they made love. But this encounter would not—could not—follow the pattern of the past two.

Today, he had to tell her the truth about his brother—and that might change everything. So he sat a bit longer, trying to rehearse what he would say, before he put aside the unread papers and walked from his club to Number 5 Upper Seymour Street.

The butler promptly admitted him, but Mason looked a bit doubtful and seemed to move more slowly than ever before as he led the way up the first flight of stairs.

Richard's patience, already worn, thinned to the vanishing point. "No need for you to make the entire climb," he said finally. "I'll show myself up to the sitting room."

The butler didn't seem to hear, for his pace remained steady. "Miss Mercer asked me to conduct you to the drawing room instead."

The drawing room? That was unexpected. Richard wouldn't have been surprised to find her already in bed; such an eager little mistress she was proving to be. In fact, he'd actually considered whether it might be better to satisfy her first before having their little talk... But he knew that was his own raging desire speaking and not common sense.

He was still wondering if the butler had got it wrong when Mason opened the drawing-room door and he saw Felicity arranging roses in a tall vase.

For an instant, he thought he had stepped back in time to when he had first come to see her. It hardly seemed possible that so much could have happened...

She looked up, and he was shocked—her face was pale and her eyes shadowed as if she hadn't slept. "My lord," she said, and her voice also was different—flat and hollow and lifeless.

"My dear." He went to her, hands outstretched.

She stepped aside around the table, and Richard stopped in the center of the room. "What's wrong, Felicity?"

"I've come to my senses," she said.

*What a shame.* For an instant, he was afraid he'd actually said it.

"I can't see you anymore," she went on. "I... I can't bear it anymore."

He couldn't believe what he was hearing. Never in his long and varied experience had a woman dismissed him before he was finished with her. For this minx to do so—especially after what they had shared—was incredible.

His eyes narrowed. She wasn't looking at him, he realized, but beyond him.

"Very well," he said. "It is, of course, your prerogative."

A bit of the tension went out of her body. Her shoulders no longer seemed rigid—as if she was relieved that he was taking it so well.

He watched her closely while he pretended to flick a speck of dust off his lapel, and then he issued a challenge. "Come and kiss me good-bye, Felicity, and we'll part friends."

She sucked in a breath that sounded painful. She looked terrified.

Just as he'd suspected. She couldn't do it. So what was she playing at?

His desire had never been far beneath the surface since the first time he had touched her; now it flared into an inferno, and common sense turned to ash. He advanced slowly on her, not looking away and not stopping until his body was brushing hers. Through the thin fabric of her dress, he could see the way her nipples peaked, the automatic response of a woman to her lover.

She darted a glance up at him and then looked away as if denying that he was there. His chest brushed her breasts with every breath he took. She sighed as if in surrender—and suddenly he was kissing her, his lips devouring hers, hot and fierce and demanding.

And she was answering. He plundered her mouth, and she kissed him in return as if she was starving for him. Satisfaction surged through him at her reaction, firing his desire to new heights.

His hands roamed freely over the body he had explored so fully, and she gasped and molded herself to him. "You're mine," he said harshly, "and you'll remain mine as long as I choose."

She turned to a statue in his arms. "Let me go."

"Felicity, what the *devil*—I beg your pardon. What do you mean?"

"I cannot go on. It was a mistake. I beg of you— just forget me, my lord. Forget that I was so foolish."

*Forget* her? She was standing in his arms, his kisses still hot on her lips, and she wanted him to simply forget that she had been his lover and go away quietly? Was the woman *mad*?

"Or what, my Lady Desire?" he said. "What will you do if I don't agree to… forget? What if I let a word slip to your good friend Lady Hawthorne?"

Her voice was small but determined. "Then I fear I would have to tell Lady Colford."

He smiled. "Go ahead. But I do beg that you'll allow me to be present, for I'd hate to miss the fun."

He heard a step on the stairway and then another in the carpeted hallway outside. What ailed the butler to make him forget his oh-so-convenient training at this of all moments?

Felicity tugged herself loose. "I am expecting a caller."

The butler cleared his throat outside the door, and by the time he entered the room, Felicity was sitting on the sofa, her spine very straight and her pose that of a perfect lady.

She was quick on her feet; Richard had to give her that... though of course she'd had the advantage of knowing that they would soon be interrupted. He wondered if she'd planned it that way. Was his delightful little golden mistress playing a deeper game than he'd given her credit for? What if her caller was the Countess of Hawthorne, come on purpose to discover him in a compromising position?

Then Miss Mercer was about to get a very large surprise... Though if she *had* intended to compromise him, why had she moved, rather than staying in his arms?

He turned to survey the new arrival and was startled to see that Felicity's caller was not the countess but a man. He was dark-haired, solidly built and a good six inches shorter than Richard, with square shoulders that looked far too wide for his height. His coat was fashionable, his neckcloth correct—but something about him whispered that the effect had been achieved only with much effort and great expense.

The newcomer advanced on Felicity with a wide smile. "Miss Mercer, I am glad to see you well."

Was he blind? Richard thought. She looked far from well.

"Lord Colford, may I present Mr. Rivers." Felicity's voice was colorless. "Mr. Rivers is the manager of my father's mill. I mean… my mill."

Rivers turned to face Richard. His gaze sharpened, and for a moment his face looked almost feral. Then he smiled broadly and bowed. "My lord."

Richard wished he had a quizzing glass. He didn't want a better look at this specimen. But it would be interesting to see the mill manager wilt under a close inspection—and the cad deserved it for aspiring to Felicity…

*So it comes to this,* he told himself. *Sparring over a woman.*

"Lord Colford was just leaving," Felicity said. "Thank you for delivering the message in person, my lord. Mason will see you out."

He was stunned. She actually thought she was going to *dismiss* him?

But he bowed politely and took his leave. He would let Miss Mercer—and her dandy of a mill manager—think they had routed him.

For the moment.

❧

Even after Richard was gone, his presence seemed to linger in the room. Mr. Rivers kept looking around as if expecting Lord Colford to tap him on the shoulder, and Felicity couldn't focus on the report the mill manager was giving her. When for a third time she had to ask him to repeat himself, Mr. Rivers smiled broadly and seated himself beside her on the sofa. "Perhaps we should leave discussion of business for another occasion."

"Yes," she said gratefully. "I don't seem to be able to take it all in just now."

"There's really no need for you to fret your mind about it at all."

His patronizing tone—as if he was patting her on the head and reassuring her that it was perfectly all right not to be smart enough to understand her finances—flicked Felicity raw. "I beg your pardon?"

"My dear Miss Mercer, surely you know that my greatest wish is to be of service to you. If you would but say the word, I would be honored to take over all responsibility for your financial affairs."

Felicity frowned a little. "*Say the word?*"

He seized her hand. "I should restrain myself, I know. I intended to wait until you got this London nonsense out of your head and came home to York where you belong. But I find I cannot. Seeing you again, after these few weeks apart, has confirmed the nature of my feelings. You are more beautiful, more charming than ever."

*Not today,* she almost said.

"My dear Miss Mercer, let us stop dancing around the subject. Once you have agreed to be my wife…"

"Your… wife?" Felicity said faintly.

"Then you need never concern yourself about your finances again, for all your affairs will rest comfortably in my care, and you need occupy yourself only with matters of our household and our children. You may devote yourself to making our mansion a true family home."

*Our mansion?* Was he thinking of the big, old dark house—the one she never wanted to see again—as already belonging to him?

*Children?* The mere thought of bearing a child that wasn't Richard's made her shudder. Yet...

Should she, for the sake of the child she might already be carrying, at least consider Jason Rivers' proposal? She could go home to York as a wife. Her child would have a name. No one would ever know, and she wouldn't have to make up a story about a husband who had died...

Jason Rivers had managed to get hold of her hands, and he was looking into her eyes. But his gaze, she thought, contained a great deal more calculation than soulful adoration. "And we will never speak of anything you might have done while you were here," he went on.

*As for the men of my own class,* she had told Richard, *they too put a premium on virginity.* Clearly, Jason Rivers had his suspicions. If she married him, Felicity—and ultimately her child—would pay for those suspicions. If her child was born with her own golden hair—and Richard's—rather than with Jason Rivers' dark coloring...

No. Bearing an illegitimate child and raising him or her with love would be far better than putting herself and her baby in the grip of a man who would hold that child's father over their heads forever.

Jason Rivers must have seen the hesitation in her face, for his grip tightened. And perhaps... did she see the slightest hint of desperation in his eyes? Certainly it had been clumsy of him to let slip that he suspected her of not being chaste. "I am willing to overlook many things, Miss Mercer."

But in return for what? *All your affairs will rest comfortably in my care...*

For the first time, Felicity wondered if he had

already arranged to take over her finances. Was this proposal simply the final step in a plan he'd been putting into motion for months?

When her father had died, she had still been numb from Roger's desertion—and she had been grateful to have an experienced manager in place, someone who could step into her father's shoes and take the necessary actions to keep the mill operating.

She had only started to recover from the double loss when she had heard of Roger's death, and again she had leaned on Jason Rivers. He had always been respectful and careful to consult her... but had he only been going through the motions, manipulating her while he actually acted as he pleased?

Why had she not wondered before now whether he really had her best interests at heart, or his own?

The profits from the mill had been much lower during the past year than she had expected. But she had accepted Jason Rivers' figures and his explanations. She had assumed that she must have misunderstood what her father had said—for he'd never fully explained the business to her.

*Because I never cared to listen,* she admitted.

Too caught up in her grief to ask questions, she had never thought to doubt Jason Rivers. But then, she had also never suspected that he might harbor warm feelings for her—and surely she should have seen that before, if those feelings had really existed.

Now he had proposed marriage. But why? Because finding her with another man had made him realize that he cared about her, and so he must speak quickly or risk losing her?

Or because finding her with another man made him fear that if she married, her husband might ask questions about the mill that Jason Rivers would find uncomfortable?

One thing was certain: she could not afford to let him realize that she no longer trusted him.

"This is so sudden," she said, letting a girlish quiver creep into her voice.

She saw the flare of confidence in his eyes and dropped her own gaze so he couldn't read her distaste there.

"Not sudden at all, Miss Mercer. You must know that I have admired you for years. It was only the sad loss of your father that kept me from speaking before now."

Or made it possible for him to cement his position with her... "I am very flattered, of course. But I must have a little time to consider. It would hardly be proper of me to accept a proposal immediately." He gave her a wide, toothy smile and pressed her hand between his. Felicity didn't know how she managed not to shake off his touch.

"Then I shall leave you to consider," he said warmly. "I will call on you again tomorrow, and I beg that you will be ready to give me the answer I crave."

❧

Felicity's butler—or perhaps to be more accurate, Thorne's butler—might be elderly, but he certainly hadn't lost his touch. As Richard came down the stairs, Mason moved into position by the front door, already holding Richard's hat—quite as if he'd been expecting Richard to get his marching orders.

Richard noted a tinge of sympathy in the old man's

rheumy eyes, and annoyance trickled through him. What business was it of the butler's what went on above stairs, anyway? On the other hand...

He took his hat and dropped a gold sovereign into Mason's hand. "The... person... who is upstairs with Miss Mercer," he said. "Has he visited her before?"

The sovereign vanished into the butler's pocket as neatly as if he were a magician. "No, my lord."

But Felicity had obviously been expecting him...

As if he had read Richard's mind, Mason said, a bit too loudly, "He sent a message this morning."

"Was she pleased to receive it?"

Mason looked thoughtful. "I would say not. She seemed... resigned."

"Yet she agreed to meet with him alone?"

"It seems to be a matter of business, my lord, at least on her side. Mr. Rivers is in trade."

Richard raised an eyebrow. "When it comes right down to it, Mason, so is Miss Mercer. He runs the factory—but she owns it."

Mason's jaw set tightly. "Miss Mercer may own a factory, my lord, but despite that she is a lady through and through."

*My Lady Desire...* "Indeed she is," Richard murmured. "Being one thing does not mean she can't be the other as well. But you said, *at least on her side.* I wonder what he is after."

The butler cleared his throat. "I should say, my lord, that he had the look of a man who is about to make an offer of marriage."

Richard couldn't say he was surprised; the same thought had occurred to him when Rivers had started posturing. But the fact that the butler had picked up the identical signals shook Richard to his core. His hand tightened on the brim of his hat, and he had to force himself not to turn on his heel, run back up the stairs, and burst into the drawing room to—if necessary—tear Felicity from the cad's arms and plant Rivers a facer while he was about it.

"You know that look well, do you, Mason?" he asked lightly.

But the butler answered quite seriously. "I have seen it many times, my lord."

Not in Thorne's household, Richard would bet. He smiled at the thought.

"As I have seen the look of a lady who is uncertain how she will answer, my lord."

Mason sounded so somber—so concerned—that Richard also sobered. Surely Felicity wasn't going to entertain an offer from a man like Jason Rivers!

Yet she had told Richard their affair was over, that she had come to her senses, that she couldn't see him anymore.

Had she begged him to forget her because she was going to marry Rivers? Surely not of her own free will… for she didn't seem to be very happy about it. Was the cad blackmailing her somehow?

Something of the sort must be going on, Richard thought, because Felicity Mercer would not, absolutely *could not* prefer Jason Rivers to himself.

❧

As soon as she saw Jason Rivers climb into a hack and drive away, Felicity ran down the stairs, calling for her cloak and a maid to accompany her around the corner to the Hawthornes' town house. Perhaps Lord Hawthorne would be at home, and she could ask his advice. Or failing that, perhaps Perkins could help her. There *must* be a way to determine whether Jason Rivers was defrauding her.

A carriage waited in front of the Hawthorne house—the one Anne habitually used, Felicity thought. The Hawthornes' butler admitted her to the front hall, and as Felicity's eyes adjusted to the dimmer light inside, she saw that Anne was at the foot of the stairway, carefully pulling on her gloves.

She came over to greet Felicity. "How perfectly wonderful! I wanted you, and here you are."

"But you're going out."

"Yes, I am—but will you do me the greatest favor and come calling with me?"

"I don't mean to be a trouble to you. In fact, I really wish to speak with his lordship—or with Mr. Perkins."

Anne shook her head. "They're both out, I believe. Something to do with a canal."

Felicity's heart dropped. But it had been silly to expect that Lord Hawthorne would be free to see her at a moment's notice, even if he had been in the house.

"Come calling with me now," Anne offered, "and after we return, you can speak with Thorne at dinner."

"I'm not dressed to pay calls."

"Nonsense. You're always perfectly well turned out."

"Anne, I'm not up to your style of society."

"This is hardly society. I'm to pick up Lady Stone at Grosvenor Square, and we're only visiting Thorne's aunt, who's an old friend of Lady Stone's."

If she went back to Upper Seymour Street, Felicity thought, she would no doubt simply pace the floor—so she might as well be occupied. And she liked Lady Stone.

Besides, it would be just as well for Felicity not to be at home, in case Richard decided to return to finish their interrupted conversation. Not that she expected he would, for she had surely made her point. All that nonsense about her remaining his mistress until he decided otherwise and the threat to tell Anne about their affair were simply manifestations of his pride.

At least, she was *almost* certain of that.

She had barely agreed before Anne was sending the maid back to Upper Seymour Street and sweeping Felicity out to the waiting carriage.

"Anne," Felicity said as they threaded their way through traffic on Oxford Street and down toward Grosvenor Square, "you've coped with your share of unwelcome suitors, haven't you?"

"A few. Why?"

"I don't know how to handle Jason Rivers. He proposed marriage to me this afternoon."

"Felicity, that's…" Anne went very still. "You said he's an *unwanted* suitor?"

"Yes. I think he only offered for me because he doesn't want me to realize he's been stealing my money."

Anne stared at her. "*Stealing*… but Fliss, how awful! You had no idea?"

"I've… I've found it difficult to concentrate on the business of late."

"Is this why you decided to sell your house?"

Anne's face was warm, full of concern. "Are things so very bad that you can't afford it any longer?"

"Oh, no—I was going to do that anyway. I'm not impoverished, Anne. Since my father died, the profits from the mill have been smaller, yes—but I thought it was because customers who were used to dealing with Papa might have been drifting away..." She shrugged. "It sounds foolish, I know, not to have asked questions."

"Not at all. When you lost your father, of course you didn't have a thought to spare for the mill. But... You mean it *wasn't* him? Jason Rivers, I mean. He wasn't the man who had you so flustered? But then who...?"

Just then, to Felicity's relief, the carriage pulled up in front of a huge house on Grosvenor Square. A footman swung down and went to the door, and Felicity shifted over to the rear-facing seat to leave room for Lady Stone beside Anne in the forward-facing one.

Noting Anne's thoughtful gaze, Felicity said hastily, "No doubt this entire thing is largely my own fault. I should have been paying more attention—learning about the mill and stepping in to run it myself. It's my responsibility, after all."

"You might rely on a husband to look after it for you," Anne said gently.

Felicity shook her head, trying to keep her face calm. Marrying someone who wasn't Richard? Pain stabbed through her heart at the very idea. "I thought his lordship might advise me about how to proceed."

"Of course Thorne will help you, Fliss. He'll be as incensed as I am at the idea of Mr. Rivers taking advantage of a woman who's alone in the world...

only he'll be a great deal more effective than I would be at solving the problem. Husbands are sometimes not a bad thing, my dear." Anne's voice softened. "But I know, of course, why you would hesitate. Is he the toad, Fliss? Jason Rivers, I mean. Is he the man who hurt you so badly?"

*No,* Felicity wanted to say. *And Roger wasn't a toad, either.* But she decided it would be better not to answer that particular question. Once Anne got her teeth in something, persuading her to let go was hard enough without giving her extra reasons to hang on. So Felicity simply shook her head and tried to deflect the conversation. "I have no proof that he's stealing, you see. Only suspicions."

Lady Stone hoisted herself into the carriage, leaning heavily on two footmen.

Felicity finished, "And I've no idea how to find out the facts."

"Suspicions? Who are we being suspicious of?" Lady Stone asked brightly as she sank into the cushions and waved the footmen away.

"I thought you made it a point to be suspicious of everyone, Lucinda," Anne said lightly.

"But of course I do, my dear. Even Lady Alice."

Anne glanced at Felicity. "Thorne's aunt," she explained.

"For what possible reason would she summon *me* to call on her," Lady Stone went on, sounding a bit querulous, "at almost the very moment she arrives in the city for her first visit in a year? To ask *you* to come calling makes perfect sense, Anne. You're family now, since you captured her infamous rake of a nephew.

And since she's been in mourning at Collinswood for months, it's the first chance she's had to meet you."

"You're old friends," Anne said.

Lady Stone gave a cackle of a laugh. "I'd much prefer it if you said *longtime* instead of *old*. But the fact is we're not friends—not really. I've seldom even seen her since she married Colford. So why she wants to renew our acquaintance now…"

*Colford*. Lord Hawthorne's aunt was named *Colford*? And she was a friend—an old friend—of Lady Stone's? But Anne was Lady Stone's friend, too, so it didn't necessarily follow that Lady Alice was old… Felicity's head was spinning as she tried to make sense of it all. "I thought Lady Colford's name was Blanche," she said feebly.

"That's the younger one," Lady Stone said. "With any luck, she won't be there. Lady Alice is my generation—in fact, we made our come-out together forty years ago. But I haven't seen her in a decade at least."

Felicity closed her eyes in pain. She was on her way to meet Richard's *mother*—and Roger's, of course—and potentially his wife as well? What horrid sequence of events had brought her to this pass?

Felicity had never dreamed that she might one day come face-to-face with the woman who had, Roger had told her, made it quite clear that he could never dream of marrying the daughter of a mill owner…

This was going to be bad. Very, very bad.

But before Felicity could think of a reason that would convince Anne that she absolutely couldn't go into the house, the carriage had pulled up—and the footman was helping them down.

Long ago, Felicity had formed a mental picture of what Roger's parents must look like, based on what he had told her about them. His mother, she had decided, would be tall and aristocratic, gray-haired, and painfully thin—with a nose like a hawk, a spine so straight it made one hurt to look at her posture, and eyes the same cold shade of gray as tired winter ice…

The woman who rose from behind the tea table to greet them did indeed have wonderfully good posture—but that was her only resemblance to Felicity's mental picture. Lady Alice was small and dainty, with fluffy white hair and a pink-and-white complexion that showed hardly a line. Her eyes were the same brilliant sapphire as Richard's, and she smiled with apparent delight at her old friend Lady Stone; her new niece, Lady Hawthorne; and Felicity…

Anne introduced her. "Lady Alice, may I present my good friend Miss Mercer?"

Lady Alice's eyebrows rose by the barest fraction. "What a happy circumstance that you could join us, Miss Mercer."

Felicity could have sunk through the floor. Had Lady Alice recognized her name? Richard hadn't seemed to know it; perhaps his mother also had forgotten… or she might have never cared to find out. But that didn't mean Felicity could let her guard down for even an instant—for it was equally possible that Lady Alice *did* remember, and perhaps she thought that Felicity had seized this opportunity to force her way into an introduction.

"I'm very pleased to meet you," Lady Alice went on.

*You wouldn't be if you knew that I've been your son's mistress.* Felicity tried her best to sink into the upholstery and disappear.

Lady Stone stirred her tea, sat back in her chair, and asked pugnaciously, "What brings you to London just now, Alice?"

"I've come to help Blanche pack," Lady Alice said calmly.

*Pack?* Felicity could hardly believe her ears. Surely Lady Colford's servants would do that. Now that the Season was coming to an end, they'd no doubt be expecting to do so. In any case, no one of Lady Alice's rank would pack anything herself or even supervise…

Lady Stone let out a bark of laughter. "Help her pack? *Send* her packing, more like. Where's she going? I don't see Blanche living in the dower house at Collinswood."

"Of course not. *I* live in the dower house, and I have no intention of sharing my home with Blanche. I believe she's going to Venice first. She can finish out her two years of mourning there—or not, as she chooses. But at least Richard will be able to finally take possession of his property. He's a bit soft-hearted, my son—not wanting to evict her from this house."

Felicity's head was swimming. A man didn't evict his wife… or did he? If Blanche was truly the horror that Lady Stone thought her…

"Soft-*headed*, I'd say," Lady Stone proclaimed. "He's the last of the line now. It's well past time to move her out and set up his own nursery."

"There's nothing official as yet, of course," Lady Alice said, "but I believe that is his intention. A cream cake, Lucinda? Our chef does such a lovely job of making them."

Anne looked delighted. "Colford's to be married? He's been in and out of our house quite a lot of late, but he hasn't breathed a word of this!"

*Colford's to be married…*

Felicity could feel the blood pounding in her head. In an instant, her hopes had been raised—and dashed. If Richard wasn't married after all… But he soon would be. So really, nothing had changed at all—and nothing could change now. If Felicity was already pregnant, her child would be illegitimate all the same—for he was as far out of her reach as if he *had* already been married.

*You're mine, and you'll remain mine as long as I choose.*

But even though he might be free for the moment, he would never consider marrying Felicity—for she was his mistress and the daughter of a mill owner.

But where on earth, she asked herself, did Blanche fit in?

༄

Lady Alice lived up to her title. She asked gentle questions, shared bits of small talk and gossip, and politely made certain no one was overlooked or left out of the conversation—until Felicity could have screamed with the tension. Every time Lady Alice looked at her or directed a comment toward her, Felicity braced herself and waited for sarcasm or accusation. But each time, Lady Alice treated her precisely as she would any other young woman who had come to call.

One moment, she had almost convinced herself

that Lady Alice had never let Roger get far enough in describing the girl he wished to marry to share Felicity's name. The next moment, she was certain that Lady Alice had simply dismissed that information as of no importance and no longer recalled it.

Felicity's body was humming with relief by the time they finally left Lady Alice at the Colford town house. But she knew better than to relax, because she still had Lady Stone to contend with, along with Anne, on the drive home.

"Do you suppose she'll really be able to remove Blanche?" Anne wondered.

Lady Stone snorted. "I expect so. Once a duke's daughter, always a duke's daughter—I doubt Alice has lost her touch. She brought Colford round her finger easily enough all those years ago, and a stiff-necked sort he was."

So Lady Alice was not only an earl's widow but a duke's daughter? Richard was a duke's grandson? Felicity's head hurt. She had always known she was out of her depth—but she'd had no idea just how far.

They delivered Lady Stone to her home. "What a very wearing afternoon," Anne said as the carriage pulled away from Grosvenor Square. "I do like Lucinda, but I must admit it's difficult to always be trying to sidetrack that disastrous tongue of hers."

Felicity was silently grateful that Lady Stone's erratic nature had served to distract Anne's attention from Felicity herself. "They do seem an odd pair of friends, don't they?"

"Very odd—though Lady Alice isn't nearly as stuffy as I'd expected she might be. How fortunate for me, since she's family." Anne sighed. "And now home—for a bit of a rest before dinner. Thorne will surely have returned by now, so you can tell him your suspicions and he'll know exactly what to do. If Mr. Rivers is truly stealing from you, the sooner you act, the better."

When the carriage pulled up in front of the Hawthornes' town house, Felicity meekly climbed down and followed Anne inside.

"Is Lord Hawthorne at home?" Anne asked the butler.

When Carson told her that his lordship was in his library, Anne swept across the hallway. She was already through the door by the time the butler finished, "With Lord Colford, my lady." Felicity, half a step behind her, stopped dead on the threshold.

But it was too late to back out, for the two gentlemen were rising from their chairs and setting down their wineglasses. "Thorne, darling," Anne said, as she planted a soft kiss on his cheek. "Felicity needs your advice—and she may well require the loan of Perkins for a while as well. Hello, Colford. You remember my friend Miss Mercer, do you not?"

Richard's gaze slid slowly over Felicity—as if, she thought warily, he was remembering every curve and every time he had ever touched her. Felicity tried not to look at him, but she couldn't stop herself. He looked magnificent in midnight blue—he always did look wonderful, but there was something about him today that was even more commanding, more dominating, and more compelling than ever before. Perhaps it was only that she knew now that he was the grandson of a duke.

"My lord," she said.

"Miss Mercer." His voice was level and cool, but Felicity felt warmth sweep over her at the reminder of other times when he had called her that—with passion, rather than detachment. He brushed the back of her hand with his lips, and Felicity needed all of her self-control to keep from turning her hand over to cup his cheek in her palm.

Very deliberately, to remind herself that she must not give in to that impulse, she said, "I understand we are to wish you happy, my lord."

Richard raised an eyebrow. "Where did you hear that?"

"Fliss, darling," Anne said hastily. "One must never tease a gentleman about such a thing. They're all skittish enough about marriage as it is, without making it appear anyone has noticed they might actually be contemplating the subject."

Even before the rebuke, Felicity had felt herself turning pink. What a nonsensical thing it had been to say! So much for Lady Stone's disastrous tongue; Felicity's could be even more troublesome.

"As for how the question of marriage came up," Anne went on, "we've just come from calling on your mother, Colford."

Richard's gaze had never left Felicity. But was that a challenge springing to life in his eyes? Was he about to demand how she had dared to visit his mother?

Felicity swallowed hard. Tension seemed to crackle through the air.

"Lady Alice is looking wonderfully well," Anne went on. "And she said only that she believed it time for you to give thought to the succession."

"As indeed it is," Richard said softly.

Felicity realized that her hands had come to rest on her stomach, cupped protectively over where her child might already be starting to grow. Quickly— with a jerk—she folded her fingers on the back of a chair instead.

The gentlemen were still standing—and likely wondering, Felicity thought, how long this trouble-some woman would take to come to the point. But she couldn't just blurt out her problem in front of Richard. It was one thing to confide in Lord Hawthorne how Jason Rivers' proposal of marriage had led her to ques-tion whether he truly had her interests at heart, or his own. It was something else to reveal all that to her lover.

Anne cleared her throat, breaking the short and uncomfortable silence. "How fortunate for you, Felicity, to have Colford here as well. Between them, the gentlemen can certainly give you the best possible advice about how you should respond to Mr. Rivers."

Felicity's heart froze. "I do not wish to trouble you, my lord. You have a guest, and I believe I must not intrude on your conversation."

Lord Hawthorne's gaze seemed understanding, almost gentle. "Perhaps after dinner?" he suggested.

Sit across the table from Richard through a long and elaborate dinner, keeping up a stream of bright and cheery social chatter? Felicity tried not to shudder at the idea. "Truly, my lord, I am exhausted, and I wish only to be at home."

Even Anne seemed to understand—for her gaze flicked between Felicity and Richard, but she didn't press the invitation. She had obviously felt the strain in the air.

"Tomorrow, then," Lord Hawthorne said. "I will await your convenience in the morning, Miss Mercer. And—did I understand you to say that Perkins might be required, my love? I shall have him at our disposal as well."

"Thank you, my lord." Felicity curtseyed. "Anne… my lord Colford…" She wouldn't let herself look at Richard for fear of what her eyes might give away. Her heart was breaking already at the idea that this had been their final good-bye—formal and chilly and polite, under the gaze of observers and without a hint of the passion they had shared.

❧

Richard had been lying in wait for an opportunity since the instant Felicity had walked into the library, but he could scarcely believe his ears when she handed it to him. "I will see you home, Miss Mercer."

Panic lit Felicity's eyes. "Oh, no. I must not take you away from your friends—and there is no need for you to escort me."

Her voice was too high, too fast, to sound natural. Lady Hawthorne was looking quite intrigued, Richard thought. "It's late," he said calmly, "and you shouldn't walk out alone."

"It's only a step through the garden. I wouldn't wish to inconvenience you or make your hosts wait dinner on your return."

*If I have anything to say about it, they'd be waiting a long time.* "It's no inconvenience, as I am not staying for dinner. In fact, I was just leaving when you and Lady Hawthorne came in." He'd been intending to go

to Upper Seymour Street and wait for her to return…
but that, right now, was beside the point. She had
delivered herself directly into his arms—so to speak—
and Richard intended to take advantage of the fact.

"An excellent plan," Thorne said. "You can have
the groom bring your horse around to Number 5
instead easily enough…" A note of very mild amuse-
ment crept into his voice. "…whenever you're ready
for it."

Richard watched the play of emotions across
Felicity's face. She was thoroughly stuck in a mare's
nest of her own making. She couldn't change her mind
about staying for dinner without causing more questions than any lady wanted to answer; and she couldn't
decline a gentleman's offered escort without causing
serious offense.

He saw the precise instant when she concluded that
the only thing she could possibly do was to accept his
assistance, make her way home in silence, and dismiss
him at her door.

Not that he would let her get rid of him so easily as
*that*. But if the thought made her feel better, he'd let
her believe it for a minute or two.

❧

The evening was cool and cloudy, bringing dusk a bit
earlier than usual. The air was misty, and the carriages
passing along Portman Square already had their lamps
lit. Richard offered his arm as they descended the steps
in front of the Hawthornes' town house, and Felicity
took it reluctantly, letting her fingertips rest lightly on
his sleeve.

At least he had tucked her hand into the crook of his arm, rather than taking hold of her elbow. Not that it made much difference exactly which part of her body he was touching... She could feel the heat of him through her cloak and through her gloves.

He shifted his hold, pulling her hand so closely to his side that her breast brushed against his sleeve... That could not be accidental. Part of her wanted—*needed*—to pull free, but that, she thought, would only amuse him. The other part of her wanted to lean into him, to savor his warmth and inhale his scent—but if she did, that would feed his arrogant certainty...

His voice echoed in her mind. *"You'll remain mine as long as I choose."*

Felicity's breath was coming with difficulty, as if she'd been laced into the tightest corset ever invented. *It's just around the corner,* she told herself. *It's a two-minute walk. How much can be said in two minutes?*

As it happened, they reached the corner without speaking at all. Only the clatter of the carriages on the square, the occasional nicker of horses, the muffled patter of a vender down the street, and the click of their own footsteps broke the silence. Now there were only three doors between her and her own house... two doors...

She was torn between wanting this agony to be over and not wanting it to end at all. If only she could walk on with him forever...

"Lady Hawthorne seemed hesitant to allow me to escort you," Richard said calmly. "Perhaps I should have reassured her that I have always taken the greatest care for your safety—as well as for your contentment and the satisfaction of your most personal desires."

Felicity glared up at him. "You wouldn't!"

"I *didn't*," he corrected. "But I certainly *would*— and I will, if you press the point."

She had the oddest combination of feelings at the very idea. Outrage, certainly, that he would manipulate or threaten her—perhaps even blackmail her into remaining his mistress. Yet she felt a sort of singing happiness that he cared enough—that he wanted her enough—to use such tactics.

She told herself briskly not to be a fool. It wasn't a matter of him caring for her; it was simply his pride that was at stake. She had ended their affair before he was ready to do so; that was all. In any case, she had already made up her mind, with good reason for her decision. Whatever methods he intended to use would not move her from her determination.

*Remember,* she told herself, *you cannot take the risk.*

Unless she already was carrying his child. Then there would be nothing more to lose by remaining his mistress…

*Except what remains of your heart,* she reminded herself.

They had reached the steps of Number 5 Upper Seymour Street. Mason swung the door open, and with difficulty Felicity removed her hand from Richard's arm. Her glove seemed to want to stick to the midnight-blue wool of his sleeve, and she tried to peel her fingers away without making it obvious that she really did not wish to break the contact. "Good evening, my lord. Thank you for seeing me home."

"I'm coming in."

"I beg your pardon?" She put on her haughtiest tone. "You were not invited."

He smiled at her, and as if she hadn't spoken, he ushered her up the steps, nodding politely to the butler.

Mason bowed and closed the door behind them. He took Felicity's cloak and Richard's hat and murmured, "There is a freshly laid fire in the green sitting room, Miss Mercer."

The green sitting room. The cozy little room next to the main bedroom... as if the servants had expected she would want to receive a caller there tonight...

Felicity led the way to the drawing room instead, where a fire also burned. Her heart had begun to pound erratically. Why had he insisted on coming into the house? "Bring his lordship a glass of port, Mason," she murmured.

"Don't bother, Mason," Richard said. "And don't come back."

"Very good, my lord." The butler bowed and went away.

Felicity stared after him. "Now even my servants obey *you*, rather than me?"

He didn't answer. Instead, as soon as the door closed firmly behind Mason, Richard came across the room to her.

"Our affair is over, my lord," she said. She fumbled at the neckline of her dress and unfastened the thin gold chain that held Roger's ring. She held it in her palm for an instant and then thrust it toward him. "Here. This was never mine. I meant to give it to you this afternoon, but I forgot."

Richard took the ring, looked at it for a long

moment, and dropped it into his pocket. "By rights, it belongs to the Earl of Colford's heir. I will hold it in trust until the next one is ready for it."

The Earl of Colford's heir... a boy who would be Richard's son—but not Felicity's. Everything around her suddenly looked dreary and flat. "Now it is truly finished, and I wish to put all this behind me. So please go."

Richard slipped an arm around her. "Why, Felicity? Why are you ending our affair?"

She tried to hold herself rigid. "I don't believe I need to give you a reason."

"And that is where you're wrong. Tell me you didn't enjoy our lovemaking, and I'll stop."

"I didn't enjoy—"

"You're lying through your teeth." He brushed the corner of her mouth with his fingertip, and Felicity quivered at the reminder of other caresses. "What was it you wanted to discuss with Thorne tonight, Felicity?"

"That is none of your business, my lord."

"*Richard*," he said softly, and let the backs of his fingers slide gently down her cheek. "You haven't said my name since we made love yesterday."

"I suppose you wanted me to call you that in front of Lord Hawthorne?"

"It would have been interesting to see Lady Hawthorne's reaction," he murmured. His mouth trailed slowly along her throat, and her breath caught. "I thought perhaps you were interested in Thorne's views of appropriate marriage settlements."

"It is not my concern whom you marry, my lord.

I regret if my foolish comment led you to believe I was interested."

He smiled down at her. "But I wasn't referring to *my* marriage settlements. I was asking about yours. Is it your intention to marry Jason Rivers?"

She was startled. How could he possibly have known that she had received an offer? Jason Rivers' intentions had not been obvious to her; how could Richard have seen, in the fleeting moments when both men had been in her drawing room, what was going to unfold?

"Why should I not?" Felicity asked tartly. "You yourself suggested that I look among men of my own class for a husband."

"I did say that, didn't I?"

That was not at all the answer Felicity had hoped for—which would have been something like, *Because I want you to marry me instead...* Richard didn't seem to be concerned by the recollection, though the casual way he said it stabbed into Felicity's heart.

"I think it is time for you to go, my lord."

"*Richard,*" he repeated, and nibbled at the corner of her mouth. "Say it, Felicity—or I'm never going away."

"Richard," she breathed, with a catch in her voice. "Now will you go?"

"No," he whispered against her lips.

"You told me you'd leave."

"I lied. Because when you say my name, it inflames me, my Lady Desire. It makes me want you under me, begging me to repeat everything I've ever done to you and then to find new ways to delight us both." He pulled her closer, letting her feel the strength of his arousal. "And I think you want that, too."

"That will not happen." She had to grit her teeth against the rush of wanting, the heat that pooled at her very center.

"Because you think to marry Rivers? I won't let you, you know."

"Why?" she snapped. "Because it would be too inconvenient to have a married mistress? I can't think why *that* would stand in your way."

He smiled at her. "Not at all. It's not scruples about you being married that would deter me, Felicity, for I know that Rivers could never be truly in your heart. It's merely the distance. York would be such a long way to go when I'm hungry for you... especially when I'm hungry for you all the time." He was stroking her back from shoulder to thigh, each touch of his hand bringing her even closer to melting into his body. "Tell me why you're so anxious to end our affair. Do you believe you're already with child and your goal has been achieved?"

"I've changed my mind."

"You don't want a child anymore?"

She seized hold of the last of her self-control, braced herself, and thrust out at him. "I do not wish to bear *your* child, my lord."

"Because it would not be Roger's child?" he asked softly.

She had expected that her cruel words would make him go cold and even more patrician than before, that he might thrust her from himself and turn away in disgust. Instead, he held her more closely still, but this time he was cradling her with comfort rather than sensuality. And something about his voice made her tell the truth. "No, not that. I… I cannot give my child the burden of being nameless. Of never knowing his father."

"Then the answer is clear." His eyes were suddenly brilliant again. "You must marry me."

The room seemed to sway around Felicity. "That's impossible. Your mother would never allow…"

"My mother has nothing to say about who I marry— any more than she did when Roger married Blanche. Or than she would have had to say about his choice if Roger had wanted to marry you."

"He *did* want…" She stopped dead as the full import of his words registered. Blanche had been *Roger's* wife? But Anne and Lady Stone had called her Lady Colford—how was that possible? Unless…

Richard's voice was gentle. "I had no idea until last night that Roger had told you he was the younger son, rather than the heir. He must have thought that would make you believe that his choices and his life were not his own."

"*Roger* was the Earl of Colford?"

"After our father's death, yes. I can only conclude that he believed if you had known he was actually next in line for the title, it might have been more difficult to persuade you that his supposed love for you was a forlorn and hopeless thing."

"Roger lied to me." Her lips felt stiff, cold. Saying the words seemed to make them sink into her soul— and made Roger feel more distant from her than even his death had done.

"I was going to break it to you as gently as possible this afternoon, but you offered me no opportunity to do so. The fact is there was no discussion of you in the family. I knew nothing of you—of any of Roger's activities in York. My parents did not forbid him to marry you—or any other woman, come to that. My mother did not object to you as a potential bride—in fact, she had no idea you existed until last night."

"*You told her?*"

"It's a great deal more than Roger did," Richard said coolly. "My mother has given me her word that he never mentioned you, and I believe her—for I knew Roger. He didn't return from York until after our father died, and he said nothing to our mother about having fallen in love there. He married Blanche shortly thereafter."

"While he was in mourning for your father?" Felicity was shocked.

Richard nodded. "Blanche was not able to have fancy festivities nor an elaborate wedding gown—but she did gain a title. Just a few months afterward, Roger himself died."

"So just as poor Blanche was about to take off her black gloves for the old Earl, she found herself suddenly a widow. No wonder…" Felicity stopped short, remembering Lady Stone's words. *Just because she's weary of being in mourning is no excuse for making Richard's life a living hell when he's grieving for his brother.* So Blanche had become tired of mourning for her husband? Felicity was very glad the woman hadn't been receiving with Lady Alice that afternoon.

"So of course you didn't ask her to leave the town house," Felicity said softly. "Because even after Roger died, there was a chance she might still have his child—and a boy would have been the heir."

"It quickly became apparent that was not the case," Richard said, a little stiffly. "But it had been her home. She had every reason to want to stay there for a while."

Curiosity swept over her. "What did you do? Where have you lived?"

"I had—still have—my bachelor quarters, but I have always spent most of my time at Collinswood, managing the estate for my father and then for Roger. I understood Blanche's shock, for I shared it. I was in no great hurry to step into my brother's shoes and assume duties that I had never expected to be mine. I was happy with the way things were before... But we have wandered from the point." He rubbed his cheek against her hair.

"The point being that even if Roger didn't tell your mother about his trollop in York," she said crisply, "you wanted to make sure she knew about me." So much for that grandiose offer to marry her. Whatever Richard thought, Lady Alice would have a few things to say about that.

He drew back a little and looked down at her, his gaze level and almost stern. "I merely asked her if Roger had ever contemplated marrying anyone other than Blanche, and she said he had never discussed any other match—or any other young woman at all—with her."

She felt the truth sink into her bones. Roger had lied when he told her how furious his mother had been and how she had forbidden him to marry Felicity. She felt sad—but not surprised. In truth, it seemed, Roger *was* the toad that Anne had once accused him of being.

"So I've been a plaything for both of you," she said finally. She stepped away from him and felt chilly when he let her go. "How very unoriginal of me. Thank you, my lord, for telling me. I shall pray tonight that I am not carrying your child."

"And I shall pray that you are."

The floor seemed to quake under Felicity's feet, and she had to reach out to the nearest chair, bracing her hand on the back to hold herself upright. "Let us have the truth between us at least, my lord. You don't wish to marry me."

"The truth?" His mouth twisted a bit. "Very well, then. Why do you think I agreed to your ridiculous bargain, Felicity?"

"Because..." She stumbled to a halt, suddenly confused. *Because I threatened you*, she had started to say—but Richard was not the sort of man who could be threatened. She hadn't realized that at the start, but she knew now that threats—even blackmail—would never have moved him. So why had he agreed?

"Because you desired me," she said finally.

"Yes. I desired you." He came up behind her, resting his hands on her shoulders and bending his head to kiss the nape of her neck. "You are very desirable. I was captivated. I wanted to make love to you, yet I knew that you didn't see me in your bed—you saw Roger."

*Not for long,* she thought.

"At first it was only desire," he admitted. "And then pride. But soon... I found myself caught, wanting—needing—you. I believed that if I attempted to destroy your feelings for Roger, you would hate me, but I feared if I let you continue to idolize him, you would never move beyond loving him to consider whether another man might fill the empty spot in your heart."

Her throat was tight.

"I didn't wish to hurt you by taking away the image you had of him—yet every time you said his name, I wanted to tear him down, to make you realize that he hadn't been all the wonderful things you thought he was. The fact was, even before I realized what was happening to me, I desperately wanted you for myself. That was why I selfishly tried my utmost to give you the child you said you wanted. Because then you would have to marry me to assure that our child would have a name."

She wanted to be convinced, but she could not. "It's a very pretty story. One would almost think you mean every word of it… But you let me believe you were married already."

"My family situation is hardly a secret. It never occurred to me that Lady Hawthorne hadn't told you… or Lady Stone. She's the most notorious gossip in London. Until you let slip that Roger had lied to you, I thought you must know he'd married Blanche."

He had a point, Felicity admitted. How could she hold Richard responsible for keeping secrets when everyone in London—save her—had known the truth?

"Felicity," he said quietly, and her name was like music on his lips. "If your desires truly have changed, and you do not wish to have my child, then I am sorry for what I have done. But if you are already carrying a child, then I must insist that you marry me."

Her heart was skittering madly. "But *only* if I'm carrying your child," she said quietly. "And if I'm not? Will you consider it a fortunate escape?"

"No," he said. "Not fortunate at all, for I do not wish to escape. I fell in love with you, and I intend to…" He paused. "I *want* to marry you, Felicity. I know you told me once that you have no desire to marry at all—that you had learned the hard way what to expect from gentlemen. I should not call those men *gentlemen* myself—my brother among them. And I am not like them. Is it wrong of me to hope that you will reconsider and marry me?"

He seemed to mean it—and perhaps he did, right at this moment. But he could not have thought of the consequences… of what society would say. "The grandson of a duke," she said flatly, "marrying the daughter of a mill owner?"

Richard smiled. "I believe you must be speaking of a man who was never supposed to be anything more than the manager of the family estate marrying the woman he loves. There's not as much contrast between us as you think, my dear. I've been in trade my whole life, too—it's just a slightly different product."

Nothing he could have said would have touched her more. Felicity could barely speak for the tears of joy that threatened to choke her. "It would be the greatest wish of my heart to have your child. But more than that, I want *you*, Richard."

He drew her close, and his mouth claimed hers gently, almost reverently—as if they were standing at the altar before a crowd of witnesses. But very quickly, restraint gave way to passion, which burned straight through self-control until Felicity was only marginally aware that they were still in her drawing room.

"Would you like…" She gestured toward the stairs and felt herself coloring at her own forwardness.

Richard laughed. "I thought you said you didn't enjoy our lovemaking." Before she could add a word, he had stopped teasing to pick her up and carry her up to the sitting room and on to the velvet-draped bedroom beyond.

"Are you certain you won't have second thoughts?" she asked, as he began to undress her. "My father often said he regretted sending me to that boarding school for girls because he thought it had ruined me. He said it left me feeling I was too good for the men of my own class, while in fact I wasn't nearly good enough for any others."

"You're perfectly fine just as you are," he said, and kissed her hair. "When will you like to pay a formal visit to my mother?"

"A formal call?" Felicity was aghast. "I barely survived the informal one this afternoon."

"I doubt it was really such a trial as you thought it. I told my mother that you have chosen not to go into society. So she invited the very unconventional Lady Stone and your good friend, Lady Hawthorne, in the hope that she could manage to arrange a meeting with you sooner rather than later."

"She did know my name, then?"

"Indeed she did. She knew, in fact, that you were the woman I intended to marry… I admit I'd like to have seen her face, however, when the two ladies she was planning to manipulate innocently delivered you straight into her hands without her making any effort at all." He was unwinding Felicity's hair as he spoke, and he stopped long enough to bury his lips in the golden mass. "I would never have let you marry Rivers, you know. Not only isn't he nearly good enough for you, but he's stealing from you. Skimming profits, diverting goods…"

She was stunned at the certainty in his tone. She had known Jason Rivers for years, but only today had she begun to question his honesty. Richard had been in the same room with the man for mere minutes, but he had seen through him.

"I'm not absolutely certain of that myself," she said, "so how do you know that he's cheating me?"

"I had my suspicions the moment I saw him. He was dressed very expensively for a man in his position."

"Perhaps he simply wanted to impress me," she argued.

"After I left here today, I looked into his affairs, and I talked to some of the men he had come to London to do business with. And I found a man who sells cartloads of goods for him—goods that are made in your factory but not entered on the books."

"Why would such a man tell *you* what he had done?"

"Because Rivers cheated him, too, and he wants his revenge." He pulled off his cravat. "I must apologize, however. Because I spent the afternoon looking into Rivers' affairs, I did not have time to retrieve the Colford engagement ring or to procure a special license. Tomorrow will have to do for those things, I'm afraid."

"The engagement ring," she said slowly. "Will you have to get it from Blanche? Because…"

"You'd just as soon not share that with her? No, my dear. She refused to wear the family sapphires—she wanted diamonds instead."

"I'm not surprised."

"What is it Lady Hawthorne calls you? Fliss? I like that." He came up behind her, slipping his arms around her waist. "I think we must also send Rivers packing tomorrow and put someone in charge who will take proper care of your very considerable property. I'd hire Perkins if I thought I could talk him into leaving Thorne and giving up this fascination with canals—but I don't suppose he'd be willing to move to York."

"So now that you know there's money after all, I'm a suitable bride?" Felicity tried to keep her tone teasing, but despite her best efforts, her voice trembled a little.

"Oh, there's plenty of money. You are—or at least you will be—quite a wealthy woman." He kissed the nape of her neck and added, sounding almost absentminded, "One of the things I was asking Thorne about today was how best to arrange it so that your money remains unquestionably yours."

Felicity's body went rigid in shock. He would watch over her possessions for her—yet he did not intend to use her wealth to increase his own? As her husband, he would have every right to whatever she owned—to use it however he deemed fit. "You would do that?" she whispered. "I would never have dreamed..."

"That a man could wish to marry you for anything but your money? Felicity, my dear..." He turned her round to face him and began unfastening her chemise, his fingers impatient against the soft white fabric. "No, it's entirely yours... Unless you decide you'd rather put it in trust for our children. The younger children, that is," he added dryly as the chemise dropped to the floor. "The heir will have Collinswood and all that goes with the title—which is enough to spoil any young man, if we don't raise him carefully." He tucked her into the velvet-draped bed with exaggerated care.

"Younger children?" she asked demurely.

"Several of them, I shouldn't doubt." He joined her in the bed and kissed her long and deeply. "But for now, let's concentrate on the first one… You know, it really is a good thing I don't have scruples about taking a married lady as my mistress," he added thoughtfully. "Because you'll always be my mistress, Felicity. You'll always be my Lady Desire."

# *Five*

## The Earl Meets His Ward

As the butler opened the door of the Hawthorne town house to admit the two gentlemen, Thorne heard a shriek echoing through the entrance hall from the small reception room nearest the front door. An angry shriek. A *feminine* shriek.

"I thought Lady Hawthorne went home to Surrey," Lord Colford said.

"She did. And Anne never in her life sounded like that anyway. What's happening, Carson?"

Before the butler could answer, Perkins came out of the reception room and closed the door firmly behind him. His face was the deep purple of a ripe plum, and Thorne wouldn't have been surprised to see steam rising from his head.

"Are you in some difficulty, Perkins?" Thorne asked cheerfully.

"No, my lord. At least not personally."

"That sounded quite personal to me," Colford commented.

Perkins ignored him. "The young… lady… says her business is with you, my lord," he told Thorne. "She says, in fact, that she is your ward." Doubt dripped from Perkins' voice.

"Ward," Thorne said thoughtfully. "My *ward*? No, nothing comes to mind. What's the young lady's name?"

"She seems to have none. At least, she has refused to confide in me with that information, my lord."

"One of your indiscretions coming home to roost, Thorne?" Colford asked jovially.

Just then the door opened again and a small whirlwind came out—a very young woman dressed in frilly pale-pink muslin that made her curly red hair look like a wildfire. She marched up to Perkins and put her small face right into his. "You can't keep me locked up in here. I *must* see Lord Hawthorne right now. I am his ward, and I have every right…" Belatedly, she seemed to notice the newcomers. "Oh. That's all right then. I forgive you."

"I live to serve," Perkins said under his breath.

The whirlwind paused. "I *do* tend to ride roughshod, don't I? My apologies, Perkins." She bestowed a smile on him. Suddenly her eyes sparkled, her elfin face shifted from striking to uncommonly beautiful, and warmth swept over the group. Even her hair seemed to stop bristling.

Thorne noticed that Colford had rocked back on his heels. Even Perkins looked quite dazed—for a moment.

The whirlwind turned to Thorne and Colford. "My lord…" Doubt sprang into her eyes. "Er… which of you is Lord Hawthorne?"

Thorne bowed. "At your service, Miss…"

"Baxter. Georgiana Baxter. I'm your ward."

"Now I remember," Thorne said. "But actually—no, you're not."

Perkins nodded as if to say, *I knew it.* Then, as a myriad of other possible relationships—each one more scandalous than the last—obviously occurred to him, he drew himself up even straighter.

"I'm the trustee of your property, Miss Baxter," Thorne said, "but not the guardian of your person. That would be—if I remember correctly—Sir Rufus Baxter."

"That is true," the whirlwind, now somewhat muted, said. "But my Uncle Rufus has proven completely incompetent, which is why I've come to you. You must save me, my lord!"

"From what?" Thorne eyed her warily. "Where is your maid?" He didn't wait for an answer. Without taking his eyes off her, he said, "Perkins, go over to Number 5 Upper Seymour Street, and request Mrs. Mason to come here immediately."

Perkins looked outraged. Thorne wondered if he objected to being sent on an errand that would normally be delegated to a footman or if he was irritated at being required to leave before finding out exactly what the whirlwind wanted. But he said, "Yes, my lord," and departed.

"I hardly need a chaperone present to consult with my guardian," the whirlwind said. "Oh, very well, *trustee.*"

"Nevertheless," Thorne said firmly, "since you have shown the bad judgment to mislay your maid somewhere, you shall have a chaperone."

"I didn't mislay her. I sneaked away from her so she couldn't report to Uncle Rufus where I was going."

"My point precisely. Have the goodness to wait in

the reception room until Mrs. Mason arrives, and then she will bring you to me."

"But I've been waiting hours already!"

"Therefore, another ten minutes need not distress you unduly," Thorne said.

The whirlwind stamped her foot, crossed her arms, and seemed to take root in the hallway. Thorne ignored her and gestured Colford ahead of him into the library.

"So *is* she one of your indiscretions, Thorne? I wouldn't have thought you old enough. She must be seventeen, at least."

Thorne refused to take the bait. "Her father was Colonel Baxter. I served under him at the War Office for a while. He died at Waterloo."

"And left you saddled with that termagant?"

"In company with her Uncle Rufus, of course," Thorne mused. "I seem to have got the better end of the deal—until now."

"Her Uncle Rufus, the *completely incompetent*. I wonder what he did to gain that title. Cut back on her pin money? Prevent her from eloping with the music master? Give away her puppy?" Colford shook his head. "You have my sympathies."

"Thank you, Colford. They are much appreciated."

Perkins knocked on the library door and came in.

"And to think I've actually said I would *like* to have daughters," Thorne mused.

Perkins' face went rigid with disapproval. His mind had obviously followed the same track as Colford's had, for he seemed to think Thorne was admitting that Miss Baxter *was* his daughter.

Thorne considered straightening out Perkins'

misapprehension, but he decided not to bother. If Perkins was contemplating his employer's moral lapses, at least he'd stop prosing on about canals—for a few minutes, at least. "Are they all such dramatic creatures at that age? What on earth was I thinking, wanting a couple of *those* around the house?"

"That," Colford said, "is why there are boarding schools for young ladies."

"I'll remember that. I wonder why this chit isn't in one. Yes, Perkins?"

"Mrs. Mason has just arrived, and is with the—with Miss Baxter. Will there be anything else, my lord?"

"Yes… find out what's happened to Sir Rufus Baxter and whether he is indeed completely incompetent as charged."

"Yes, my lord." Perkins cleared his throat. "Will the young lady be remaining long?"

"I have no idea, Perkins." Thorne poured himself a brandy. "Care for one, Colford?"

"Certainly. But I thought you weren't drinking brandy anymore," Colford said.

"Anne's in Surrey, and I need a bracer. I have a feeling I'm in for a siege." Thorne drained his glass and faced Perkins. "Now you may send Mrs. Mason in—with the whirlwind."

# *Six*

## My Lady Flame

LONDON HAD CHANGED A GREAT DEAL—AND NOT ALL
for the better—since the last time Julian had been
home. The streets were busier, the smell of horses was
stronger, and the tradesmen hawking their wares were
noisier. He was relieved to reach Portman Square,
where he summoned a street urchin to hold his horse
while he strode up the stairs to the glossy, red front door
of the Earl of Hawthorne's town house. Thorne could
hardly be expected to be at home at this hour of the
afternoon, of course—or even in London at this time of
year. But if Julian was lucky, the butler would tell him
where his lordship could be found.

On the other hand, the butler was just as likely
to take one look at Julian and inform him that
tramps and other undesirables weren't welcome—
or that he should present himself at the kitchen
entrance instead, if he was begging for a handout.
Unless Mason hadn't yet retired; Mason would surely
remember him…

Julian tried to brush off his uniform, but there was
no removing the grime of a long day in the saddle,

much less the wear of four years of war, with the wave of a hand.

However, only by the merest flicker of an eyelash did the butler—not Mason, Julian was sorry to see—betray his consternation at finding a road-worn soldier on the step. "Yes, sir?"

"I'm Major Hampton. Is my cousin, Lord Hawthorne, at home?"

"I shall enquire," the butler said. "If the major will follow me?"

Julian was shown into a small reception room that he remembered from his last visit to this house. It had been a dark, formal little hole, chilly even on the warmest of days. Now, at the very end of summer, a fire blazed on the hearth; a bunch of orange and yellow flowers stood on a table in the center of the room; and comfortable chairs were scattered about. Better and better, Julian thought, warming himself at the fire. It seemed the gossip was right—and if so, perhaps this new wife of Thorne's wasn't such a bad thing after all.

The door opened, and Thorne burst in. "Julian! About time you showed up. It's taken you an age to get home. Come into the library." With an arm around Julian's shoulders, Thorne ushered him across the hall, gave him a glass of wine and a chair by the fire, and sat down across from him. "That street urchin of yours is taking your horse around to the stables... You told Carson you're Major Hampton?"

"It's still my name." Julian knew he sounded defensive. "It's hard to remember the other."

"Well, yes. But you'll get used to it soon enough."

"And it's still my rank, at least for a while—half pay and all."

"I imagine our grandfather has made it clear he expects you to sell out."

"No doubt he has. Just not directly to me."

Thorne looked astounded. "The Old Man has held his tongue on that topic?"

"I haven't seen him," Julian admitted. "I stopped at the War Office and then came straight here. I'm just not up to seeing the Old Man right away—and I didn't go all the way across the Peninsula on Wellington's staff without learning to choose my battlegrounds."

"I should think not. Where are you staying?"

"I was going to beg to join your bachelor establishment, if I found you at home. Then the gossips at the War Office told me you've gone and gotten married—so I sent my batman to the Red Dragon on the Islington Road. Remember when you and I used to go there with a couple of very eager ladies?"

Thorne smiled.

It was, Julian thought, an amused, nostalgic smile—as if he was reliving the days before marriage had tied him down. Julian smothered a sigh to see Thorne with his wings clipped. "I see you do. Those were the days, Thorne. Now you're married, and I'm…"

But Thorne had reached for the bellpull, and the butler came in just then. "Send James out to the Red Dragon," Thorne told him, "to inform Major Hampton's batman that the major will be staying in Portman Square, so he's to bring the baggage along at his earliest convenience. Then have a guest suite prepared for the major and a room for his batman."

The butler bowed and went away.

Julian said, "Your wife won't mind you acquiring an uninvited houseguest?"

"As it happens, this *is* a bachelor establishment. Anne's in Surrey—she'll be there until after the baby arrives at Christmastime—and I only came back to London for a few days to transact some business."

"It's a lucky thing I found you, then. But if you'll only be here a few days…"

"The business has turned out to be a bit more complex than I expected," Thorne said ruefully. "If Anne discovers you're here, she'll be posting straight back to town and pounding on the door, despite the doctor's orders. And if I were to let you stay at an inn, she'd be pounding on me."

"You're letting the muslin company set the rules? You amaze me."

"Times change." Thorne contemplated his cousin. "I'm sorry, Julian. I know it's not what you planned—Cousin Aubrey sticking his spoon in the wall."

"Oh, I'm sure there are advantages to the situation. Someday I may even think of one or two." Julian scowled. "Why couldn't it have been you instead of me, Thorne?"

"I presume you're not asking me to explain the laws of inheritance?"

"Of course not. But you look the part—especially when you put your head back and sneer down your nose like that."

"I practice," Thorne said dryly.

"It shows." Julian couldn't stop himself from yawning. "Sorry. It's been a long day."

Thorne stood up. "Your room will be ready by now. I'll send my valet along to—"

"I don't need help to get out of my coat for a catnap, Thorne. Lord knows I've slept in my uniform—when I've slept at all—for days on end sometimes."

"Then I'll see you at dinner. Eight o'clock."

The butler showed Julian up to a guest suite. Like the reception room, it had a new, lighter look than Julian had remembered. Lord, had four years really passed since he'd last been in London?

Julian dropped his coat on the back of a chair, struggled to pull off his boots, and sank with a sigh of relief onto the bed, still wearing the rest of his clothes. He'd barely been still for days. The trip across France had been long, the Channel crossing had been a rough one, and he'd scarcely set foot on land again before he'd climbed onto a horse and started for London.

Not that there was any enormous hurry in getting home. Aubrey Silsby had died nearly two months earlier. The funeral had been over long before word had reached the distant post where Julian had been stationed since Waterloo. The black-edged letter from his grandfather had been delivered by the same courier who had brought Julian's official orders from the War Office to return to England.

So he had come home… though he wasn't quite certain whether he was obeying his commanding officer or his grandfather. He supposed it didn't really matter. The result was the same.

The bed felt as if it was rocking—as though he were still on horseback or even on the Channel. Julian closed his eyes and knew no more.

They dined casually, to Julian's great relief. A short
nap had taken the edge off his exhaustion, a bath
had restored his spirits, and a uniform that had
been sponged and pressed by Thorne's valet made
him feel a new man—at least until he reached the
drawing room and compared himself to his elegant
cousin. His best uniform looked painfully weather-
beaten next to Thorne's dark blue coat and flawless
white linen.

It was clear to Julian that he had better visit both
a tailor and a barber before presenting himself to his
grandfather. For that worthy gentleman, even the war
would be no excuse for careless grooming.

Still, it was good to be home and with Thorne, who
had always been his favorite cousin—though the man
seemed to have just one topic of conversation these
days. No, that wasn't fair, Julian told himself. Thorne
could—and did—talk quite sensibly about horses,
estates, canals, and society gossip, in between references
to his wife. The Countess wasn't even in London, but
she seemed to be right there in the dining room with
them—even after the brandy and the cigars came in,
when any lady of quality would have fled to her private
parlor and any normal husband would have been
relieved to speak of other things.

"Charming though your countess sounds," Julian
said as he sampled the brandy, "I'm still amazed you let
yourself get caught in parson's mousetrap."

Thorne shook his head. "I walked straight in with
my eyes open. You'll be looking for a bride soon
yourself, I expect."

Julian sighed. "I imagine that will be the next thing on the Old Man's list, after selling my commission."

"Or possibly even before. Anne could help you there—she seems to know every young woman in the *ton*."

"I'll keep that in mind when I decide to put my head in the noose." Morosely, Julian watched the brandy swirl in his glass. *When,* he'd said. Not *if*. But though that had been a slip of the tongue, it was also a fact—he would have to marry. "Tell her not to get in any hurry to bring me to the ladies' attention. I'll look around when I'm good and ready."

"I didn't mean she'd try to marry you off, Julian, for she won't. It's just that you'd be wise to ask her counsel before making your choice. Young women can be remarkably sweet in masculine company before the wedding and then turn into shrews the moment they leave the altar. Anne can spot things like that."

Julian couldn't bear thinking of altars and weddings just now. "I'll keep that in mind. But at the moment I have other priorities."

"Probably wise. With the Season over, you'd have to look long and hard anyway. Most of this year's debutantes have been spoken for, or else they never will be. Let the word spread that you're home, and by next spring when the Marriage Mart is in full swing, you'll be able to dance at Almack's and take your pick of the next crop."

"The very idea of all those matchmaking mamas terrifies me more than facing a cavalry regiment."

"You could go to Bath for the autumn, I suppose—it's a lot less intense than the London

Season. And there's something to be said for getting it over with quickly."

Julian shuddered. "No, thanks. I'm going to enjoy being unfettered while I still can. In fact, if you don't mind forgoing my company for the rest of the evening, I think I'll go for a walk and shake some fidgets. That nap left me feeling restless."

"Be careful, Julian. After dark, a man wandering the streets alone is a target, even in Portman Square."

"And wandering around Waterloo was safe?"

"Point taken. Make yourself at home." Thorne stubbed out his half-smoked cigar. "I have some letters to finish. If all goes well, I'll be leaving for Surrey by the end of the week—but you're welcome to stay as long as you like. It appears I'll be coming back and forth all through the autumn to deal with loose ends." He sounded irritated by the prospect.

Julian couldn't decide whether to be amused or concerned. It wasn't natural for a man to be so impatient to get back to his new wife... at least, not a man like Thorne.

After his cousin had gone back to his library, Julian took his glass of brandy over to the long windows. If he stood close enough to the window, he could see beyond the reflected candlelight to the garden beyond. Trees swayed gently, and banks of light-colored flowers ruffled in the early autumn breeze. And beyond the flowers...

He leaned closer yet to the glass. Someone was out there between the flower beds. All he could really see was a pale oval, something that might be a face and that seemed to float across the lawn. He might have thought it a ghostly apparition, except that he didn't believe in spirits.

Something drew him to take a closer look. Quietly and impulsively, he opened the window and stepped over the low sash into the soft silt of the flower bed beneath. His boot heel sank and almost overset him, and he did considerable damage to a lilac bush before he regained his balance. By then, the apparition had moved along the garden path to a spot farther from the house. But from this angle he could see it wasn't just a head but a woman—judging by the size of the form and the sway of the step.

A housemaid, perhaps, who had slipped out for a quick break and a breath of air? But what maid would dare to wander around her employer's garden at an hour when someone looking out of the public rooms might see her?

The stealth he had learned on reconnaissance missions served him well, for he was within a few feet of her before she noticed him. She was bending to smell a flower on a small bush when Julian's boot cracked a stick underfoot and she jerked upright.

The pale oval of her face was surrounded by red-gold hair that fell in perfect, springy ringlets to her shoulders. Her face had seemed to float because she was wrapped in a cloak, but the hood had fallen back, leaving her head bare. Her wrap was velvet, so dark and rich a color that it seemed to swallow the moonlight, and the fastening at her throat was gold. Clearly not a servant, then.

One of Thorne's mistresses, perhaps? There had been plenty of them. But surely Thorne wouldn't be meeting one in his own garden...

"Good evening," Julian said.

The mysterious lady drew her cloak closer. But there was frank interest in her eyes and not a hint of fear. Did that mean Thorne was going to be along any minute, expecting to meet her here?

"Good evening." Her voice sounded like honey flowing across warm bread.

"We have not been introduced," Julian began.

Her laugh was low and rich, rippling across his skin like the touch of a gentle hand. "Yes, I'd noticed that. If it offends your sense of propriety, sir—"

He felt like a fool. "It does not. You're wandering around my cousin's garden in the middle of the night, so I think that could be taken as introduction enough."

"It's just gone eleven—I heard the church bells only a moment ago. That's hardly the middle of the night." Her tone was light, careless. "Lord Hawthorne is your cousin?"

Wariness licked at Julian's bones. Danger lurked as surely along this peaceful garden path as it ever had on the roads of Spain. The danger was of a different sort, that was all—couched in the cultured voice of a young woman who had just identified potential prey. If he was the cousin of an earl, then he might be someone important, too. Perhaps even someone worth pursuing…

And he had very neatly sprung the trap on himself. He wanted to curse.

"A cousin, yes." He kept his voice casual. "One of many. His branch of the family is senior to mine—I'm just the son of a younger son." That was all quite accurate, he thought, proud of himself for turning the tide and deflecting her interest—even if it wasn't the entire truth.

She didn't seem disappointed. "I thought perhaps you meant Lady Hawthorne was your cousin."

He was annoyed with himself. That long, involved explanation had been entirely unnecessary—she'd only been asking which of the Hawthornes he was claiming. Unless she was a better politician than any other woman he'd ever met. It wouldn't be the only way she was different from the women he had known...

In the moonlight, her face was as smooth and pale as ivory. At the moment she looked quite serious, but he hadn't forgotten the sparkle in her eyes and the way her generous mouth had quirked right before she laughed. Something inside him longed to make her do it again so he could watch more carefully this time and catch each telltale sign before she burst into that rippling, sensual laugh. So he could enjoy every single moment...

*By doing what, Hampton? Telling her a joke?* He pulled himself back to the moment. "Julian Hampton, at your service."

Her gaze summed up his appearance. "A pleasure, Major Hampton."

She was a very close observer, this mysterious lady, to so easily spot his rank despite the uncertain light and the disrepair of his uniform. Now he was especially glad of his faded coat and his worn boots. In case she hadn't really been convinced by his recital of the family tree, it was just as well that he looked the part of an impoverished younger son barely making do on Army pay. Besides, at the moment it was mostly true.

"He has many cousins, you said?"

"Litters of them," Julian lied. "And you? You know my name, but I do not know yours."

She shrugged, and the velvet cloak rippled in the moonlight, making him wonder what lay underneath. Was she really as slender and fragile as she seemed to be? "Oh, I'm no one, really."

"Wise of you not to give your name," he admitted. "Your mama would be very unhappy to hear of you wandering at night alone."

She sidestepped the hinted invitation to tell him about her family. "But I'm not alone," she said with that low, sensual laugh. "You're with me."

The frisson of impending peril licked at him again. That, he thought grimly, was precisely the problem. If he was found with her in Hawthorne's garden in the dead of night, there would be hell to pay.

But now that he'd got himself into the situation, he couldn't just walk off and leave her out there by herself. "I'll see you home."

"My garden is just through there." She waved a hand vaguely. "But it's quite small, so I trespass now and then to enjoy Lord Hawthorne's. I do beg you not to tell him we met here."

"You think he would be angry at you? It seems unlikely to me that he would be unwilling to share the scent of his flowers."

"The thought of facing his wrath terrifies me."

She didn't sound terrified. A bit cautious, perhaps. Even a trifle concerned that she might be discovered. *But no more concerned than I am that someone will find us here, alone together.* "You need have no fears on that subject," he said dryly. "I shall not tell him."

"Thank you." She rewarded him with a smile that seemed to make the moonlight a little brighter and a little warmer. "But since my presence makes you ill at ease—"

Julian wanted to protest, which was utterly foolish. She was uncomfortably perceptive in recognizing his concern, and he suspected she wouldn't hesitate to laugh at him if he denied it.

"—and as I have no wish to cause a gentleman to stand about in the night air on guard duty while I take my exercise, I shall return to my home. Good night."

Before he could answer, she pulled her hood over her bright hair, stepped behind an azalea bush into the shadow of a huge, old elm tree, and seemed to vanish into nowhere.

❧

Meeting a scruffy, threadbare soldier in the garden was quite the most excitement Georgiana had experienced in the entire long week since she had confronted Lord Hawthorne and demanded his assistance in dealing with Uncle Rufus. She almost wished that she had stayed out a little longer and asked Major Hampton to tell her about the battles and campaigns he had fought in.

But as Hawthorne's cousin, Julian Hampton probably had the same sort of starched-up soul as the Earl, despite the worn-out uniform. "*We have not been introduced.*" "*I'll see you home.*" Yes, he sounded exactly like the Earl. It was just as well that she hadn't stayed. The temptation to tweak him would have been irresistible, and who knew what complications that might have led to. If he happened to mention her to his cousin...

He had said she need not fear, and she had no reason to think he was not a man of his word. Still, it was only sensible not to push his sense of propriety too far.

He was the son of a younger son, he had said. Perhaps he had come to Lord Hawthorne for financial help. He certainly looked as though he could use it. A scruffy, threadbare soldier... and not just because of his mangy uniform, battle-scarred boots, and unkempt black hair.

He looked too thin for his height. He was also too brown in the face, as if he had been in the sun for months on end. And his eyes—blue, she thought, though it was hard to tell in the moonlight—looked far too tired. Yet his expression had held kindness, along with a bit of wariness.

She paused to think about that. Major Hampton, she concluded, had been just the slightest bit afraid—of *her*.

A thrill of feminine power surged through Georgiana. How very interesting that she could actually frighten a tried-and-true soldier, a man who had faced Napoleon's army...

Yes, meeting Major Hampton was by far the most entertaining thing that had happened to her all week.

Not that he should feel particularly flattered by the honor, for he didn't face much competition. In fact, this had—until now—been the dullest week of Georgiana's life. Worse by far than being stuck in Dorset with Uncle Rufus and his dogs.

She'd believed that once she was in London, things would get better—but they'd no sooner arrived in the city than Uncle Rufus had told her of his latest lunatic plan. Then she'd convinced herself that once she managed to reach Lord Hawthorne and explain to him what Uncle Rufus had in mind for her, he would make everything all right.

And to be fair, Lord Hawthorne *had* helped—a little. At least Uncle Rufus wasn't haranguing her every day about what she owed the family and how easy life would be for her if only she did as he wanted. What he meant, of course, was that it would be easy for *him*. She sniffed at the very idea.

And she did have a nice place to stay—for Number 5 Upper Seymour Street was quite the loveliest house Georgiana had ever seen, much less lived in. The bedroom she was using made her feel like a princess. Being surrounded by all that green velvet and lace made her feel elegant from the moment she woke up each morning.

But however nice it was, the town house didn't make up for being hidden away from the world, told not to even set a foot out of doors. And however much she appreciated not having to listen to Uncle Rufus rattling on, that didn't make up for being ordered not to talk to anyone except the servants.

Plus, Lord Hawthorne seemed to have forgotten all about her. He hadn't even come round to call, to tell her how matters were progressing or what Uncle Rufus had to say. The only visitor she'd had was Perkins—and he hadn't said a single word that mattered. He'd brought her a couple of novels that she didn't want to read, and he'd rattled off a whole lot of drivel about *patience* and *forbearance* and *due time*, and then he'd gone away again. Luckily for him, he'd made his escape just as she'd gotten seriously near to losing her temper and throwing a book at his head.

She knew she should be happy that she was some-where safe and quiet, and where Uncle Rufus wasn't kicking up a dust. But everything was so dull at Number 5 Upper Seymour Street that Georgiana was about to go mad.

Spending a few minutes in the garden with Julian Hampton had been a nice change. And, if he happened to walk out there again, it might be fun to see if she could scare him just a little more.

∽

The sun was brilliant in the morning, and from the breakfast room, Julian could see no shadows flitting in the garden. But then, his mysterious lady with no name was likely still abed. Julian himself had been up since before dawn, as he always was. That habit from long years of campaigning was hard to break; the moment the first light of day crept into the eastern sky, he was alert.

The butler brought in the morning post. Thorne glanced through it and tossed a letter across the table to Julian. "It didn't take the Old Man long to discover you're here. His spy network seems to be as good as ever."

"The government should have adopted it during the war. We'd have beaten Boney in a year." Julian broke the wafer and spread the page open. The letter was short and to the point. "It's a summons, of course. I'm to appear for dinner this evening to account for myself."

"At least we have a few hours to get you into shape."

Julian felt mulish. "I think I'll go just as I am."

Thorne pushed his plate aside. "It's only a step to my tailor. Sooner or later you'll have to put the uniform away, so we may as well start the process. And it looks to be a pleasant day. If you don't mind the walk…"

Julian pulled his mind back to the breakfast table and finished his coffee. "As long as you don't expect me to carry a pack and a rifle," he said dryly, "I think I can manage it. The tailor first? Let's go, then, and get started."

It was not only a beautiful morning but a fine one. A warm breeze stirred the oak leaves in Portman Square and teased a too-long lock of hair loose over Julian's ear. As they strode off down the square and then turned the corner onto Upper Seymour Street, he found himself watching the houses. From the vague wave of the mysterious lady's hand last night, she must have been indicating a house somewhere along here…

He saw a carriage pull up before a nearby house to wait. The front door opened, and his pace slowed so he could observe as a family came out to climb into the carriage. But there was no bright-haired young woman among them.

On Oxford Street, he saw a girl with reddish hair, but she was too young and obviously a servant—and in any case her hair was straight, rather than in ringlets. On Bond Street there was a lady who walked with the same sort of glide in her step as his mysterious lady, but her hair was dark and she was far too old.

Thorne was watching him thoughtfully, and for an instant Julian almost asked whether he had noticed a stunning young woman with curly red-gold hair anywhere in the neighborhood. But he couldn't, of course—for how would he explain how he'd happened to meet this lady of mystery? Tell Thorne that a neighbor was making a habit of trespassing in his garden? At any rate, Julian had given her the promise of a gentleman that he would not breathe a word to his cousin. And he was a man of honor.

No. He would simply have to figure out the mysterious lady on his own.

❧

It was nearly ten that evening when Julian came into Thorne's library and headed straight for the brandy decanter. Thorne put down his pen, tented his fingers together, and observed, "The Old Man was in fine fettle tonight, I see?"

Julian drained his glass in a gulp. "He started off the evening by scolding me for not having a proper visiting card to present. I told him it was a trifle hard to find a printer in the section of France where I've been stationed. And it became increasingly sticky from there." He refilled the glass and raised it to his lips.

"You might want to go easy on that, Julian. Aubrey was already well on his way to ruining his digestion with alcohol long before he took that corner too fast and upset his curricle."

"I can see why he drank," Julian said grimly, but he put the glass down. "I was prepared—among other things—for the Old Man to tell me to choose a wife and be brisk about it. But instead he announced he's already chosen one for me."

"Well, that's tidy of him."

"Tidy? It's an unholy mess! The Old Man arranged a betrothal for Aubrey just weeks before he died.

The settlements were agreed to and the marriage contract already drawn up. Then Aubrey cracked up his curricle—"

"Which ended the betrothal and voided the contract, of course."

"Not as far as the Old Man's concerned. I didn't actually see the paperwork, but he's apparently just had the lawyers scratch out poor Aubrey's name and insert mine. And if I don't agree to the plan, he has an entire list of unpleasant consequences for me."

"Starting by cutting off the allowance he hasn't yet agreed to give you?" Thorne leaned back in his chair. "You know, I feel sorry for the Old Man. He's got no idea how to deal with you, so he barks orders and expects them to be obeyed—never realizing that you're far too much like him to respond to his threats."

"What do you mean, I'm like him? I should call you out for that insult, Thorne."

"Pistols at dawn?" Thorne suggested cheerfully. "If you insist. But I think it would be more productive if you took your irritation out on me at Gentleman Jackson's in the morning. I don't mind."

"Thanks, but I'll just draw the Old Man's face on a punching bag instead. If I throw enough jabs at that hooked nose of his, I might feel better."

"A punching bag won't give you enough of a challenge to be satisfying."

"Very well then—I'll give you the beating you deserve." Julian flung himself in a chair and stretched his feet out to the fire.

"What did you think of the woman?"

Julian didn't look up. "We didn't meet."

"That's odd. I'd have expected the Old Man to have had her there tonight. If you're to be betrothed…"

Julian shuddered. "He probably didn't want to give me any extra ammunition that might prompt me to refuse the match. It seems—from what I was able to pick up from the servants—that she's something of a shrew. But the Old Man's story was that she's been indisposed ever since Aubrey died."

"Indisposed? That's an all-purpose excuse. Perhaps she's not any happier about the arrangement than you are."

"You mean that she was attached to Aubrey, and now she's mourning for him? It seems not—they'd barely met. It appears she agrees with the Old Man that Aubrey and I are completely interchangeable. There's no question she's getting the better end of the bargain, and she knows it. It seems she's inherited a tiny corner of land practically next door to the Abbey. God knows why, but the Old Man wants it at any cost—and her price is marriage."

"I suppose you told him that in that case, he should marry her himself."

"I would have done so, if I'd thought of it." Julian contemplated his glass and sipped. "No wonder Aubrey drank too much and drove too fast. Even the Old Man couldn't make this woman—do you know, I don't think he ever told me her name—sound like anything but a virago. If I can't find a way out of this, I may have to throw myself *under* the curricle, not just fall out of it—because I might survive a simple fall!"

If he hadn't been stuck in the middle of London, Julian would have saddled his horse and gone for a bruising ride. He considered it anyway, for he was far too wrought up to sleep. But he knew the city's streets, never quiet, would not provide the freedom he needed to take his mind off his problems.

Instead, he stripped off his coat and boots and paced the floor of his bedroom, still too furious over the way the Old Man had so callously arranged his life to even sit down. Being swapped off for a few acres of land… For *this*, he had fought his way across Portugal, Spain, and France? To preserve the English way of life… what a cruel jest that was.

His measured step brought him close to the window, and he paused to look out over the garden. Far below, light glinted and shifted, and his heart leaped. But it was only a statue that had caught the moonlight. A swaying bough had made the statue look as if it had moved…

No—there *was* someone out there. He could feel it.

He reached automatically for the red uniform coat he had just removed and tucked his boots under his arm as he crept down the stairs, avoiding the servants who were still moving around the lower floor as they extinguished fires and candles and lamps, and readied the house for the night. He sat down in the dining room to pull on his boots before once more stepping through the window that so conveniently overlooked the garden.

She was nowhere to be found, and he would have given up except for the unshakable sense that she was there. Was it the barest hint of her scent along the paths, or just a simple feeling? Then he saw movement in a secluded corner.

His mysterious lady had retreated to the shelter of the grape arbor, her dark cloak closely wrapped around her. The hood was pulled up—it was cooler tonight—and the light of the moon fell in bars across her face. For an instant as he approached, she seemed to be wearing a mask.

"You look as if you've just come from a masquerade ball," he said.

"I've never been to one." For a moment, she sounded sad, almost wistful; then her rich voice curled around him like a warm blanket on a cold winter's night as she went on. "Good evening, Major Hampton. I wondered if you would dare to come tonight."

So much for the warm blanket. *Wet* blanket, more like. "*Dare?*" he asked. "Miss... I still don't know your name."

"I know. Quite exciting, isn't it? Very... illicit."

There was an undertone of laughter in her tone now. A woman of many moods, he thought, a little dazed at the speed with which she could shift from one to the next.

She patted the bench next to her, and he sat down. "May I call you Julian?"

"You may not—and if you don't give me your name, I'll call you Lady Mysterious."

She smiled, and a dimple he hadn't spotted before, just at the corner of her mouth, teased his senses. "Oh, that's quite lovely. I'm not a lady, you see—only a Miss."

"And not a lady in the *other* sense of the word, either, if you're meeting a man in a garden at this hour."

"Why, Major Hampton—it's not as if we planned this assignation." She reached up to a cluster of grapes hanging just above her head and plucked one, popping it in her mouth.

The bunch looked sadly depleted, as if she'd been sitting there quite a while. So she had waited for him, had she? Julian felt a sizzle of warmth at the idea but sternly suppressed it. "You dare steal my cousin's grapes?" he asked in mock indignation.

"Why not?" She reached up for another and smiled at him. "If he notices at all, he'll think *you* ate them. And you would tell him that you did, wouldn't you? Rather than give me away? Because you promised."

"Yes, minx, I would." Julian dug a small knife from his pocket and cut a larger bunch from the vine, setting it on the bench between them.

She pulled a grape from the cluster he'd cut, and he watched as she savored it. "That one tasted much better than the ones I chose." She took another grape and leaned closer, holding it close to his mouth. "Here—see if you don't agree."

He started to suggest that her flirtatious behavior was both inappropriate and unwise, but she popped the grape into his mouth before he could get the words out. Her fingertip brushed his lips, and the velvety touch sent a surge of hot blood through him. He bit down on the grape, and the sweet, cool juice flowed over his tongue.

She would taste like grapes if he kissed her right now… and oh, how he wanted to kiss her, to taste her sweetness mixed with that of the grapes…

He tamped down the thought and tried to focus on the fruit. His stomach growled.

"I'm teasing you about grapes when you haven't had dinner." She looked concerned, and the sparkle vanished from her eyes. He hadn't been able to see their color the night before, and he still wasn't certain—but he thought they were dark, unusually so for a woman with hair so bright.

"I had dinner. I just didn't enjoy it." In fact, Julian wasn't certain he'd actually managed to swallow anything at that ill-fated meal. "My grandfather spent it lecturing me about marriage."

She pulled another grape from the stem and ate it. "You'll be looking for an heiress to wed, I suppose."

"You sound quite matter-of-fact about it."

She shrugged. "I'm just very practical, I'm afraid. Since you're from a younger branch of the family and you're a soldier, it seemed a likely guess that you haven't any money of your own."

"I don't," he said.

"Then an heiress it must be. Unless you don't wish to marry at all?"

"Not particularly, no."

She fed him another grape. "But your grandfather is leaving you no choice? You have my sympathies. I'm in the same straits as you, actually. I've no money of my own, so my uncle is trying to sell me off to the highest bidder."

"Rich, old, and unpleasant, I suppose, or he wouldn't have to buy a wife." Julian gritted his teeth at the idea.

"He's certainly no prize," she agreed. "But he *is* rich—and my friends say that surely one can fall in love with a rich man just as easily as with a pauper."

"You're very young." *And naïve and innocent.* Julian felt old himself as he said it.

"Exactly." She seemed to have taken the comment as a compliment—which was not at all the way he had meant it. "However, I don't wish to marry, either. No matter how rich he is... what if he's like my uncle and raises dogs right in the house?" She shuddered. "I want to travel. I want to be free. I want to do good deeds... and I want to publish my memoirs someday for an adoring audience."

"And the money to support you and your good causes, and pay for your travel, will come from where?"

"Well, that is a bit of a poser," she admitted. "But I've been thinking—and I've decided I shall be a mistress. I will collect diamonds and houses and carriages from my lovers, and then whenever I wish to travel or do a good deed, I'll sell something."

Julian's jaw dropped.

She poked another grape into his mouth, and the dimple in her cheek peeked out again. "And you could give me lessons," she went on blithely just as he bit down on the grape.

Julian choked.

"Don't expect me to believe you're inexperienced, Major Hampton."

"Not exactly, but..." He had to stop to clear his throat, and finally his wits returned. "This is not a conversation one has with a..."

"All soldiers have lovers from time to time," she said as if he hadn't interrupted. "My father, for instance—"

"Your *father* told you that all soldiers have lovers?"

Her eyebrows raised a little. "No, but Uncle

Rufus sort of did. Not that I needed telling. My
mother died when I was very small, and my father
was away a great deal before he was killed during the
war. Of course he must have had lovers. But that's
beside the point, really. As I was saying, you could
give me lessons."

He caught her wrist just as she was conveying
another grape toward his mouth. The wrist felt delicate,
dainty, as if he could crush her bones simply by closing
his hand tight. "Lessons in how to be a courtesan." It
seemed to Julian that she was doing quite well already
for an amateur.

"Yes. Though I think I'd rather just be called a
mistress. Still, it's no different, really. Don't all mistresses
do the same things?"

She had tipped her face up to his and was watching
him earnestly. A single drop of purple grape juice was
lurking at the corner of her lips, and it was all Julian
could do not to lick it off and call it Lesson One…

He swallowed hard and looked away. "Not
precisely. And certainly not in the same ways."

"You see? That's why I need a teacher who knows
these things." Her voice was blithe, her face bright.
"I assure you I'm a very good student. Well—not so
much when it comes to music and drawing. And I'm
simply *terrible* at embroidery. But when it's something
I *want* to learn, like geography or…"

"Or being a mistress." He was doomed to burn
for this, Julian knew. Not that he was going to do as
she asked. He had some common sense left, after all,
and more self-discipline than the average man. He
could—he *would* resist the temptation.

But just thinking of her stretched out on a bed taking lessons in seduction… and then practicing her homework… left his mouth dry with desire and his body tense with the urge to take her right here and now on a hard bench in a grape arbor.

He had to do something—say *something*—to distract himself from the image. "If you really want lessons in being a mistress, you should talk to Thorne. Lord Hawthorne, I mean."

She wrinkled her nose. "Lord Hawthorne has a mistress? But he's so *old*."

"Only two years older than I am," he pointed out. "And not *a* mistress—he's had rafts of them." His tongue seemed to have a mind of its own. Telling a girl who was barely out of the schoolroom about mistresses—what was wrong with him?

She shook her head very definitely. "Oh, no. I couldn't do that. At least… Well, from what I've heard about him, I cannot think that we would be a suitable combination."

"Mistresses don't always have a lot of choice, you know. Men who have the money to keep a mistress in style and buy her diamonds and houses and carriages aren't always the young and handsome ones. They're sometimes just as old and unpleasant as the man your uncle wants you to marry—and they might raise dogs in the house to boot."

"I didn't say Lord Hawthorne wasn't handsome," she said judiciously.

Julian felt as if he'd taken a punch in the gut. So she thought Thorne was good-looking, did she?

"And anyway, I would have plenty of choices, as

long as I'm a very *good* mistress. Please, Julian, do help me. Wouldn't you like to be able to say someday that you were the very first lover of the notorious and oh-so-famous… hmm. What name shall I use?"

"*The very first?*"

"Well, yes." She looked at him as if he'd just fallen off a hay wagon. "Someone has to be first."

"You're a *virgin?*"

"Of course I'm a virgin, but that doesn't mean I intend to remain one."

"How old are you?"

"Eighteen. I've been out of the schoolroom for nearly two years. Hmm. What shall I call myself, do you think?"

His head was swimming. His throat was still tight from choking on that last grape, and his eyes didn't quite want to focus. He watched as moonlight peeked out from behind a cloud and touched her hair. For a moment, she looked as if a fire had sprung up around her head… "Flame," he said. "Lady Flame."

"Oh, I like that." She rewarded him with a smile that made his insides twist. "See? You're absolutely the perfect choice."

"I'm absolutely *not*."

He thought for a moment she was going to stamp her foot, but she simply drew back her hand—she'd been about to feed him another grape—and said, "If you won't help me, perhaps I *will* have to ask Lord Hawthorne to train me. Perhaps I can overlook his advanced age because of his extra experience."

He wished he could believe that she was possessed or demented. Turning her down would be so much easier if he thought she honestly had no idea what she was saying. But she'd told him herself that she was practical—and damned if he didn't believe she meant it. She intended to do this... one way or another. His blood ran cold at some of the possible ways she could carry out her plan.

So now what did he do? He should never have mentioned Thorne's name, of course, even in half jest... but now that he had done so, he couldn't live with himself if he was responsible for turning this sensual armful of temptation loose on Thorne. He seemed intent on sticking to his marriage vows, but Thorne was vulnerable just now, on his own in London with a pregnant wife all the way out in Surrey...

*Oh, hell, Julian, at least tell the truth. It's not Thorne's morals you're worried about.*

The truth was that he couldn't stand the idea of any other man *training* her... taking advantage of her... perhaps hurting her. She was far too innocent to have any idea what she was doing.

At the least, he could teach her why she shouldn't take risks like this...

He felt dizzy at the enormity of what he was contemplating. She was far from being a child, and yet her artlessness, her absolute certainty of the path she had chosen, made her seem very young.

"You're serious?" His voice felt raspy.

This time, she didn't smile. There were no dimples peeking out. He looked down at her hands, clutched in her lap. Her knuckles were white, and she apparently hadn't noticed a grape crushed and oozing from her fingers. "Never more so."

He looked into her eyes. There was no mischievous sparkle, no teasing light. Just somber consideration and something that was almost stern. There was nothing childish about her now—she was all woman, and his body responded fiercely, hungrily, to the sight.

*All right,* he told himself. *Think like a seasoned campaigner here.*

Delay—that was the battle plan. Fall back, regroup, and attack along a different front—one that she didn't expect. If she thought he was going to help her, then at least she wouldn't be looking around for some other man to do so, and she'd be safe for exactly as long as she believed that Julian simply needed time to make arrangements for her lessons. For exactly as long as her patience with him lasted.

His own patience was nonexistent. *Right now,* his body urged. *Right here.* He squashed the thought.

If she persisted in her plan and insisted on him carrying through—well, he'd deal with that when the time came. And if in the meantime she came to her senses and changed her mind... Then he would have done her a very large favor, and he could walk away with his honor unscathed.

He hoped she *would* come to her senses. Really he did.

He tried to ignore the sourness in his mouth. Telling lies—even to himself—left an aftertaste.

"Very well," he said. "There are some practical aspects to consider, of course. I'll have to think about where we can go to be completely alone and uninterrupted. Lessons like this take time, and privacy."

The Red Dragon, perhaps? He wondered if she had

a horse. He certainly couldn't borrow a lady's mount from Thorne's stable without prompting far too many questions. And she'd need to have a complaisant groom or a maid who might accompany her without immediately reporting to whomever was supposed to be safeguarding her...

*No,* he reminded himself. *You're not really planning this. You're only pretending to.*

Just getting her out of the house unnoticed would require more strategy than some of the battles he'd fought. Damn, arranging a tryst with a virgin was a whole lot more of a challenge than he'd encountered in any of his previous affairs...

She stood up, and—his attention still focused on the assignation he was *not* going to be arranging—Julian came automatically to his feet. Without a word, she reached for his hand.

She led him across the garden, behind the azalea bush and beyond the huge old elm tree, and through a small wicker gate into a garden barely the size of a pocket handkerchief. No wonder, he thought—half dazed— that she preferred Thorne's garden to her own.

Her fingers were small and cold, and he folded his hand protectively around hers. He didn't begin to recover his senses until they reached the back of the house and she led him into the shadowed entranceway. "Are you completely moonstruck?" he asked. "You can't carry on an intrigue in your own house."

"Why not? You said we needed privacy and time. We can have both right here."

"But..."

"The butler is very old and quite deaf, and the

maids sleep in the attic. How do you think I manage to walk in the garden every night at this hour? No one will know." She raised her chin and looked him directly in the eye. "You were going to put me off, weren't you? Pretend that you were making arrangements and then come back in a few days to tell me you hadn't been able to find a place that was private enough and I'd have to wait longer."

He could hardly deny it when she'd hit squarely on the truth. "Only for your own good," he muttered.

Her eyes flashed. "Why will no one believe I know exactly what I want?"

"Because you haven't any idea what you're getting yourself into, that's why!"

"So show me," she challenged.

Julian gulped. *All right,* his body said eagerly. *Let's do what the lady wants.*

"You promised me."

"I didn't." He had implied, perhaps. He had let her believe what she wanted to, certainly. But *promised*? Hardly.

"And if you don't keep your word, I... I shall think you a coward, Major Hampton!"

Julian almost smiled. He'd have knocked down a man who called him that, but when the accusation came from a very young woman who was clearly willing to use any weapon that came to hand—no, he wasn't about to take it personally.

She had pushed the door open, and somehow he'd crossed the threshold. Now how had she managed that?

"And what about your chaperone?" All he needed was a prim old lady poking her nose into her charge's

bedroom to check on her in the middle of the night—
and, upon finding him there, screaming the roof off.
Yes, that was something to remember whenever his
body threatened to take charge. Not only would there
truly be hell to pay, but the Old Man would never
speak to him again.

On the other hand, if the Old Man disowned him,
at least he wouldn't have to marry the shrew...

"No chaperone. The housekeeper believes that I
retire early each night to read."

"She's a trusting sort, I see. What are you suppos-
edly reading? Sermons?"

She gave him an elfin grin. "As a matter of fact,
yes. Each day I move the page marker—just in case
someone checks."

"What about your uncle?"

Her gaze shifted a little, and after a moment she
said, "He doesn't live here."

He wondered what she was hiding. But while he'd
been distracted, she'd pulled him through the kitchen
and up the back stairs. What was wrong with him?

*Not a thing,* his body said. *Except this infernal delay.*

Just then she pushed open a door, leading him into
a cozy sitting room and on across it to a bedroom
where a candle guttered on a bedside table and the fire
had burned down to embers.

Even in the dim light he could not fail to recognize the riches that filled the room—heavy green
velvet draperies held back with gold cords and
tassels, and white silk bed curtains drifting down
from a canopy above a graceful four-poster bed
that was big enough for pleasure. Only then did he

realize that he'd expected a schoolgirl's room, not a high-class bordello.

"You have the right surroundings for lessons, that's sure," he said dryly.

She looked around as if she'd never seen the place before. "At first, this room made me feel like a princess. But now I think it's much more than that. It makes me feel like a mistress." She unfastened her cloak. "What should I do first?"

She was trembling a bit, he noticed. From eagerness or fear? He was afraid that he knew which it was. Now that he was actually in her bedroom, and she believed it was too late to change her mind…

*It* is *too late,* his body shrieked. *It's much too late, my dear. Come here this instant and make love with me.*

"You're shaking," he said. "Are you afraid?"

"I'm shivering. It was cold in the garden—that's all." She laid the cloak aside and came closer.

For the first time, he could see her without the all-enveloping velvet cloak. She was just as small and fine-boned as he had expected, slender and delicate. He thought he could probably span her waist with his hands, and the idea of this woman submitting to some clumsy oaf—to the kind of man who believed that buying a woman a diamond bracelet would purchase any liberties he cared to exercise—made him feel ill. She could so easily be damaged by careless hands…

"Moment of truth," Julian said. His voice felt raspy, and he gritted his teeth for a moment before he could go on. But he was a man of honor…

*Of course you are,* his body jeered. *That explains why you're in her bedroom.*

"I can go back downstairs right now, and no one will ever know I was here."

She folded her arms across her chest. "You *promised*. And if you don't make love to me right now, I'll seduce a footman by tomorrow." She sounded quite sincere.

Julian swallowed hard. How, exactly, had he lost control of the situation? How had he gone from planning how to protect her to being blackmailed into making love with her? A *footman*, for the love of God…

If she'd said she would turn to another gentleman if Julian refused her, he wouldn't have been nearly so concerned. She wasn't likely to run across any man but him walking in Thorne's garden late at night. In fact, Julian would make certain of it—even if he had to sleep in the grape arbor every night. And for a young woman to get outside her home and meet up with a gentleman long enough to seduce him would be much more difficult during the day; someone would be keeping a very close eye on her.

But a footman… Damnation. The moment he left her, she could ring her bell to wake up one of the menservants—and the deed would be done by midnight. So much for his plans to give her time to reconsider…

*Stop yammering and get on with it,* his body urged.

She came closer. "Should I kiss you?" She didn't wait for an answer but rested her hands lightly on his shoulders and let her lips brush his. Indeed she was chilly to the touch; the cold out in the garden had filtered deep inside her… but the same could not be said of him. The innocent touch of her mouth—her lips closed and almost firm—was enough to heat his blood.

He cupped her face in his hands and flicked his

tongue against the corner of her mouth, capturing the drop of grape juice that had tantalized him in the garden.

She drew a quick breath and let her head fall back against his shoulder. The feel of her in his arms—slim and fragile and trusting—set him on fire. He was beyond thought, beyond guilt, beyond remorse for what he was about to do...

*It's about time,* his body whispered.

"Open your mouth," he murmured, and when she did, he let his tongue slowly invade. Her eyes widened in surprise and then drifted shut. He thought about counting her long, silky eyelashes—because the exercise might take his mind off what he wanted to do right now. Perhaps he could slow himself down and extend his self-control.

*Oh, God, what have you got yourself into?* One inexpert kiss, and he had turned into a rutting stag, barely able to keep himself from ripping her clothes off and having her right then and there.

Speaking of clumsy oafs, he was rapidly turning into the prize. Julian took a deep breath and held her just an inch away from him.

Her eyelids fluttered. "Did I do it wrong?"

"No." His voice was rough. "What's your name?"

"Does it matter? My father called me Georgie, sometimes."

Her father called her Georgie. Her *father*, Julian thought, and wanted to swear. Was the girl trying to sound naïve? Mentioning the man who—if he were still alive and could see what Julian was doing right now—would slice him up with the nearest carving knife was hardly the way to stimulate a lover...

Her innocent comment should have cooled his ardor right down to the freezing point, but just then Georgie snuggled closer and kissed him, and oh God, she *was* an apt pupil—for this time her lips were soft and warm and mobile, and her tongue slipped shyly into his mouth and toyed with his...

His fingers were clumsy as he unfastened her dress and let it drop to the floor and then stepped back to look at her. Her chemise was pure white and so dainty that he could see straight through it—but somehow the shadowed curves were even more arousing than if she had been naked.

He had been right; she was perfectly made—but so delicate that a man could break her with a careless touch.

Julian took a deep breath and struggled for control. Her breasts were just the right size to fill his palms, and the nipples swelled to his touch, sending painful darts of desire to his groin. Her legs were so endlessly long that he felt light-headed at the thought of them wrapped around him, pulling him close. And her scent... He could smell eagerness on her, and his own lust multiplied.

He stripped off his coat, ripped his cravat loose, and almost tore his shirt. He maintained enough presence of mind to set his boots down carefully rather than tossing them aside, for a loud thump might bring someone to investigate. But that was almost the last coherent thought he had.

She watched as he undressed, her face alive with interest, her eyes widening at her first view of him as he stepped out of his breeches. Only then did he remove her chemise and lift her onto the bed.

She wasn't chilly anymore. Her skin was flushed with warmth, her breasts taut against his chest. He settled himself over her, and she wrapped her legs around him as if instinctively trying to draw him inside her.

"Not yet," he whispered, and kissed her. He slipped a hand between them, his finger mimicking the thrusts of his tongue against hers. She urged him closer, and he wanted nothing more than to bury himself inside her—but she wasn't ready yet; she couldn't be, not so quickly.

He had to stop—had to shift his attention elsewhere for a while. She whimpered when he withdrew his hand, and Julian clenched his jaw and set about exploring the safer bits of her body.

The trouble was that no part of Georgie was any less sensual. The curve of her hip, the lushness of her breasts, the angle of her collarbone, the satin of her skin, the enticing hollow of her navel... He caught her hand as she cupped her palm over his jaw, and he kissed each perfect fingertip. He nuzzled her throat and found that she had a ticklish triangle directly under her right ear. He wound ringlets of her hair around his fingers, and traced her lips and the arch of her eyebrow with the tip of his tongue.

And when he finally dared to slip his hand between her legs again, she was wet and slick and hot... so ready for him that the mere thought of sliding deep inside her was almost enough to drive him past reason.

He shifted until he was poised over her, nudging the head of his shaft between her legs, inching into her, holding himself with rigid control to keep from going too fast. But soon he could feel her maidenhead, and there was no going back. He could not stop—and he was honest enough not to pretend, even to himself, that he might.

"I'm sorry," he whispered. "This is going to hurt a little." He thrust firmly past her barrier and caught her squeak of protest with his lips. With his teeth gritted, he stayed still, letting her accustom herself to the feel of him inside her, and only when he felt her ease a little did he start to move.

He slid slowly in and out once, waiting for her response. She began to move with him, raising her hips to welcome him. Each thrust was a little stronger than the last, and with each, she drew him just a little deeper. He lost track of himself; he'd had no idea he could last so long, but Georgie's pleasure was what mattered, not his own. When at last he felt her muscles start to quiver, he slowed once more, stroking her carefully, timing himself to her rhythm, and watching as her eyes filled with wary wonder. His own desire was sublimated in the need to satisfy her, to make her first experience a wonder she would always remember. He would wait until she was ready…

"Don't be afraid," he said. "Let yourself go. It won't hurt anymore, I promise." When ultimately she tensed around him, he was poised, and with a long, deep, intense thrust he took her over the edge, caught her cry of satisfaction with his lips, and followed her into the maelstrom.

❧

Despite what Julian had told her, that last frenzy of feeling *had* hurt—it had been so intense that her teeth

ached, and her body felt as if it would never stop
trembling. Not that the feeling hadn't been worth
the pain: Georgiana had never felt anything like the
wave of well-being that swept over her in the after-
math as her breathing slowly returned to normal. She
lay quite still for a while, basking in the satisfaction.
She could feel Julian's heart still pounding against her
breast, but eventually it also slowed to something like
a regular rhythm.

She smiled and raised a hand—slowly, because the
action seemed to take a lot of strength—to pat his
cheek. "Lesson One. That *did* work out nicely. I knew
you would be a great deal of help, Julian."

He frowned as if she'd done something wrong.
"Don't go thinking you know it all, Georgie. Not all
lovemaking is like that."

"Oh, I know there must be an immense amount to
learn," she assured him. "And I'm quite ready to…"

He raised himself away from her.

"Julian?" she said.

"Dammit, Georgie. Being a mistress is nothing for
you to aspire to."

She surveyed him thoughtfully. "You thought *that*
would make me change my mind?"

He gave a rueful laugh. "Obviously a miscalculation."

"Yes," she agreed. "It was awfully nice, in fact. I
know I need more lessons. I mean, I didn't really *do*
anything this time. Aren't mistresses supposed to…
I mean…"

"Take an active and energetic role."

"Exactly. You need to show me how." Of course,
he would do so, she told herself. He'd agreed to tutor

her, hadn't he? Why was she feeling unaccountably frightened that he might not carry through with his promise?

"Later, perhaps."

"But… You *are* going to teach me, aren't you?"

"I suppose if I don't, you'll call on the footman?" He sighed. "The truth is, you might feel ready for a second lesson, my dear Georgie, but I am not." He kissed her softly, nuzzled her breast, and pulled away from her. As if he couldn't bear to move any farther, he sagged back against the pillows with one arm draped casually across her.

Not quite certain whether to believe him, Georgiana turned onto her side and curled up, one hand propping up her face so she could inspect him. He lay with his eyes closed. His arm felt heavy over her waist; every muscle must be relaxed, she thought, for he hadn't weighed nearly that much earlier even though his entire body had been on top of her. Her gaze wandered down the length of him. Yes, definitely he'd relaxed… or else she'd done something wrong.

His breathing was slow and heavy, as if he was asleep. She reached out a gentle fingertip and prodded his penis.

"That," he said without opening his eyes, "will be covered in Lesson Two—in due time. How to stir a man when he's reluctant or tired."

Due time, again. How tired she was of men telling her to wait until *due time*. "That would be a most useful thing to know," Georgiana agreed, "because if a mistress is to be truly desirable, she mustn't always wait for the gentleman to come to her. She must make

him want her. Then he'll be more likely to give her
diamonds and houses and…"

"Georgie, where do you get your information
about the proper behavior of mistresses?"

"I don't think I should tell you that."

"My dear, we've just slept together. You can tell
me anything."

"I don't *think* I went to sleep," she said doubtfully.

He smiled. "It's a manner of speaking. Another
name for making love."

"Oh. Then it's apparent I do need more lessons."
She hesitated. "Are you tired, Julian?"

"Extremely."

"Then this would be the perfect time for Lesson
Two." She sat up, suddenly eager. "How to stir a man
when he's reluctant, you said, or tired. Let me think…
No, don't tell me. Let me figure this out on my own."

"I have no intention of telling you. I'm going to
sleep for a few minutes, and then I'm going to sneak
back across the garden."

"And you'll visit me again tomorrow? I'll be sure
to unlock the door after the butler goes to bed—unless
you'd like me to meet you in the grape arbor again."

Julian opened one eye. "I could almost feel sympa-
thetic for your guardian."

He hadn't promised, Georgiana noticed. Definitely
she was going to have to take matters into her own
hands. "I understand being tired. But reluctant…?
No, I don't see why anyone would ever be reluctant,
Julian, because what we did was awfully nice. I liked
it a great deal."

"I noticed that, urchin."

"And I'd really like to do it again." With tentative fingers, she began to explore, tracing the angles of his face, the arch of his throat, the outline of the muscles on his upper arms, the fine dark hair on his chest where it arrowed down across a narrow waist and flat belly. She stroked the head of his penis. "It's so velvety. And so soft. Not at all like it was before."

He gave a bark of laughter. "Georgie, you hellborn brat, stop it!"

She was obscurely pleased. "Does that mean I'm doing well with my lesson?"

"Too well, minx."

She watched as he seemed to stir and grow under her touch, and then, quite happily, she applied herself to learning exactly what worked best... until he growled and pulled her under him once more and demonstrated that he was neither tired nor reluctant.

Yes, she thought. Lesson Two had gone *quite* nicely. And... in due time... Lesson Three did, as well.

It was hours later—not long before dawn—when Julian slipped back across the garden. Blessedly, no one in Thorne's household had discovered the unlocked dining-room window, so he climbed back in, sat down to take off his boots, and tiptoed up the stairs to his room, where he dozed a bit—and thought about Georgie.

He felt like a cad—yet he couldn't quite bring himself to regret what he'd done. Since Georgie had been absolutely set on losing her virginity, he'd thought he could at least ensure that she was with a man who wouldn't hurt her in the process. Once she had experienced making love, he'd told himself, she would understand how vulnerable a woman was when she gave herself to a man in that way, and she would let go of her truly lunatic notion to choose lovers based on their ability to give her jewels and fund her travels.

Except it hadn't turned out that way at all. He supposed if he'd been thinking clearly—something that he could see now wasn't likely to happen anytime Georgie was in the vicinity—he'd have threatened her with rape instead of making love to her. Scaring her half to death might have given her second thoughts. Making love to her certainly hadn't.

For, as it happened, Georgie was a natural at love-making. She was as sensual as a kitten—and every bit as cunning in gaining her own pleasure. He couldn't remember the last time he'd been so easily aroused.

Yes, he was a cad, no question about it. Making love to her even once had been reprehensible; he'd had absolutely no intention of repeating the process. But Georgie's eagerness was a stimulant like no other, and so Julian had compounded his lapse in judgment by staying with her. And allowing her to seduce him again.

She'd worn him out, in fact—but she had still been going strong, making plans for Lesson Four, when he'd finally forced himself to leave her. Walking away from her had not been easy; she'd been curled temptingly in that velvet-draped bed, an innocently seductive siren. But if he'd waited any longer, he might as well have sat down on the back step and waited for the scullery maid to take him in with the milk.

Damned if he didn't think Georgie was right about the potential for success in her chosen career. All she'd have to do would be to walk around Hyde Park and give limpid looks to gentlemen, and she'd have them lined up on her doorstep. They'd be bidding for the honor of giving her diamonds and houses and carriages...

It made him feel ill.

Except... there was no reason she couldn't be *his* mistress. True, his income—such as it was—wouldn't run to diamonds and houses and carriages anytime soon, but surely he could convince Georgie that there were compensations to having him as her only lover...

Something about that didn't feel quite right, but he hadn't figured it out yet when his batman came in to open the drapes. Julian yawned and sat up, and as soon as he had bathed and shaved, he went downstairs to breakfast.

He wasn't aware he was whistling until Thorne eyed him suspiciously and said, "You're in an unexpectedly good mood, considering the black cloud the Old Man left you in last night."

"Oh, that," Julian said. "Actually, it's just that whistling... uh... keeps me from yawning. I haven't slept well since the war started—always the need to be alert, you know. That's why, when I can't sleep, I walk around at night."

"The war's over, Julian."

"It gets to be a habit. Plus I'm a bit worried about what the Old Man will think up next." Julian put a slab of ham and a spoonful of deviled kidneys on his plate, selected a slice of toast from the rack, and sat down. Damn, he was hungry. "I hate to keep the servants up waiting for me while I'm out walking. Might I have a key? Just in case." *In case next time someone finds a window open and locks me out.*

The butler poured his coffee. Without taking his eyes off Julian, Thorne said, "Carson, give my cousin a key so he can come and go as he likes."

"Yes, my lord," the butler murmured, and went away.

"I've been thinking about your problem, Julian."

*My problem?* For an instant, Julian felt a mad urge to ask Thorne's advice on what a mistress should know. But of course *that* couldn't be the problem Thorne was referring to.

"Yes?" he managed. "My problem?"

"The Old Man and the shrew," Thorne said patiently. "She wasn't just a bad dream, Julian. Pull yourself together. I'm going home to Surrey at the end of the week. I want you to come with me."

Leave London? Leave Georgie? Not bloody likely. Julian shook his head. "The tailor said it would be next week before he had all my order finished."

Thorne's eyes narrowed. "You didn't seem so concerned about clothes yesterday."

"That was yesterday. What's in Surrey, anyway?"

"You'll be able to visit around the neighborhood, and get to know a few people. Start to establish yourself in society. Then you can go and stay with Colford for a while and do the same thing."

It sounded deadly dull to Julian.

"Let people know you're home. Hint that you'll be looking for a wife. Then as soon as hunting season starts, you'll be invited to some house parties, and you can begin to meet a few young women."

"What good will that do? The Old Man—"

"The Old Man is being very shortsighted. You need to take a longer view of things—and if you make your case like a reasonable man, you can bring him around."

Julian looked at Thorne with astonishment. "Maybe it's easier to deal with him when you're an earl in your own right, Thorne, but I'm telling you—"

"When you find someone you like, you'll simply come back to town and discuss it with the Old Man. Remind him that you're the last remaining heir—and tell him if he insists on marrying you off to the shrew, he can whistle the idea down the wind of you having a legitimate son to carry on the line. But if he lets you marry someone you don't mind seeing in the bedroom, you'll make sure he has a half-dozen great-grandchildren to bounce on his knee. If you handle him right, you can get what you want."

*Someone you don't mind seeing in the bedroom...* Yes, that would make a good topic for a lesson sometime. Being a mistress entailed always looking attractive and appealing and tempting...

Of course, there were far more important subjects to take up first, and Georgie didn't need much help in being attractive and appealing, anyway. That chemise she'd been wearing last night might have been virginal white, but the way it fit hadn't just been tempting, it had been downright wicked.

He wondered what she'd look like wearing blue, the same color as the Dorset sky...

"Julian!"

"*What?* Oh, Surrey. I don't think so, Thorne.

You'll be billing and cooing with your bride, and I haven't been in London for so long that I really want to stay a while."

Thorne rubbed two fingers across the line between his eyebrows as if his head hurt. "You know you're taking a chance this young woman will turn up at Seaborne House some night for dinner."

"She's indisposed."

"Indispositions end, Julian. Or the Old Man may summon her, just as he did you last night—and I wouldn't put it past him to have a special license in his pocket so he can take care of the matter right then."

"I'll deal with that when the time comes." Julian polished off his ham and went back to the sideboard for more, along with a pile of eggs and bacon. He wondered what Georgie was having for breakfast—or if she was even awake yet. More likely she was still curled up in bed like the kitten she so resembled... sleeping off an exhaustion that would look far more innocent than it really was.

❧

Georgiana, however, was wide awake. After Julian left her, she had napped for a while and then remembered that the maid would be coming sooner or later with her morning chocolate, and there would certainly be questions if she found Georgiana snuggled up without a nightgown on. So she'd scrambled to pick up her discarded clothes, made sure Julian hadn't left anything behind, and then put on the nightgown that had been laid out for her the previous evening and started to climb back into bed.

When she pulled back the sheets, however, she realized that not all of the traces of their night together could be as easily removed as a chemise that had been discarded on the floor.

Julian hadn't warned her of this. Of course, he had been rather busy all night—and he'd left in a bit of a hurry near dawn—so perhaps it had simply slipped his mind.

But if the upstairs maid did a thorough job of bed-making this morning and saw bloodstains on the sheets, she would have to go to the housekeeper and report. And Mrs. Mason would have to go to Lord Hawthorne and tell him. And Lord Hawthorne—he of the many mistresses—would certainly know what had happened, and he would summon Georgiana and yell at her. Or even worse, he might send Perkins to yell at her. They would demand to know who the man had been, but of course Georgiana would refuse to tell. Even if they were to torment her, she still wouldn't talk...

But the important point was that she'd be watched far more carefully in the future. No more late-night walks in the garden, and certainly no more visits from gentlemen. Julian wouldn't be able to come to see her again tonight—but she had no way to warn him to stay away. And if Lord Hawthorne found out that Julian had been the one in her bedroom, the Earl might throw him out of the house and refuse to help him financially...

Julian wouldn't have any choice then but to marry an heiress. Even thinking about that made her feel sad—especially since it would be partly her fault.

Besides, Georgiana had no intention of giving up her lessons. So obviously she had to act—and quickly.

She stared at the stained sheet, thinking hard. She could say that her monthlies had started—but she could hardly keep up that pretense for long.

She could say that she'd cut herself—but she didn't have a wound nor the strength of mind to actually pick up her scissors and create one.

She stood for a moment, thinking quickly—for the maid might come in at any moment—and then she reached for her inkwell. Just in time, too, for the glossy black ink was still spreading over the spots on the fine linen when she heard steps outside her door.

She tugged the sheets off the bed and was standing in the midst of a maelstrom when the door opened.

The maid looked around in confusion. "Miss Georgiana, what's the matter?"

"I was writing a letter, Mary," Georgiana improvised. "And I tipped over the inkwell."

"In your bed?" The maid sounded horrified.

"I know—it was so careless of me. The sheets are ruined, I'm afraid, but I think I got them off the bed before the ink soaked through and into the mattress… I hope Mrs. Mason won't be too angry with me." Her voice trembled a little—and not intentionally.

Mary's gaze slid from the stained sheet to Georgiana. "Begging your pardon, Miss, but how did you get so much ink on the sheets and none at all on you?"

Georgiana bit her lip. Why hadn't she thought of that? Not that she would have liked to stain her nightgown, for it was her very favorite. But she could at least have coated her fingers… "Just lucky, I guess?" she offered tentatively.

Mary made her way around the heap of linen to set Georgiana's tray on a small table by the fireplace. "Accidents happen," she said finally. "I'll just put the sheets in the rag bin."

Remorse tugged at Georgiana. "Do you think Mrs. Mason will be angry? They were very nice sheets."

"Mrs. Mason has seen worse than ink on sheets. I mean…" Mary's face went red. "I beg pardon, Miss. I shouldn't speak to you of…" She gulped and went to open the draperies. Then she swept up the bundle of sheets and went hastily away.

Worse things than ink? That was certainly interesting, Georgiana thought, and sat down to drink her chocolate.

In the off-season, there were few visitors to Gentleman Jackson's club, and Julian enjoyed the attention of the famous boxer himself for a while, basking in a couple of restrained compliments and taking to heart some advice on how to better protect himself in a street brawl.

When he was finished—and feeling both winded and hot—he wandered over to where Thorne was sparring with their cousin Lord Colford. Neither was really putting his heart into the bout, Julian thought. In fact, they seemed to be doing far more talking than fighting.

"Maybe York," Colford said as Julian walked up. "That should be far enough. Felicity could…"

"No." Thorne sidestepped what looked like a

half-hearted jab. "I'm breaking the rules as it is. I can't just ship…"

Colford cleared his throat.

"…the package out of town. Not 'til I hear from the… owner."

"A package?" Julian observed lightly. "Or a baggage?" Was Thorne disposing of another mistress? Heaven knew he'd done it often enough; Thorne had never had a mistress who lasted for more than a few months. Julian was just glad Georgie wasn't going to be one of that long line…

"A bit of both," Thorne admitted. "How did your instruction go?"

"I'm too tired to take you on this morning. Which is exactly what you intended, I'm sure—because you know I still owe you a beating for that insult."

"What insult was that?" Colford asked.

"He told me I'm just like the Old Man."

"And so you are."

"I'll have to fight you both if you keep that up, Richard." Then Julian grinned. "Excuse me—I should say, Colford."

"Only if you want me to call you Silsby."

"Let's stick to first names, in that case." Julian mopped his brow. "I'm ready to go, if you two are."

"A friendly game of cards at White's?" Colford asked.

Why not? Julian thought. He had nothing better to do—and the rest of the day to kill before he could go back to Georgie.

They walked from Gentleman Jackson's to Colford's club, and on the way a carriage pulled up, blocking the traffic on Oxford Street while a beady-eyed old lady leaned out to quiz them. "What are you doing back in town?" she asked Thorne, but without waiting for his answer she moved on. "Colford, nice to see you." Her gaze came to rest on Julian. "And you must be the new heir. What a good-looking trio Seaborne's grandsons have turned out to be. If I were thirty years younger…"

More like forty, Julian thought, from the weather-beaten look of her. Possibly even fifty. But he made his bow nonetheless.

"Lady Stone," Thorne said.

She looked him in the eye. "Sir Rufus Baxter was asking about you last night. You haven't compromised his ward, have you?"

"Certainly not," Thorne said coolly.

"Well, I'm glad to hear it. I'd hate to have to write your wife and tell her you've been up to no good. If it's about that silly canal project of yours instead, I have to warn you he's got no money to invest." Shouts were starting to rise from the carriages that her ladyship's barouche was blocking, but she didn't seem to notice. Her gaze had drifted back to Julian. "I understand we're to wish you happy, Silsby."

"Not just yet, my lady," Julian said.

Her gaze grew even beadier. "Seaborne's found someone who'll stand up to him, eh? That ought to be interesting."

But finally even Lady Stone's selective deafness had to admit the protests around her, and she waved to her coachman to proceed. As the traffic jam began to break up, the three cousins walked on.

"A canal?" Julian said. "You're actually thinking of sinking good money into a muddy ditch?"

"Perkins swears it's the next sure-fire investment."

"I'll wager you don't see *him* putting money into a long hole in the ground."

Thorne looked intrigued by that idea. "It's not a bad notion, at that. I'll be interested to hear what you think after he tells you his reasoning."

"I didn't say I wanted to listen to him," Julian protested. "If I had any spare cash to invest—which I don't—I'd put it in steam engines." Unless he was putting it into houses and diamonds and carriages for Georgie.

In any case, he could hardly refuse to do Thorne a favor by hearing his man of business out. And if the scheme turned out not to be solid, he might save his cousin a great deal of money and grief.

Besides, what else did he have to do this afternoon? Cards would fill an hour or two, but what about the rest of the day? He calculated the hours until he could meet Georgie once more in the garden and sighed. At least thinking about a canal might keep his mind off her for a while.

❧

Georgiana was standing on the top step of the library ladder, peering into the shadowed bookcase to see what other interesting volumes might be hiding in the very back of the uppermost shelf, when the housekeeper came into the library.

"Miss Georgiana? I can summon Mason for you, if you need something taken down from the top shelf. He's a great deal taller and could reach more easily."

Georgiana almost fell off the ladder. "Oh, no, that's

fine, Mrs. Mason. There doesn't seem to be much up here." She let the book she'd just snagged slip back into place.

"If you need another volume of sermons," Mrs. Mason said, "I believe they're on the other side of the fireplace."

Georgiana peeked down at her and was relieved to see a twinkle in the housekeeper's eyes. She gave a discreet little push to the books she'd already selected, shoving them back on the shelf where—she hoped—the housekeeper couldn't see. She'd simply have to come back for them later. "I thought perhaps some variety in my reading material would be better for me."

"I should think so, dear. Mary tells me you were writing letters this morning and had a bit of an accident."

Was there an edge to the housekeeper's voice? "I beg your pardon—I should have told you myself. I'm sorry about the sheets. It was so very careless of me."

"The sheets don't matter. But I was just wondering, dear—who were you writing to?"

Georgiana goggled for a moment. How had she managed to forget that she wasn't supposed to communicate with anyone outside the house? Writing letters—letting anyone know where she was… no wonder Mrs. Mason was checking on her. "Oh, no one, really."

Mrs. Mason's eyes narrowed.

"I mean, I *was* writing a long letter to a friend, pages and pages—just to pass the time. It's more like a diary, in fact. I didn't intend to send it—at least not until Lord Hawthorne has talked to my uncle and straightened everything out. But I thought perhaps if he made arrangements for me to go somewhere else, instead of back to my uncle, I should have a letter ready so my friends would know where to reach me."

"I see," Mrs. Mason said slowly.

"Then I'd only have to add the address of where I'd be staying."

"Yes, dear. Well, give it to me when it's ready, and I'll send it over to Lord Hawthorne to be franked."

And read as well, Georgiana knew. But since the letter was entirely fictional, there was no sense in feeling irate at the idea of her trustee reading her mail…

Though perhaps she should write a long letter, just in case Mrs. Mason went looking for it in her room… Oh, why had she said *pages and pages*? Could she perhaps say it had been ruined by the spilled ink so she'd tossed it into the fire?

"As it happens, dear, I came in to tell you that Mr. Perkins has called to see you. Perhaps he has news about your situation."

Perkins? *Now?* Georgiana could have kicked the nearest chair. After almost a week with no word at all, of course Perkins would have to show up today. If he had come to tell her that she had to go home… or that Lord Hawthorne had reached an agreement with Uncle Rufus and was sending her somewhere else instead…

Well, she wouldn't go, that was all. She simply wouldn't go. She didn't want to leave Upper Seymour Street, and she didn't want to leave Julian…

Only because of her lessons, of course. Certainly not because she'd been foolish enough to grow fond of him. Mistresses didn't get attached to their lovers. The only way to be successful in her chosen field was to keep her head and never, *ever* fall in love...

No. She was absolutely not in love with Julian. She was going to be a mistress. And he was going to marry an heiress.

Her problem right now wasn't nearly so complicated as falling in love. It was simply that she couldn't possibly leave before she'd finished these most interesting—and useful—lessons...

Of course, if Julian was to marry a very rich heiress, then he could afford to keep a mistress as well as a wife.

The thought of continuing to be Julian's mistress should have been an inviting one, but it tasted like dust on her tongue.

Georgiana brushed her hands over her skirt and came down from the ladder. "I'll see Mr. Perkins here," she said quietly. "Ask Mason to show him in, please."

With any luck, she told herself, Perkins had only come to make another speech to her about *patience* and *due time*. If that was the case, he'd no doubt be quite impressed with how well she took the news.

❦

Colford joined them in the afternoon for Perkins' droning and interminable analysis of the latest data on the canals—he had expanded from one muddy ditch, it seemed, to an entire network of them, and much to Julian's surprise, the man actually made sense—and then stayed for dinner.

The meal, it seemed to Julian, was even more extended than the discussion of canals had been. It appeared likely to go on until midnight. Not that there was anything wrong with it, as far as dinners went. The dining room was cozy, the roast well cooked, the port and brandy excellent, and the conversation among the three cousins lively.

But Julian's gaze kept wandering to the window that so conveniently overlooked the garden. Its blank glass reflected the branches of candles on the table, as though there was no garden outside. No flower beds and graveled paths. No grape arbor. No Georgie...

Was she out there waiting for him? He wondered if she'd be in the grape arbor tonight, or if she'd discovered some other sheltered spot. He thought he'd seen a pear tree—and though he wouldn't have thought of pears as a tool of seduction before now, he was learning that in Georgie's hands, anything was possible.

He hoped she wouldn't stay out there too long; he didn't want her to get cold.

But if she gave up and thought he wasn't coming... what then? Should he follow her into the house and up to her bedroom, looking for her? But how would he know if she was really waiting for him or if she'd changed her mind? What if she hadn't gone out to the garden to meet him at all? What if the door was locked?

What if she didn't want him to come to her tonight?

But if she *did* want him, and he didn't come... he couldn't bear for her to think that he hadn't wished to be with her.

The clock in the hallway struck half past ten, and Julian pushed back his chair. "I don't mean to be rude, but I'm about to doze off in my port. You two wore me out at Gentleman Jackson's today. I think I'll take a quick walk and then go to bed." *Just not to sleep.*

He made his escape without giving the other two a chance to comment.

The moon was past full now. The garden was quiet, and the air was still. He could smell grapes as he approached the arbor, and the aroma caught at his senses and sent a surge of arousal through him. He would never smell grapes again without thinking of Georgie... and wanting her.

The arbor lay in shadow, and he couldn't see whether she was there. But as he approached, a breeze seemed to stir, and suddenly she was there in his arms. He almost staggered at the impact as she flung herself against him, the velvet of her cloak swirling around him and caressing his entire body—enveloping him in her scent. Her lips were cool against his—but only for a moment, and then the heat of her seared his mouth as she pulled him closer.

*A mistress makes sure her lover knows that she finds him desirable.* Well, that particular topic could be scratched off his list of lessons for Georgie.

*Any time she wants to refine her technique,* his body announced, *I'm available.*

He held her away from him. The moonlight shifted just then, so he could see the reproachful look she gave him.

"You don't like the way I kissed you?" she demanded.

"Very much, my dear. But I don't want you to bruise yourself on my coat buttons."

She smiled. "Then let's go inside and take them off."

Her tone was only slightly naughty—but the mere

hint of mischief left him suddenly as hard as he'd ever been in his life, so eager for her that he almost stumbled as she led him through the garden. The strength of his reaction startled him—and something deep inside him twisted oddly. The night before, she had been shy, tentative, an innocent girl. Tonight Georgie was a woman—totally in control of herself—and her incredibly sensual nature was at full heat.

He didn't like it. *Because she thinks she doesn't need lessons anymore,* he thought. *She thinks she's learned it all.*

And that could be very dangerous for her. If she were to share herself so quickly, so enthusiastically, with a man who wasn't inclined to be gentle with her, she might as well ask to be mistreated. So the next lesson she needed to learn was an important one— though perhaps not one that either of them would particularly enjoy.

Damnation, he thought. All he wanted was to be with her, inside her, toying with and teasing her—but for her own sake, he first had to make sure she understood this basic rule. And clearly he would have to demonstrate, since Georgie didn't take well to explanations…

Once in her bedroom, she dropped her cloak on the floor and danced around him. "Come *on*, Julian. Hurry!"

He lifted an eyebrow at her. "What's the rush?"

*Have you lost your mind?* his body asked. *Let's rush!*

"I want to practice."

*Oh, good,* his body murmured. *Where shall we begin?*

"Then practice patience, my dear. Not only is it a virtue, but you have a lot more to learn about making love."

"Exactly," she said. "So let's get started." She was stripping off her clothes as she spoke. Not that she had much on to start with, Julian saw; he thought she must have chosen her dress for the sheer ease of getting out of it.

*Big buttons,* his body noted. *And not many of them. Very convenient…*

He observed her out of the corner of his eye—he didn't dare really watch, or he'd never keep control of himself long enough to make the point he needed her to understand—as he stripped his own clothes off. She was already in bed by the time he was naked, which suited him fine. He rolled on top of her, letting her feel his full weight. He nudged her legs apart, settled himself comfortably, probed a little…

She jerked away, ever so slightly. "Julian." Her voice was very small. "Aren't you even going to kiss me first?"

"Why should I? You seemed to be in a hurry."

"Not *that* much of a hurry."

"Well, I'm in a hurry, and you certainly led me to think you were. At any rate, since I'm ready, what does it matter if you're not? All a mistress has to do is lie still."

She bit her lip, and he thought he saw the glint of tears in her big hazel eyes. "That's not what you said last night."

"There, there, sweetheart." He rolled onto his side and snuggled her against him, kissing her softly. Even in her confusion, her body was warm and yielding, her skin silky against his, and desire flooded through him.

*That's the way,* his body mused. *Enough with the restraint.*

"It's all right, Georgie; I'm not really that much of a cad."

She blinked, and he watched her throat flutter as she swallowed.

"Not very romantic, was it—that approach?" he said.

"Well—no. Why...?"

Her voice, little more than a husky whisper, set him aflame, and he had to clench his jaw for a moment to keep control of himself. She was far from being ready—and so he would wait, trying to distract himself from the glorious softness of her breasts rising and falling against his chest with every breath she took. "Men are generally unromantic creatures, Georgie. They're quick to arousal and quick to action. If you wish to be treated with restraint and care and patience, then you must not encourage your lover to be in a rush."

"Oh. You mean I shouldn't..."

He traced her profile with his fingertip. "You shouldn't strip your clothes off as if they're on fire, for one thing," he said gently. "And don't bound into bed like that. Require him to tempt you into making love—Lady Flame."

"Even if I *am* ready?" she said doubtfully.

"You'll never be so ready that a little tenderness won't make you more so." He kissed her, long and slowly. She hadn't been eating grapes tonight, but her taste was just as sweet, just as exotic, even though it was entirely her. He let his tongue trace the even white line of her teeth. He wasn't a bit surprised—but he was delighted—when she bit him, very gently, and sent an arc of heat straight to his groin. He groaned a little and tried to remember the point he'd been making. Something about tenderness... and being ready to make love...

*I'm ready,* his body announced.

"Encouragement, but not impatience." He moved just a fraction away so he could palm her breast and toy with her nipple. "Men are hunters. When it's too easy to bring the quarry down, they lose interest and move on to the next prey." She moved ever so slightly, pushing against his palm, and suddenly he could barely hear his own words through the rush of blood in his ears.

"So you're saying if I'm to keep a lover..."

Julian's voice was thick. "Make him seduce you."

*Any time,* his body agreed. *Now's good for me.*

She reached up to run her fingers through his hair and pull him down to her. "Like this? Kiss me, Julian..."

He kissed her, and fireworks went off behind his eyes as she responded. What was it he'd been saying? "That's good. Show him that you're interested—but make him work to have you." His hand wandered down until his fingers spread over the warm, flat plane of her belly. He could feel the ebb and flow of her breathing, and the rhythm—mimicking the pattern of making love—made his groin ache.

She arched against him. He cupped her hip, and his fingers seemed to burn from the heat of her. His hand slipped over her thigh and slowly worked its way up the inside of her leg. Very slowly, because he didn't dare go faster. He wanted to plunge into her, to plunder, to take... and he was barely hanging on to his self-control as it was.

"Otherwise," he managed to say, "he'll just spread

your legs, thrust a few times, and be done. And if that's all he needs to do, then any woman can satisfy him."

"But you're not like that," Georgie observed. "You could have done anything you wanted just now—but you didn't." She nestled against him and smiled. "I bet you never have to." She took his hand and—almost carelessly—moved it up a bit until his palm rested over her mound.

He groaned.

Georgie said innocently, "I'm just showing you what I like."

*That's torture,* said his body.

He slipped a fingertip inside her, and she moved just a little to make it easier for him to touch her. "What about this?" He probed a bit further. His chest was getting tight, making it difficult to breathe properly.

"Quite nice," she said. She sounded very relaxed.

He eyed her suspiciously. Yes, the dimple had peeked out. She really was a star student... who was already applying this newest lesson against him.

Her fingers curled gently, almost lazily, around his penis, cupping him so lightly it was almost as if she hadn't noticed. Not that he believed for an instant that she didn't know precisely what she was doing.

*All right, now pride is at stake,* his body agreed.

It was time for a serious change of tactics, Julian thought, or the minx would have him begging—and he would never hear the last of that.

❧

No doubt he was correct that patience was a virtue, Georgiana thought, even though when he said it he sounded a great deal too much like priggish old Perkins for her taste. But maintaining an attitude of forbearance was extraordinarily difficult when he was being so very tempting. Didn't he understand that she was aching, longing to have him inside her?

What had he said she should do? Oh, yes—*encouragement, but not impatience*. Well, she'd encourage a little more and see what happened. She let her fingers tighten just a little on that most interesting part of him, and she slowly began to stroke…

Suddenly, he pulled away from her. Her head, which had been resting quite comfortably on his shoulder, almost bounced on the pillow. "Julian—"

"I'm not leaving you," he said. He sounded a little hoarse. "Just beginning Lesson Four."

"I thought that *was* Lesson—"

"Lesson Five, then." Suddenly his voice was muffled against her most private place, and the vibrations of his words sent shivers through her body.

"Oh…" Georgiana said helplessly.

He used his thumbs to gently open her and bent his head to nuzzle at her. She bucked against him, and he said, "Now, now. Lie still. A mistress' job is to please her lover."

She gripped the pillow with both fists. "I'm supposed to just hold still while you do that?"

He raised his head long enough to grin at her. "You can try," he said sweetly. He blew gently on her, and Georgiana shuddered under the sensation of his warm breath. He was driving her past the point of reason, and the emptiness inside her had become a gnawing ache.

She unclenched one hand from the pillow and wrapped it into his hair instead.

"I'm busy right now," Julian said, a bit breathlessly.

"I'll yell."

"Blackmail? But Georgie—think, dear heart. If you yell, someone will come in, and then you'll never get what you want. What is it you want, by the way?"

She could feel the low rumble of his voice all the way through her. "You—inside me. *Now*."

"Just another minute," Julian murmured.

It didn't take another minute. As the quivers grew to a tumult, Georgiana bit down on her hand to keep from screaming. As if knowing that she would shatter if he pushed her any further, Julian shifted until he was beside her again, holding her gently as the shudders of satisfaction ripped through her. As the last ripples calmed, he slid firmly inside her and began to move. She moaned once with relief at having him where he belonged. But that comfort didn't last long, for she was so sensitive now that his every touch created havoc.

Her hunger rose with each stroke, her frustration with each withdrawal. She met each thrust fiercely, drawing him more deeply inside her until ultimately even he could resist no longer. He smothered a hoarse cry against her throat and exploded inside her just as she also toppled over the edge.

❧

Georgie had locked her legs around him—the girl's flexibility was quite remarkable—so even if he'd wanted to pull away, he couldn't have done so. Julian figured it would be wise to let her have that much of a victory; he was fairly sure he'd made his point.

Except that he couldn't remember exactly what he'd been trying to prove.

To tell the truth, he couldn't have moved even if he'd been completely free. He wanted never to withdraw, never to leave her. More to the point, he could barely lift his head enough to watch her. The effort was worthwhile, though, just to see Georgie's distant, unfocused stare as she slowly came back to earth.

She gave a little hiccup of a sigh, shook her head as if to clear it, and eventually relaxed, freeing him. "That was nice, Julian."

"Just nice?" he teased. Reluctantly, he pulled away and then shifted a little and drew her close to his side.

She didn't answer.

"What's wrong, Georgie?" He watched her eyes. "Are you having second thoughts about this plan of yours?"

"No…" But her voice was uncertain.

"Well, you should be."

"Not all gentlemen are like you, are they, Julian? I mean they aren't careful with women."

He kissed her hair and snuggled her closer. Though disillusioning her had been necessary for her own good, and he was very glad that she'd finally gotten the point, he wished he hadn't had to demonstrate. "Some men don't see any reason they should care what their partners feel. That's true."

"Well, then," she said firmly, "you'll just have to help me decide which lovers to accept."

Julian was speechless. Exactly where had his

oh-so-careful lesson gone wrong? She was supposed to still be shuddering in horror at the thought of finding herself in bed with some cruel libertine. She was supposed to give up the entire idea—not try to turn him into her procurer!

"Georgie, if you think I'm going to arrange…" He swallowed hard and forced a laugh. "Sorry… I was a bit muzzy for a moment there. I didn't realize you were teasing."

"I wasn't," she said firmly.

"Well, I won't do it. How the hell would I know, anyway? I'm not in the habit of watching people make love."

"But you know what kind of men they are. Your friends, I mean."

"Being honorable in a card game or a boxing ring isn't the same thing, Georgie." And if she thought for a single moment that he would run down a list of his friends, choosing which one of them should make love to her next…

The thought made his head spin. It was bad enough just to know that she intended to take lovers; the very idea of helping to select who and when was enough to choke him.

"You know which ones are gentle and thoughtful and kind—like you." She smiled brightly at him and reached under the pillow. "*That's* all settled, then. I found something today that I want you to look at."

"Nothing's settled—and what are you up to now? You haven't already made a list, have you?"

"No, because I don't know who to put on it. But that's a really good idea, Julian—I'll start collecting names, shall I? My friends talk about gentlemen all the time. And then you can help rank them."

He stared at her, his jaw slack.

She held out a book, a small, slender, calf-bound volume. "I found this down in the library today. I thought it was the most amazing thing."

Obviously they weren't done yet with the idea of her list—but Julian was too boggled to even try to make her see sense just now.

*Keep her too busy to make a list,* his body suggested.

He sat up just enough to flip through the pages. She wasn't joking about the book being amazing; it was full of woodcut illustrations of couples in intimate embraces. "I'm surprised this was in the library at all. It's not the sort of book you want some aged relation's eyes to fall on when they come to visit."

"It was on the top shelf, pushed way into the back."

"I see. And I suppose you stumbled across this only because you were ransacking the room for more sermons to improve your mind?"

He was beginning to anticipate exactly when her dimples would flash, and he wasn't disappointed. "I was checking for dust," she said demurely.

"Of course you were. Such a good little house-wife." The image of her in an apron and cap—and nothing else—tantalized him. To take his mind off it, he deliberately returned his attention to the book.

*That's not going to help,* his body warned.

He turned a page. "Does this belong to your uncle?"

"No, I'm quite certain it doesn't." Her voice was airy.

"Oh, that's right. You told me he doesn't live here. Where does he live?"

Georgie didn't answer. "I had to sneak the book out of the library tucked in my unmentionables, and I've been reading it all day. Well, looking at it, actually, because there's not much to read."

The mental image of Georgie's method of smuggling would have been enough to stir a dead man to lust; what it did to Julian was downright painful. He turned the book sideways and looked more closely, trying to distract himself from his arousal. It didn't help, though, for the book had fallen open to a position he'd never heard of before—and one he wouldn't mind trying. If anyone could bend into that particular shape, it would be Georgie...

No wonder she'd been such an eager little thing tonight, after spending all day with this sort of literature.

"But I don't understand how some of these things work. I mean, look at this one." She flipped through the pages and held the book out to him again. "How can they possibly enjoy this? They're not even looking at each other."

He felt himself growing harder at the very idea.

*All right, there are limits,* his body whispered. *I'm past mine.*

"Like this, minx." He set the book aside and spooned her into his body, her back nestled firmly against his chest, his hands cupping her breasts as he shifted her to just the right angle and entered her once more.

"Oh," she said. "Yes, now I see. That's quite an interesting..." Her breath caught. "...sensation. Oh, Julian!"

He had to admit he liked that one himself, for he found it marginally easier to maintain control. He could go on making love to her all night, like this—except that she was right; not being able to look directly into her face, to kiss her and catch her words on his lips, to see her eyes dilate as she climaxed, robbed him of the best part of the joy of making love to her.

He interrupted their play and pulled her on top of him instead, so he could teach her how to take charge of her own satisfaction. And only after she had once more come apart in his arms did he roll her onto her back and very slowly take everything he wanted, building to the strongest release he had felt in his entire life.

Nothing, he thought, could ever be as fulfilling.

He was almost dozing when Georgie said, "Once I'm established as a mistress, I'll hear all the gossip, and I'll know all about everyone—so I can even help you find your heiress."

He'd forgotten that particular notion of hers—that he needed to marry someone who would bring money with her. Not that it was a bad idea, he thought. At least if he married an heiress he wouldn't have to fret about what demands the Old Man might make of him next.

He wondered, for an instant, if his grandfather was playing an even deeper game than he'd realized. The fact that the shrew didn't have a fortune might actually be a benefit in the Old Man's estimation—for the match meant that not only would he get hold of the corner of land he wanted so badly, but his heir would remain financially dependent on him... and therefore could be pressured for anything else the Old Man wanted.

*I'll think about that some other time,* Julian told himself. Right now he was utterly exhausted... He'd rest just a little, and then perhaps he should go back across the garden. Surely by now Colford would have gone home and Thorne would be sound asleep…

But his body rebelled at the idea of leaving her.

"And perhaps," Georgie went on brightly, "your wife won't mind if you have a mistress. Most women don't, my uncle says. So you can keep right on teaching me."

"Your uncle shouldn't tell you these things." Every time she said something about her plan, Julian got a bad taste in his mouth—and it was getting worse every time she mentioned the scheme.

It wasn't that he didn't want Georgie to be his mistress—and he was rather sure that if he ended up married to the shrew he'd *need* a mistress. But what really made him feel ill was that he didn't want Georgie to take lovers. Ever. No matter what.

He tried to open his eyes. "Your uncle is right, you know. Perhaps when he looked around for a husband for you, he could have made a better choice—but one man would be much safer for you than a string of lovers. You really should…"

She really should what? *Marry?* What was he thinking? That door was closed; he'd shut it for her himself the moment he'd climbed into her bed…

Remorse slammed through him.

*Better me than the footman,* he reminded himself. But the excuse didn't help; he was the one who was responsible.

Surely there were men who were open-minded enough to understand. And Georgie was such a taking little thing—there would be a gentleman who would marry her anyway. Probably hordes of them, Julian thought.

But could her husband forget that she hadn't been a virgin? Would he overlook her lapse, or would he throw it up to her? Blame her? Even punish her for it?

And no matter who she chose—even if her husband was a lamb who never blamed her for a moment—Julian had to admit that outcome wouldn't satisfy him, either.

It wasn't just that he wanted Georgie to be safe from harm—though of course he did. The truth was that he didn't want her using her new knowledge with any other man, even with a husband. He didn't want any man to know Georgie's sensual side, to experience her playfulness, her humor, and that all-gone look in her eyes as she climaxed...

*Any* man... except for him.

That was the fact. The plain, simple, undeniable truth. It didn't come as a shock; he supposed he had known it all along—perhaps ever since she'd made her crazy proposal. He just hadn't wanted to think about it in quite those terms.

The problem was, what was he going to do about it?

There was only one course of action—only one thing that an honorable man could do. In the morning, he would talk to his grandfather. Perhaps Thorne was right, and if Julian made his case in a reasonable way, the Old Man would go along. He could get the land by some other means, after all—including marrying the shrew himself, if he felt so strongly about it.

Then, once he'd settled matters with the Old Man,

Julian would hunt down Georgie's uncle for a long talk about her future.

Only then—after he'd eliminated all the obstacles—could he come back to Upper Seymour Street and ask Georgie to marry him.

With his mind at ease, he snuggled her close. He would close his eyes and rest for a bit, and then he'd go back to Thorne's house. Unless, of course, Georgie found another illustration in that incredible book and wanted it explained...

Maybe he'd buy her a copy of her own to keep under her pillow. As a wedding gift.

❧

Georgiana nestled close against Julian's warmth, but her heart felt chilly.

*Your uncle could have made a better choice,* he had said. *One man would be safer for you... You really should...*

*Marry,* he'd almost said. He might as well have spoken the word, Georgiana thought; the meaning was clear enough. His tone had been casual, as if he'd been giving her advice about a horse or a new dress. Of course, the idea of who she married probably mattered just as little to him as those other things would. Even less, perhaps, than the horse.

This, she told herself firmly, was exactly why mistresses were not supposed to get attached to their lovers.

Maybe it wasn't such a good idea for her to help him find an heiress to marry so he could afford a mistress, too. Because if he was to care more about his wife than he cared about Georgiana...

He *should* care more for the woman he married

than for a mistress, she told herself fiercely. But though she believed that with all her heart, she wasn't sure she could put the idea into practice. She wasn't at all certain she could make love with him whenever he was free to come to her, and then smile and pretend it didn't matter as she watched him go back to his wife and perhaps give *her* a child…

No. She couldn't do it.

She had been taken off guard; she had never dreamed that she would come to care so deeply for Julian. Her lack of experience had worked against her. So she would simply have to be more careful in the future and never allow herself to become so involved again. And when the time came that Julian married, she would have to say good-bye to him.

But that time was not yet. For right now, he was still hers.

At least she'd thought ahead today. She had told Mary that she would want to sleep late in the morning and not to hurry about bringing her chocolate. Of course, Julian would still need to be out of the house before the kitchen staff began to stir, but Georgiana would have a bit more time to figure out what to do about things like sheets. She certainly couldn't use the ink trick again, but she had no idea what she would do instead.

At any rate, she wasn't going to worry about that until dawn came and he left her. In the meantime…

She wriggled suggestively against him. He shifted a little, pulled her closer, and rested his chin on her hair. She twisted round and pressed her breasts against his chest. He only murmured something—she thought it sounded like "Greedy wench"—and draped an arm across her, holding her still.

Georgie tried every technique she'd learned in the past two days but ended up admitting defeat—for nothing she did won a response. Obviously she wasn't finished with lessons just yet.

So she curled up and listened to him breathe. There would be another night, she told herself. And, if she was lucky, another... and another...

She slept, secure in Julian's arms.

❧

Julian found himself walking through the pages of Georgie's book, vaguely aware that he was dreaming—for the book had somehow grown larger and come to life. All the figures in the illustrations were real now, and they were all Georgie and him. No wonder he was so tired...

He heard something rattle, and then light shot through the room and struck his face like a blow just as he dragged his eyelids open. He wanted to curse. What was his batman doing opening the curtains in the middle of the night? But if it *was* the middle of the night, why was it light already?

Someone was making an infernal amount of noise; that was sure. Were they being attacked? He couldn't for the life of him remember where he was—someplace in France, perhaps. It must be one of the rare times that they'd been billeted in decent housing, for he could swear he smelled chocolate and maybe freshly baked bread as well...

He opened his eyes. Beside him, Georgie was

sitting up, her arms crossed over her chest, with the sheet clutched in both hands and drawn up to her chin. He grinned and eased closer, stretching out an arm—and she hauled off and smacked him across the top of his head.

Julian opened his mouth to protest—but before he could get the words out, he saw the enemy drawn up in battle lines at the foot of the bed. Two women stood there—a maid, complete with apron and cap, and an elderly woman wearing black, with a ring of keys jangling at her waist.

That might have been what he'd heard rattling, he deduced—the housekeeper's keys. Unless it had been the curtain rings after all... or the china pot, cup, and saucer that sat on the tray the maid was still holding. She didn't appear to have a very good grip on it, and her hands seemed to be shaking. The rest of the commotion must have been the maid having hysterics; she was quiet now, but her mouth was still gaping open as she stared.

"*Master Julian?*" The housekeeper sounded both astonished and horrified.

But not, Julian thought, any more shaken than he was. "Mrs. Mason? I thought Thorne had pensioned you off."

"Mason and I were ready for a slower pace but not a complete..." She drew in a stern breath. "That, young man, is entirely beside the point! What are you doing *here?*"

Julian thought she probably didn't need—or even want—to hear the answer. He rubbed his chin and looked around. Full daylight was streaming in the windows. It must be at least three hours past dawn.

He'd apparently had the first thing resembling a full night's sleep he'd managed since the start of the war.

And just look where it had landed him.

"Miss Georgiana," the housekeeper went on, "what do you have to say for yourself?"

Georgie bit her lip and cowered a little.

"That's enough, Mrs. Mason," Julian said, and put his arm around Georgie. "Now if you'll take yourself away for a while…"

"And leave you in this young lady's bedroom? I should think *not*!"

From the doorway came a man's voice. "What seems to be the—Master Julian!"

Julian tucked the sheet more closely around Georgie. "Good morning, Mason. You know, I'd been wondering why Thorne has a different butler these days. Now I'm *really* wondering, since you and Mrs. Mason are obviously still in the business."

"We wanted a quieter life," Mason said. "Of course, sometimes it's not *much* quieter." He stepped aside, but only to let another newcomer in.

Julian stifled a groan. "Perkins? Is that you? What the devil are you doing here? If you've chased me down to discuss that canal of yours again…"

Perkins drew himself up straight and took in the scene. "I have not *chased you down* to discuss anything, my lord. I have come to retrieve Miss Baxter and take her to her uncle, which is what Mrs. Mason was kindly coming to tell her when she discovered… *you*." His tone made it clear that no explanation would be adequate.

Julian couldn't blame him. Still, he had to try. "Yes. About that, Perkins…"

Perkins plowed straight on. "Considering the circumstances, I have no alternative but to report what I have seen." He turned away so sharply that Julian wouldn't have been surprised to see a hole where his heel had drilled into the floor, and strode down the hall.

Julian wanted to swear. "Mason, kindly tell the troops to go away. Mrs. Mason, I'm getting out of bed now so I can catch Perkins and talk some sense into him. You can either watch or leave—it makes no difference to me."

Mrs. Mason said something under her breath, caught the maid by the arm, and retreated. Mason glowered at Julian for another moment before he left, too, closing the door behind him with a bang. Julian pushed the sheet back and rolled out of bed, reaching for his clothes.

Georgie seized a pillow and flung it at him. "Don't you *dare* leave me alone here!"

"Darling, I'll come right back, I swear. But I have to stop Perkins before he gets to your uncle. That's all there is to it."

"Mrs. Mason will scold me!" She wasn't so much angry as frightened, he realized; her eyes were huge and brimming with tears.

"I'll tell her not to. But Georgie, that'll be nothing compared to what your uncle has to say, if I don't stop Perkins." He stepped into his breeches, ignoring shirt and boots and cravat and coat, and pulled the bedroom door open.

He almost ran Mrs. Mason down right at the top of the stairs. She drew herself up tall and opened her mouth, and Julian held up both hands in surrender. "Scold me all you want," he said. "I deserve every word of it. But not her. And not me, either, 'til later—if you please. Then I'll listen for as long as you want to yell at me. Right now, I beg you—just move out of my way."

Her lips compressed to a thin, rigid line, but she moved. He ran down the stairs and stopped at the bottom, for Mason was just closing the front door.

"He's already gone?" Julian said.

"Indeed he is. And I must say that in this case I agree there was no reason to delay. Nothing you could possibly say would remove the need to inform Miss Georgiana's uncle of the situation."

Julian sighed. "No, I suppose not."

"I must say, Master Julian, I've seen a lot happen in my time in this house but never anything like this. Debauching an innocent young girl like Miss Georgiana in her own bedroom… It hurts me to think you capable of such a thing."

Obviously Mason had no idea what his innocent Miss Georgiana was capable of, Julian thought, or he wouldn't be so certain that Julian had been the one doing the debauching.

However, not only did a gentleman not kiss and tell, no matter what the circumstances, but in this case Mason was right. The fault was Julian's and only his. No matter how enticing Georgie had been, he should never have given in to the temptation. He should never have exposed Georgie to anything like the disdain, the horror, the shock that she would have to face now.

"I'll fix this," he told Mason.

"You might begin by putting on a shirt," the butler said stiffly. "I expect Mr. Perkins will be back at any moment with his lordship and Sir Rufus."

His lordship? Oh, damnation—Thorne was likely to get involved in this, too? Julian swore under his breath and went back upstairs to get dressed.

Georgie had gotten out of bed and wrapped herself in a gold brocade dressing gown that made her hair look as intensely red as a bed of glowing embers. He suspected she was just about as dangerous, too—though for the moment his Lady Flame seemed subdued.

Under other circumstances, the garment would have set Julian's blood pounding, for she'd tied it so carelessly around her waist that it kept slipping off one creamy shoulder. And it was a trifle too short, so her slender bare feet and tiny trim ankles peeked out from under the hem. Why hadn't he noticed before that her feet were as gorgeous as the rest of her? Maybe if he'd been given another night to explore, he would have worked his way there, he told himself as he put on his shirt.

Georgie sat down at the dressing table and began to brush her hair, almost as if she didn't know what else to do with her hands. "You know the Masons," she said. It didn't sound like a question.

"Yes. Have since I was a child, when I visited Thorne at his various homes to play. I used to swipe food from the kitchens, and then I'd run to one or the other of the Masons for protection when Cook got angry." The story didn't matter; he was talking to try to ease the frozen look on her face. "It's a bit of a surprise to see them here, though. I thought they'd retired to the country, since they aren't working for Thorne any longer."

"Yes, they are. Working for Lord Hawthorne, I mean."

He frowned. That was a bit of a stopper. "They're not on your uncle's staff?"

She shook her head. "No. This is Lord Hawthorne's house."

Thorne owned Number 5 Upper Seymour Street? But why? Julian's eyes fell on the velvet bed hangings and he wanted to groan. Of course. No wonder Georgie's bedroom looked like a high-class bordello.

"He called you *my lord*," Georgie said.

"What? Who?" Julian shook out his cravat. Since he hadn't actually slept in it, how could it possibly look so wrinkled?

"Perkins. He said he hadn't chased you down to talk to you about canals, and he called you *my lord*."

"Oh, that. Yes."

"You're a lord?"

"Uh, not really. It's only a courtesy title."

She was staring at him in the mirror.

"My grandfather holds the real rank. Mine is a lesser title, traditionally used by the heir."

"I thought you were a soldier."

"I was. I am. But when my cousin died—he was really the heir, you see—then I… well, I'm the Marquess of Silsby now."

She reached out blindly, and her hand closed on a crystal inkwell.

"Georgie?" he asked tentatively.

She drew back her arm. "You're Silsby?"

"Uh… yes." Wrong answer, apparently. He ducked as the inkwell shot past his head and splintered against the cream silk wallpaper. "Georgie…"

Mrs. Mason pounded on the door. "What's going on? What was that bang?"

"Nothing important," Julian called. "Miss Georgiana had a bit of an accident with the inkwell."

"*Again?*" The housekeeper stormed into the room.

Georgie burst into tears and flung herself into Mrs. Mason's arms. "I'm so sorry," she wailed. "About… about *everything!*"

That was a facer, Julian thought. Not that he didn't deserve it, of course.

Mrs. Mason patted Georgie's shoulder and smoothed her hair. "There, there, dear. You poor motherless child. No wonder you let him do this to you…" The housekeeper glared at Julian. "You *will* make this right, Master Julian. I mean—my lord."

Julian gulped and felt about six years old again. He finished tying his cravat, put on his coat, rubbed a hand over his stubbly beard, and stepped into his boots. Absentmindedly, he picked up a no-longer-hot bun from the tray the maid had hastily set down as she retreated, and pulled off a bite. He suspected he was going to need all the sustenance he could get before Thorne and the uncle showed up.

Which, judging from the racket rising from downstairs, was right about now.

He took a deep breath and started down to face the music. Perkins was just inside the door, and Thorne and a stout man with a very red face were standing in the center of the hallway.

So this was Georgie's uncle. He looked like the sort who would try to—what was it she'd told him? Sell her to the highest bidder: that was it. He'd matched her to a man who was no prize but who was quite rich…

*That doesn't matter anymore,* he reminded himself. Because she wasn't going to marry the highest bidder—she was going to marry Julian.

Of course, that whole thing about the money might be a bit of a problem, especially if the Old Man kicked up rough about this turn of events. If he refused to give Julian an allowance…

He wondered how Georgie would take to being the wife of a half-pay Army officer. Perhaps it was a good thing he hadn't sold his commission just yet… Or, instead of being able to invest in Perkins' canal, perhaps he could get a job helping to dig it.

Perkins was fluttering around the two gentlemen, and Mason was trying in vain to take their hats. Thorne looked up as Julian approached and bellowed, "What the hell do you have to say for yourself, Julian?"

The roar set Julian's teeth on edge—especially coming from Thorne, of all people. The hypocrite— he was the one who'd set up this house for a mistress in the first place.

He sauntered down the stairs. "Hello, Thorne. Best night's sleep I've had in years. No; to be absolutely accurate, it was the best *half* a night's sleep. If you all would go away—"

He shouldn't have said it, of course. The stout gentleman with Thorne was spitting, he was so angry. Julian watched him warily. It was hard to tell with the big fellows; some of them were nothing more than windbags, while others packed a considerable punch.

Julian maintained a cautious distance and bowed. "Sir, I regret that we meet under these circumstances. I wish to assure you that I have the greatest respect for your niece——"

The stout gentleman thrust out his chin and took a step forward, fists clenched. "Fine way you have of showing it, you blackguard!"

Thorne sighed and moved between them. "Julian, this is Sir Rufus Baxter. Sir Rufus, allow me to present my graceless cousin, the Marquess of Silsby."

The stout gentleman had already started to speak. He stopped mid-word and suddenly looked like a fish out of water, gasping for oxygen. "You're Silsby?" he croaked.

"Is there something funny about my title?" Julian asked. "Because your niece said exactly the same thing just a minute ago."

"He's your cousin, Hawthorne?" The stout gentleman's voice rose shrilly. "This is the first you've said about that. I thought you were acting in the best interests of our ward, but now I find that instead you were——"

"She's *your* ward, Thorne?" Julian's head was beginning to ache. Could this whole situation possibly get any worse?

"In a manner of speaking, she is," Thorne said. "Sir Rufus, much as I regret at the moment that I am required to claim him—yes, Silsby is my cousin." He turned on Julian. "*This* is why you wanted a key to my house? You *idiot*! I had her tucked away on purpose, but you——"

"Keeping her for yourself, were you?" Julian asked coldly. "Thinking to make her your mistress?"

"I should call you out for that, Julian."

Sir Rufus sputtered. "You, too, Hawthorne?"

"No," Thorne said firmly. "Do you think I'm mad? I'd slice my own throat before I'd take on that whirlwind for a mistress. You utter fool!"

"Well, then," Julian said, "if you don't want her for yourself, why did you… What do you mean, you had her tucked away on purpose?"

"The Old Man was pushing you into marriage. I was just giving you a hand—so you'd have an option."

Julian shuddered at the reminder. "I'll have to talk to him, of course," he said drearily. "As soon as possible. I don't suppose I can persuade you to stand as my friend there? I do apologize for what I said, Thorne—"

Thorne stared at him. "I stashed her here in this house, with the Masons to look after her, to keep her out of reach. To keep her away from *you,* Julian." He added bitterly, "At least, I thought that's what I was doing—giving you the chance to make your own choice of a wife."

"My own choice?" Julian said blankly. "I've made my choice."

"You certainly have," Thorne said. "You fell smack into her wiles. But come to think of it, so did I. She came to me for help, she said… and I was stupid enough to believe her. So I did what she asked and kept her away from her guardian—thinking that if I made her vanish for a while, he wouldn't be able to press for an early marriage."

Sir Rufus started gasping like a fish once more.

"You deliberately... you... Sir, I regret to inform you, you're no gentleman!"

Thorne ignored him. "But it seems that all I really did was hide her right where she could lie in ambush for you, Julian."

"I really must insist that you stop insulting Georgie, Thorne."

"*Georgie*? You're calling the whirlwind *Georgie*? Julian, you prize idiot, haven't you been listening at all? She's the shrew the Old Man picked out for you!"

Julian had been listening; he just hadn't wanted to hear what Thorne kept on saying. "Georgie's the one who owns the piece of land the Old Man wants?"

Thorne nodded. "She inherited it from her father. It's about the only thing she has, too—so it was very clever of her to turn it into a title. What I want to know is how she figured out who you are, and how she got to you."

"She didn't," Julian said slowly. "She didn't know, 'til just now."

Or had she? *He's certainly no prize,* she had said of the man her uncle had agreed she should wed. *But he is rich—and my friends say that surely one can fall in love with a rich man just as easily as with a pauper.*

No. He'd stake his life that she hadn't known, that she'd thought he was no more than the simple soldier he had pretended to be.

Thorne shook his head in disbelief. "It's all immaterial now anyway. The Old Man will be riding roughshod over you for the rest of his life if you give in on this— but you have to marry her, Julian."

Thorne was usually right about these things, Julian

thought. But if that was the price he had to pay for having Georgie… yes, he could put up with the Old Man thinking he'd won. "I have every intention of doing so."

The stout gentleman stopped in mid-sputter. "You will? Truly?"

"Of course, I shall. And I might point out that your obvious doubt is unflattering not only to me but to my future wife."

The stout gentleman looked puzzled for a moment. Then he smiled. "No matter. As long as you're married. And you will abide by all the agreements your grandfather, the duke, has made."

Something about his self-satisfied tone set Julian's back up. "I will review all the agreements before I sign anything," he said cautiously, "and abide by the ones I approve. The only really important one is that whether you get what you want or not, I'm going to marry Georgie." He added under his breath, "Because that appears to be the only way I'll ever be able to get any sleep."

The stout gentleman started to sputter again.

"Since the only thing which matters to you, I'm sure, is your niece's good name," Julian told him, "and since I've given you the word of a gentleman that I will marry her, and soon, then I believe this conversation is finished."

"Well done, Julian," Thorne said. "You were every inch a duke just then—looking down your nose and all." Then he shook his head as if it hurt. "I think it's this house. It makes people do strange things. They begin acting different—irrational, even—the very moment they take up residence." He fixed Julian with a stern eye. "Or take up with the resident."

From the corner of his eye, Julian noticed that Perkins seemed to freeze, and then after a moment he oozed slowly toward the door and disappeared. Idly, Julian wondered why, but at the moment he had more important things on his mind.

"If you'll excuse me," Julian said, and fixed both Thorne and the stout gentleman with a firm gaze, "I am going to go shave and get some fresh clothes before I propose to a lady."

❧

Georgiana had gone through the motions of getting dressed, but the maid was still fussing with her hair when a tap sounded on the bedroom door. Georgiana didn't know whether to be pleased or worried. The conversation downstairs seemed to have made progress—at least they'd all stopped yelling at each other—but what did that actually mean? If Julian would only come back upstairs, surely he could tell her what had happened and how much trouble she should expect. Was she going to have to face Uncle Rufus right away?

But if Julian was at the door, why had he knocked, rather than just coming in?

And what was she going to say to him?

They would want him to marry her, of course. But then they—the duke, and Uncle Rufus—had always wanted him to marry her. So nothing had changed, really.

Except, possibly, for what Julian wanted.

He would almost certainly offer marriage. The blow to his honor if he did not would be too much to withstand—even if the duke and Uncle Rufus and Lord Hawthorne had nothing to say about the matter.

Yes, he would offer to marry her. But would he mean it?

He had told her himself that his grandfather was forcing him into the match, that he didn't want to marry at all. Now he had no choice but to offer for her, no matter what he wanted.

And what would her answer be?

Would she accept a man who didn't want to marry her—simply because her own foolishness had left them caught in this trap? Or would she turn him down and ruin them both?

Mary went to open the door, and Mrs. Mason bustled in, carrying a fresh pot of chocolate on a tray.

For a moment, Georgiana couldn't believe that Julian wasn't the one who stood there. Her heart fell. Shouldn't he have come himself to tell her what had happened?

Of course, she *had* thrown the inkwell at him… What if he didn't want to see her again after that? Oh, *why* did he have to be Silsby?

Her gaze fell on the dull black stain on the cream silk that covered the wall. Mary had cleaned up what she could, refusing to allow Georgiana to help. "You'll get your hands all stained," she had fussed—and so Georgiana had been relegated to watching as the maid gathered up the shards of crystal and blotted the wall.

She felt like a scolded child. *Because you've acted like one,* she thought. She had seized what she wanted without thought for anyone else… That was why Julian was in this mess, being raked over the coals downstairs… What was *happening* down there, anyway?

Had Mrs. Mason come to take her downstairs to face the music? "My uncle?" Her voice trembled a little.

"Sir Rufus and Lord Hawthorne have gone."

*Gone where?* Georgiana wanted to ask.

"I thought you might like something warm while you wait, dear. Lord Silsby presents his compliments and asks if he may call on you in an hour."

An *hour?* What could possibly take as long as that? Did Julian need to be coerced into doing the honorable thing? Did he have to muster his courage before facing her? Was he trying desperately to find a way out? Or was he lying somewhere bleeding and insensible?

Surely not the last—unless he had actually not sent that message himself.

But whatever was going on, she had an hour to think about what she would say to him.

❧

Georgiana was in the library when Julian arrived; Mason showed him in, and she stood still, holding a book clutched in her hands to keep her fingers from trembling, and surveyed him from head to foot.

Lord Silsby looked very different from the Julian she was used to. His coat was new, a deep, rich blue that suited his tanned skin and his eyes. She'd never been quite sure what color his eyes were—it was so difficult to tell by candlelight, and sometimes they'd looked blue and sometimes gray. But now she could see that they were indeed blue, a light, clear shade like seawater. His boots were new and polished to a glassy gleam; his cravat was perfectly tied; he was freshly shaved and his hair was no longer falling into his eyes. He looked every inch a lord, with not a trace left of the scruffy soldier she'd fallen in love with.

She couldn't deny it any longer, and Georgiana was too honest even to try. She did love him. Probably, she thought, she'd fallen in love with him that first night in his cousin's garden—because even when he'd been all starchy and correct, he'd also been thoughtful and charming and funny...

When he'd relaxed and showed her his true self, she had loved him even more. And then when he'd made love to her and shown her what a man and a woman could be together...

"Miss Georgiana," he said, and bowed over her hand with impeccable manners.

Her world hung in the balance. She wanted to fling herself into his arms... to carry them back to the night before when things had been so much simpler.

"I have discussed the matter with your uncle, and he has given his permission for me to ask for your hand in marriage."

As if Uncle Rufus would refuse the match that he'd practically given his soul to arrange!

Georgiana waited. And waited. "Is that all?" she asked finally.

"I have not yet discussed the matter with my grand-father, but since he approved the match initially, I'm sure there will be no hesitation from that quarter, either. You'll be a marchioness..." He cleared his throat. "And one day my duchess."

He didn't sound very happy about it.

*I don't want to be a duchess,* she thought drearily. *I'd so much rather just be your lover.*

And that, she thought, was probably what he'd prefer, too. So she knew exactly what she had to do.

"Lord Silsby, I am honored by your offer," she said, her tone every bit as formal as his had been. "But I refuse."

She looked delectable, Julian thought as he was ushered into the library by a stern-faced Mason. But then Georgie always did. Today she was dressed in something that was pale blue and frilly and much more formal than he'd seen her wearing before. He doubted she could get out of this dress in a hurry, for it seemed to fasten up the back. But that was all right; he'd be more than willing to help...

He almost stumbled over his proposal. Then, with the formalities over and the rote words spoken, Julian was more than ready to draw her close and kiss her—a real kiss, too; none of this peck-on-the-cheek stuff that newly betrothed couples were allowed by society's rules—and so it took an instant for her answer to sink in. Even then, he looked at her for a long moment, expecting her dimples to appear, expecting that her warm, rich laugh would ring out at any moment as she shared the joke.

Instead, her face remained sober and her lovely sensuous mouth stayed firm.

"What the devil?" he said, shaken. "Georgie, you can't turn me down."

"I just did." She looked directly at him. "Please go away."

"You *can't*. I mean it—you really can't. You'll be ruined."

"But that's exactly what I intended," she said, sounding surprised that he had to be reminded. "I did this so no gentleman would ever want to marry me."

"Now there's an idea that was doomed to failure—as you'd know if you had just a little more experience."

"Either I'm ruined, or I'm not," she pointed out. "You can't have it both ways, Lord Silsby. So which is it to be?"

Julian felt like throwing something. "Georgie—"

She seemed to have stopped listening. "I want to travel."

"I'll take you to Italy for our honeymoon. I'll take you around the world, if you want."

"I want to be free—and I've achieved that. My uncle certainly won't try again to arrange a marriage for me after this. And I'll have my pick of the gentlemen of the *ton*, once they discover that I've been your mistress."

"Georgie, if you think I'm going to start you on your chosen career with some kind of a recommendation—"

"You won't have to, my lord. I'm sure the word will get out soon enough."

If she'd hit him over the head with a book of sermons, she couldn't have stunned him more. "It will not come from me," he said coldly.

"Of course not. But servants talk, and enough people know what happened here this morning that the news will spread. For all I know, my uncle and your grandfather are talking it over right now."

"And if that discussion of theirs *doesn't* lead to a wedding… It's not just your reputation that'll be ruined, you know. People will think I refused to marry you."

"Oh, now we reach the nub of the problem. It's *your* reputation you're concerned about."

"It is not. Dammit, Georgie—"

She raised her chin. "I shall tell them differently, of course. You need have no fear that I will blame you, Lord Silsby."

"Georgie, stop the *Lord Silsby* nonsense. You can't do this."

"Tell me why I should not." She sounded perfectly reasonable—which did not take away his urge to pick her up and shake her. Gently, of course, and only long enough to jar loose these nonsensical ideas of hers.

"Well, for one thing, my grandfather still wants that land. If you turn me down, he'll be proposing to you himself, and the Old Man doesn't take rejection any better than I do."

He was hoping she'd laugh at the sheer foolishness of the suggestion. Instead, she seemed to turn the idea over and consider it from all angles before shaking her head.

"You're angry," he said.

Something flashed in her eyes, but she said calmly, "I have considered my answer, and it is final. Good day, Lord—"

Julian took a step toward her, and she broke off mid-title. At least he'd made that much of an impression—though he felt like a brute, because he'd seen a flicker of fear in her face.

"Georgie." His voice was hoarse. "I know you don't want to marry me. I know you don't want to marry anyone—at least not right now. But you must."

"Last night," she said almost casually, "you started to tell me I should marry—as if anyone would do."

Julian frowned. "Well, yes, I suppose that's the way it could have sounded."

"And today you've proposed. Why? Because Uncle Rufus will call you out if you don't?"

"I'd like to see him try."

"I heard Lord Hawthorne yelling at you."

"He'll get over it."

"You almost sound as if you mean it. How noble of you to make the sacrifice."

This was not going at all the way he'd planned it. "It's not a sacrifice."

"Oh? Today you expect me to believe you actually *want* to marry me? After all this fuss and bother?"

"No one is forcing me into anything, Georgie."

"But left to yourself you would never have offered for me." She turned away.

Was that the very smallest quaver in her voice? Hope sprang to life inside him. After all, she hadn't actually thrown him out—quite. But what was she up to? Why was she being so obstinate? Something about this felt familiar...

Lesson Four, he thought. *Make him seduce you,* he had told her. *Show him that you're interested—but make him work to have you.* Now the wily little imp was using it against him.

He wanted to laugh, to seize her and spin her around in some crazy dance.

He knew better. He was a seasoned campaigner; it was time to change his tactics.

"Left to myself," he said softly, "I would have gone to my grandfather this morning and told him I wanted to be released from the match he had arranged for me."

Her spine had gone rigid. "Exactly. Which is why I cannot—"

"So I could offer for the woman I love instead."

She stood very still.

"You, Georgie." He watched her thoughtfully. "But you've rejected my offer, and I accept that it's your right to do so. You say you want to be a mistress. All right—but you'll be *my* mistress. Or else."

She spun to face him. "Or else what?" She sounded quite annoyed, and it took great effort not to smile at her indignation.

"Or else I'll make sure every gentleman in the *ton* knows you've got a dreadful disease and might give it to him if he gets too close to you."

She gasped. "You wouldn't!"

"I would. I intend to be your only lover. So come, darling, since you're going to be stuck with me and only me for the rest of your life, why not go the whole way and marry me? It's not such an awful fate. I'll take you to masked balls. I'll give you diamonds and carriages and houses—"

"And furs, I suppose?"

"Nobody said anything about furs—but yes, I'll give you furs. And children. Because no matter what you think, you're really not cut out to be a mistress, my Lady Flame—except to one man who will treasure

you and adore you and love you, and have no intention of sharing you ever."

"You don't really want to marry me."

"Yes, I do."

He could see in her face the struggle she was
enduring. She was torn between doubt and belief...
between wanting him and being afraid he didn't truly
want her. But he knew now how this would end—
and he could be patient for as long as it took her to
believe him.

"You can have the land," she said faintly.

"Give it to my grandfather. He's the one who wants
it. What is it, anyway, a few acres? What does it matter?
Someday we'll have an abbey... it's as big as a castle."

"I don't want an abbey."

"Are you certain? We could put up arbors all over
the place and grow as many grapes as you like."

Sparks flared in her eyes. "You lied to me—*Lord
Silsby.*"

"No, I didn't... Yes," Julian admitted slowly. "I
suppose I did, in a way, because I let you believe I
was nothing more than I appeared to be. But I wasn't
hiding it from you as much as I was trying to deny it
to myself. I wasn't meant for this, Georgie. I was never
supposed to be anything but a soldier."

She was looking doubtfully at him.

"Besides," he went on, "you lied to me as well.
You knew perfectly well Thorne would never have
touched you, but you threatened that if I didn't make
love to you, you'd go to him instead."

Her cheeks flushed ever so slightly.

"And I haven't seen a single male servant, except

Mason, in this house, Miss *If-you-don't-make-love-to-me-I'll-seduce-a-footman*."

She ducked her head a little, and Julian seized the opportunity to put his arms around her. Georgie resisted for a moment longer, but then she melted into him, and suddenly happiness surged through him.

He put his hand under her chin and looked deep into her eyes, which were filmed with tears. Happy tears, for she was smiling at him in a gentle, almost shy way that he'd never seen before—a smile that made his heart twist.

"It's you I want," he whispered. "You, and only you. I love you, Georgiana."

She started to cry in earnest, then. "Oh, Julian—I only wanted you to care about me."

"Always. More with each day that goes by." He kissed her long and slowly, and tasted such sweetness in her that it made him ache.

After awhile, he sat down on the library sofa and drew her onto his lap. "What would you have done if I hadn't obliged you, Lady Flame?" Julian nibbled the sensitive triangle right below her ear.

"I'd have kept tempting you until you did," she admitted. "I don't understand how I knew you were the man I should make love with. I just knew it. But I didn't mean to fall in love with you, Julian. I didn't want to—at first."

"I know, sweetheart. But that's all right, because you did it anyway."

She snuggled closer, and closer yet. "You don't have to go see your grandfather just yet, do you?"

He held her a few inches away from him and said

firmly, "If you're trying to seduce me, Georgie, you can stop right now. I'm not taking you back to bed until we're married."

He was expecting her dimples to flash, and he wasn't surprised. But even though he'd braced himself for the impact of her smile, he hadn't counted on it being brighter and more stunning than ever before. Her elfin grin lit up her face and made him woozy.

"Want to bet?" she said softly.

And Julian, the seasoned campaigner, knew when it was time to surrender.

# Seven

## THE EARL RECEIVES AN OFFER

LORD HAWTHORNE SCRAWLED HIS NAME ON THE LAST OF the letters Perkins had laid out on the big desk in the library, sanded his signatures, pushed his chair back and crossed the room. Thorne's hand was already on the knob, the door was half open, and the butler was waiting in the hall with his greatcoat when Perkins spoke.

"I'll see that these letters are sent out immediately, my lord. But there's one more item to call to your attention."

Thorne sighed and turned back to his man of business. "If you're still on about that bloody canal, Perkins…"

"No, my lord."

"Because I have to tell you that you've convinced us. Colford, Silsby, and I are all agreed you're correct that it will be a good investment. Purchase four shares—one for each of us."

"*Four* shares, my lord?"

Thorne grinned. "You're thinking I've forgotten how to count? The fourth one is for you, man. If we're going to have to listen to you prose on about canals for the next ten years, we thought you should be just as heavily invested as we are."

Perkins' face was a study in astonishment. "My lord!"

"Consider it a token of gratitude from each of us—for finding that incredible house on Upper Seymour Street."

Perkins cleared his throat nervously and followed Thorne into the hallway, lowering his voice. The butler retreated to a discreet distance, still holding Thorne's coat. "About the house, my lord…"

Thorne groaned. "New wallpaper again? I thought we'd already replaced the panel the whirlwind hit with the inkwell."

"Yes, my lord, we did. It's not about wallpaper or servants or the roof this time. A gentleman has expressed interest in purchasing it."

Thorne's eyebrows raised. "Does the gentleman have a name?"

"Not as yet, sir. I mean, rather, that the man of business who approached me did not divulge the gentleman's name."

"Testing the waters," Thorne mused. "Seeing if I wanted to sell before coming out in the open."

"I presumed so, my lord."

"I suppose you believe it the sensible course of action?"

Perkins coughed. "It's not for me to say, my lord. However, it would seem that you… that you…"

"Have no further need of it? Oh, I wouldn't go *that* far, Perkins. One never knows when a small, discreet, very private little hideaway will be welcome."

"But my lord…"

"It was, after all, your idea," Thorne reminded him.

Perkins stiffened as if a poker had been rammed up his spine.

Lady Hawthorne came out of the morning room

cradling her infant son, Lord Chilton, in her arms. "Say good-bye to Papa before he goes out to his club for the day," she crooned to the baby, who drooled and waved his hands. "Perkins, did I hear you speaking of Number 5 Upper Seymour Street?"

Perkins looked wildly around, as if hoping that a trap-door would open under him right there in the hallway so he could make a faster escape. He stared for a moment at Thorne, who remained silent. Then he sighed and took the fall. "Just a matter of the drains, my lady."

"I see. You always handle things so carefully for his lordship. He is fortunate to have you looking after his... interests." She bestowed a smile on Perkins and started up the main staircase.

"As for the house," Thorne said. He wasn't looking at Perkins; he was watching the sway of the Countess's skirt as she climbed the stairs. "It's really up to Lady Hawthorne to decide whether I will need it or not. Feel free to discuss it with her, Perkins. And do let me know what she says."

"Yes, my lord." Perkins' voice was hollow.

❦

Lord Hawthorne was at his club an hour later, browsing the newspapers and carrying on a desultory conversation with an old acquaintance, when a white-gloved waiter brought him a letter laid on a silver tray. "This was just delivered for you, my lord."

The paper was high quality; the address had definitely been written by a feminine hand, and the impression stamped in the sealing wax on the back was one Thorne didn't recognize.

His interest piqued, he broke the seal and glanced at the contents. He then refolded the paper and tucked it carefully into the inner breast pocket of his coat. "My apologies, Hastings," he said to the man sitting across from him. "You were saying?"

Lord Hastings didn't look surprised. "Message from a lady," he deduced. "You won't want to keep her waiting. I must say I've been wondering how long it would take you to stop living in your wife's pocket and find a new mistress."

"Indeed," Thorne murmured, and leaned back in his chair. "But there's no rush. Do, please, continue telling me about that horse."

"You're a wise man," Hastings said, seemingly unaware that he was now contradicting himself. "Never let a mistress think you're so anxious to see her that you'll come running the very moment she drops her handkerchief. Now about this bay—it's the sweetest goer I've ever seen, and…"

⁂

In due time, Thorne presented himself at the lady's door and was admitted by the butler without a word being exchanged.

She was waiting for him in her sitting room, dressed in a velvet robe of his favorite dark green. Her hair was tied back in a loose knot that made his fingers itch to take it down, to stroke the long smooth dark strands and then to brand the nape of her neck with his lips before moving on, farther and deeper, to brand the rest of her in his own most personal way.

Instead, he stood very straight in the center of the

room and said sternly, "After all these months with no word at all, you dare to summon me out of the blue with a message containing nothing more than a time and a place?"

"And a promise."

"Certain of yourself, aren't you?"

Her eyebrows arched. "You're here," she pointed out. "If you didn't wish to come, no one was forcing you."

"What sort of a mistress lets months go by without even attempting to meet her lover?" He stripped off his coat and draped it over the back of a chair.

"A mistress who has an obligation to give her husband an heir," she murmured.

"The selfish bastard," Thorne said calmly. He was taking the pins out of her hair as he spoke, and he buried his face in the rich silky strands to inhale her scent. Then he picked her up from the sofa and carried her into the adjoining bedroom. "I suppose he'll want a spare one day, too."

"I think it quite likely."

"Well, we'll worry about that when the time comes." His voice was muffled because he had unfastened her robe and was nuzzling her breast. "Maybe we'll present him with my child, instead of his. He's dim enough not to notice."

"He'll never know the difference," she whispered. Her hands were busy as well; his shirt gaped open.

"Speaking of time," he added as he sat down to pull off his boots, "it was wicked of you to give me hours to contemplate this assignation."

She shrugged. "I had no idea how long it would take my footman to find you and deliver the message."

"Minx. You knew exactly where to find me at that hour of the morning, and you deliberately gave me plenty of time to anticipate what we will do together."

She smiled, just a little.

"But you'll pay for it, because I am so hard and so hot for you that it may take all night for you to satisfy me."

"Then it's a good thing I left the heir with his nurse so he won't be screaming because I'm delayed."

"It *would* be a shame if he set the house in such an uproar that servants went out to search for you." He stepped out of his buckskins.

She looked her fill. "I see you don't exaggerate, my lord—and indeed I am pleased, for I plan to satisfy you no matter how long it may take." She reached for a decanter on a nearby tray and handed him a glass. "You'll need something for stamina, no doubt."

He took the glass, looking at her across the rim. "This is brandy, Anne," he said, and suddenly the teasing note was gone from his voice. "You don't like the taste of brandy."

"On you," she said, "I love the taste of anything. Come to bed, Thorne."

He sipped his drink and set it aside. "And I love the taste of *you*, my Lady Wilde," he said, and joined her. He reached into a drawer next to the bed and handed her a velvet box.

She toyed with the clasp. "I'm glad you decided not to sell the house."

"I couldn't. It belongs to you. But *you*, my darling, belong to me."

She smiled at him and opened the box. A necklace

and bracelet of perfectly matched rubies winked against the white velvet lining. "They're beautiful."

"The jeweler has been all this time finding them for you," Thorne said. "I told him the day we met at his shop that I wanted to drape you in rubies."

"It is a generous gift," she said thoughtfully, "and as your wife, I am most grateful for this token of your love. But as your mistress—I fear I am greedy. Rubies are not enough, my lord. Show me."

In the sitting room, Thorne's coat slid slowly from the back of the chair where he had carelessly tossed it, dislodging the letter. The paper fluttered to the carpet and lay open.

> *Four this afternoon. Number 5 Upper Seymour Street—where all your dreams will come true.*

# Acknowledgments

Special thanks to: Rachelle Chase, who encouraged, cajoled, and downright nagged me into writing this book—thank you, my friend. To my editor, Deb Werksman, whose enthusiasm for this story is everything an author could ask for. To my incredibly involved and responsive agent, Christine Witthohn of Book Cents Literary Agency, for reasons beyond number. To Jacqui Bianchi, who forgot more about writing and editing than most authors and editors ever knew. To Horst and Renate, who gave me seven weeks in London, and to Kate and Biddy, who shared their love of British history. To my extraordinary friends Elaine Orr and Margaret Trucano and to my sweet sister, Linda Smith, for listening. And to my readers everywhere—thank you for making this journey with me.

# About the Author

Leigh Michaels is the author of eighty contemporary romance novels and a half dozen nonfiction books, including *On Writing Romance* and *Creating Romantic Characters*. More than 35 million copies of her books have been published. She is a six-time finalist in the RITA contest sponsored by Romance Writers of America, and has received two Reviewer's Choice awards from *Romantic Times* magazine. She teaches romance writing online for Gotham Writers Workshop (www.writingclasses.com). She wrote her first romance novel when she was a teenager and burned it, then wrote and burned five more complete manuscripts before submitting to a publisher.

She lives in Iowa with her artist/photographer husband, Michael W. Lemberger, where she enjoys taking long walks and watching wildlife in her garden.

Her website is www.leighmichaels.com, and she can be contacted at leigh@leighmichaels.com.

# *One*

THE TOWN ASSEMBLIES WERE TOO SMALL TO HAVE much of an orchestra, so the music was most often provided by Miss Minchin at the piano. But this was all the young people had ever known, so they didn't miss the elegance of a London ballroom. Most of them would never have a London Season.

Including, Miranda thought with a wisp of sadness, the belle of tonight's ball.

Miranda's gaze rested on her daughter. Sophie's dark-gold hair was a striking spot of color as she moved through the steps of the country dance. Miranda admitted she was partial to her own daughter. Still, everyone else faded into the background when compared to Sophie.

If only it was possible to get her to London... Even there, among the assembled lovelies of the nation, Miranda was certain that Sophie would stand out.

Sophie smiled up at her partner. It was a truly breathtaking smile, and Miranda wasn't surprised when the young man looked dazed, turned red, and missed a step.

Next to Miranda, Lord Ryecroft shifted his broad

shoulders against a pillar. "I see my sister is at it again, Mama. That will make three young popinjays whose pretensions I'll have depressed this month alone."

"It's only a dance. That doesn't mean he'll come to ask your permission to call on Sophie."

Rye looked down at her, one eyebrow raised. "If not, it will be because his father saw that smile too and put his foot down. You know as well as I do that Newstead wants someone with more dowry than our Sophie has, when it's time to marry off his younger son."

"I wish..." Miranda bit her tongue, too late.

But it didn't matter, for the same thought was obviously already in Rye's head. "You can't wish it any more than I do, Mama. Get Sophie to London and she'd take the town by storm, marry a Croesus, and save us all."

He was joking, of course, Miranda knew. At least, he was mostly joking. But there was truth in what he said. Not that she wanted Sophie to choose a husband based only on wealth. But rich men fell in love too— and a young woman with Sophie's warm heart could surely find a wealthy man she could care about.

*If only I could get her to London...*

Rye smiled down at his mother—but though his expression was reminiscent of his sister's brilliance, she could see the shadow in his eyes. "I haven't the blunt to lay out for a London Season," he said, "and with the best will in the world, I can't find it this year."

"I know you can't, my dear." *But perhaps I can,* Miranda thought.

It would take sacrifice, and she would have to be careful not to let Rye and Sophie know. But for the sake of her children, Miranda would do anything.

Rye bowed to his mother and moved toward the refreshment room, where he helped an elderly lady to punch. She sipped the watery concoction and looked at him speculatively over the rim of her cup, her black eyes beady. "You're Viscount Ryecroft, aren't you?"

Rye admitted, warily, that he was.

She didn't favor him with her name. Instead, she looked him up and down and asked, "Why isn't a young buck like you in the assembly room flirting with the young ladies? Not lack of interest from the chits, I'll be bound. Is there no one here tonight with enough juice to be worth your while to court?"

The comment stung Rye's pride—the more so because, in part at least, it was true. What sense was there in raising hopes among the young ladies at this assembly by dancing and flirting, when he would never be able to form an attachment to one of them? Even worse, what if he were to meet a woman he could care about, but could not afford to marry? Better to stay on the fringes.

What was true of his sister Sophie was equally true of him. If anything, his case was even more desperate—for Sophie needed only to marry a man who had enough money to support her. Rye needed to marry a woman who had enough money to support his estate and all the responsibilities that came along with it—including the tenant farmers, the servants, the retainers, his mother... In short, he needed an heiress of great magnitude—and generosity. Someone he was not likely to meet at this rural assembly.

Only in London...